Erin failed
pushing against the wall of Storm's chest.

Seizing both her hands in one of his, he compelled her to admit the uselessness of her effort. . . . When she once again stood quietly under his touch, he tipped back her chin and coaxed her into meeting his gaze.

"You can't escape me, Erin. You were always meant to be mine."

His implacable determination frightened her almost as much as the clamor of her own body. What for her would be the supreme act of love would be for him no more than a weapon for achieving vengeance. How could she look into his eyes afterward and see the callous satisfaction she was certain would be there?

Yet even as she tried again to flee, she sensed that he was right. There would be no escape.

Dear Reader,

We, the editors of Tapestry Romances, are committed to bringing you two outstanding original romantic historical novels each and every month.

From Kentucky in the 1850s to the court of Louis XIII, from the deck of a pirate ship within sight of Gibraltar to a mining camp high in the Sierra Nevadas, our heroines experience life and love, romance and adventure.

Our aim is to give you the kind of historical romances that you want to read. We would enjoy hearing your thoughts about this book and all future Tapestry Romances. Please write to us at the address below.

The Editors
Tapestry Romances
POCKET BOOKS
1230 Avenue of the Americas
Box TAP
New York, N.Y. 10020

Flame on the Sun

Maura Seger

A TAPESTRY BOOK
PUBLISHED BY POCKET BOOKS NEW YORK

Books by Maura Seger

Defiant Love
Rebellious Love
Forbidden Love
Flame on the Sun

Published by TAPESTRY BOOKS

This novel is a work of historical fiction. Names, characters, places and incidents relating to non-historical figures are either the product of the author's imagination or are used fictitiously. Any resemblance of such non-historical incidents, places or figures to actual events or locales or persons, living or dead, is entirely coincidental.

An *Original* publication of TAPESTRY BOOKS

A Tapestry Book published by
POCKET BOOKS, a division of Simon & Schuster, Inc.
1230 Avenue of the Americas, New York, N.Y. 10020

Copyright © 1983 by Seger, Inc.

ISBN: 0-671-49395-7

First Tapestry Books printing September, 1983

10 9 8 7 6 5 4 3 2 1

POCKET and colophon are registered trademarks of Simon & Schuster, Inc.

TAPESTRY is a trademark of Simon & Schuster, Inc.

Printed in the U.S.A.

For Anne and Brendan Jones,
my parents,
who never said,
"Stop daydreaming."

Flame
on the Sun

Chapter One

"I WISH YOU WOULD RECONSIDER, MISS. YOKO-
hama is no place for a lady on her own."
Captain Foster stroked his trim white beard
anxiously as he spoke. Beneath his peaked
naval cap, his gray eyes darkened with worry.

Not even the excitement of a successful
voyage or the prospect of shortly going ashore
in a fabled land few Westerners had ever
visited could improve his mood.

During the long months at sea, he had done
his best to convince his lovely young passen-
ger that she was embarked on a futile and
dangerous journey. It was unlikely that having failed to convince her in the past, he
would do so now. But for the sake of his
conscience he had to try one last time.

Erin Conroy listened to him patiently despite all the distractions offered by the harbor teeming with proud clipper ships and square-sailed junks. She understood that the captain spoke from genuine doubt about her safety, so she did not resent his well-meant advice. But neither did she have any intention of following it.

Behind her lay months of arduous travel from her home in Boston to the enclave perched on the edge of Japan, between the flat green sea and the distant snow-covered peak of Mt. Fuji that seemed to guard the very edge of the world.

Ahead lay the objective that had kept her going despite grave uncertainty, exhaustion, fear, and more often than not, just plain boredom. She was not about to turn back now.

An onshore breeze redolent of salt water, fish and seaweed ruffled the ebony hair pulled back in a neat chignon at the nape of her neck. Her creamy skin held a slight, sun-warmed glow. The slender oval of her face was set off by a high brow, straight, slim nose and dimpled chin whose firmness hinted at considerable inner strength. Her mouth was wide and generous, given to frequent smiles. Crystal blue eyes set off by pure white flecks sparkled as she strove to reassure the captain.

"I appreciate your concern, but as I have explained before, there is no alternative for me but to go on. This is the only chance I have to rebuild my family's fortunes. I can't abandon it simply because there is some danger involved. Besides," she added teasingly, "I am not alone. Mrs. Gilhoully is a formidable companion."

Captain Foster snorted, not at all convinced that the middle-aged Irishwoman could keep her young mistress out of trouble. Although she did try. He had to give her credit for that.

His first glimpse of the pair had been on the dock at San Francisco harbor when Erin came to negotiate their passage on the *Pacific Star*. A gin-sodden young sailor had declared his desire to spend some time—and money—in the young lady's company. For that, he had earned a sharp crack from Mrs. Gilhoully's parasol and the warning, rendered in unmistakable terms, of what would happen to him if he didn't retreat at once.

As a loving husband with three daughters of his own, Captain Foster had no patience for such low-life. But he could at least understand the n'er-do-well's infatuation. Erin Conroy was an enthrallingly beautiful young woman.

Despite the austerity of her navy-blue serge skirt, plain white blouse and maroon pelisse, the perfection of her tall, slender body was impossible to hide. Perhaps in part because she steadfastly refused to lace, a fact which the captain privately applauded. All too many young women seemed bent on constricting themselves to the point where they could do little but lie about on settees and occasionally swoon.

3

Not Miss Conroy. Each morning of the voyage, no matter what the weather, she had walked the deck eagerly. She became such a familiar sight to the crew that they even grew somewhat accustomed to her stunning good looks. At least enough to engage her in friendly conversation under the watchful eye of the captain. To the horror of the formidable Mrs. Gilhoully, she soon joined them in practicing knot tying, fishing, singing sea chanties, and the few other diversions available in the midst of the seemingly endless Pacific.

By the time they had made port the day before, there was not a man aboard who hadn't developed a soft spot for the beautiful young girl. More than a few had approached the captain to ask if he might not be able to convince her of the foolhardiness of her venture. But it seemed that was not to be the case.

Giving in with ill grace, Captain Foster muttered, "Aye, the two of you must surely be a match for whatever this godforsaken country can serve up. That poor fellow—the shogun, is it?—had better watch out. You'll charm his rice fields right out from under him while Mrs. Gilhoully holds off a whole army of those samaritans I hear are supposed to be so tough."

"Samurai," Erin corrected gently. "At least that's what the book I've been reading calls them. It's by Mr. C. P. Hodgson, the British consul in Nagasaki."

Captain Foster's scowl deepened. The English had earned his undying enmity when they sided with the Confederacy during the Civil War. More than two years after the conclusion of that blood-soaked blot on the nation's history, he was still not prepared to forgive them.

"Whoever they be, do you think you might at least allow me to provide you with an escort to the consulate?"

Erin was not dismayed by his gruffness. She suspected the captain used much the same tone with his daughters. At twenty-four, with her parents dead at the beginning of the war and her last remaining uncle in his grave almost a year, she was not opposed to a little cosseting.

"I would be most pleased, sir. Mrs. Gilhoully seems about to join us, so we should be able to leave whenever you choose."

The iron-haired, amply built woman who plodded purposefully toward them across the deck was completely swathed in black. Her plump face with its red cheeks, small mouth and piercing eyes appeared unrelentingly stern.

Out of long habit, she frowned at her mistress. But there was no malice in the look, as quickly became apparent when she murmured, "Here you are standing in the sun and wind again, like as not adding more freckles to your collection. Can you never remember to put on your bonnet?"

Erin shook her head cheerfully. "I've been leaving it off for the last eight years, Meg. You should be willing to admit by now that I'm a lost cause."

The older woman sighed mournfully. "The good Lord alone knows what will become of you, Erin Conroy. Traipsing halfway across the world to this heathen country." She shivered as delicately as her considerable bulk allowed. "Twenty-four years old and still no sign of getting yourself a husband and settling down to have the children I should already be looking after. It was bad enough when we were in Boston, but now . . ."

She broke off, distracted by the appearance of several people on the dock beside the clipper ship. "Oh, sweet heaven, there's some of those yellow devils now! Mary and all the saints protect us!" Determinedly imposing herself in front of the younger woman, she did her best to shelter her from the unseemly sight.

Erin peered around her shoulder eagerly. Months of reading everything she could get her hands on about the mysterious inhabitants of the Kingdom of the Rising Sun had only fueled her desire to see them for herself. But at first glance, they were undeniably disappointing.

There was nothing in the least exotic about the half-dozen men approaching the ship. The large number of Chinese thronging San Francisco had accustomed her to the idea that people came in other shades besides white, black and red. So although the men did not precisely resemble the Orientals she had seen, their color and the almond shape of their eyes were no great surprise.

Neither were the black trousers, frock coats and top hats they wore, which would have looked perfectly at home in Boston's Quincy Street. Even their expressions were recognizable. They glanced up at the clipper ship with shuttered gazes that did not quite mask a hint of great excitement and interest. She had seen that same look on her father and uncles when they were contemplating an attractive business opportunity.

A sigh escaped her as she took in the final, all-too-familiar detail of their accouterments. Each carried an overstuffed briefcase undoubtedly full of forms.

"Customs officials," Captain Foster grumbled. "They'll be wanting to levy tariffs on my cargo."

"Can they do that?" Erin asked.

"Aye, according to the treaties negotiated with the various Western countries that trade here now, a portion of each cargo's worth goes to the shogun. In return, he keeps the port open and maintains order." Grudgingly he admitted, "I suppose it's a fair arrangement. Leastways, there seems to be plenty of money being made on both sides, so I don't rightly see how anyone can complain."

Erin was glad to hear it, since she had come

to Japan precisely for the purpose of making enough money to prevent the bankruptcy of the Conroy shipping line. Her task would be difficult enough; if there was any breakdown in the local markets, it might become impossible.

"I'm sure you'll be busy for some time, Captain, so I won't keep you." Graciously thanking him for making the long voyage both safe and pleasant, she took her leave. It was difficult to say good-bye to a man she had become genuinely fond of, but over the last few years she had learned to accept such farewells as an inevitable part of life. With his final admonitions fading behind her, she stepped lightly down the gangplank.

"Will you look at this?" Meg muttered as they settled into the jinrikisha a young officer had secured for them. Her disapproving gaze focused on the backs of the two men pulling the conveyance. "Whoever heard of using humans to do the work of horses?"

Erin had to agree that the sight was distressing. But she was well aware that knowing as little as she did about conditions in Japan, and Yokohama in particular, she was in no position to complain.

"Perhaps it's a question of having to make do with what is available," she suggested. "There does seem to be a great deal going on here."

That was putting it mildly. Single-story

8

wooden buildings were packed so closely together that their sloping tiled roofs nearly touched. They framed the narrow street crowded with merchants, sailors, missionaries, diplomats and unabashed opportunists, all looking to benefit from the inevitable chaos created by the confrontation of two vastly different cultures.

Tantalizing aromas wafted from the closely packed buildings and stalls they passed. Erin recognized the scents of tea and rice, jasmine and hyacinth mingling with the other, less pleasant odors that were inevitable in any place of dense human habitation.

Almost all the people they passed were either peasants dressed in simple homespun cotton garments, straw hats and sandals, or both Japanese and Western businessmen dressed in subdued suits of black or gray wool. Only a few of the more obviously affluent merchants preferred the robelike garments she had learned were called kimonos, made of crimson, yellow and indigo silk richly embroidered with gold and silver threads. Along with the vibrant banners advertising wares and the displays of goods artfully arranged on outdoor counters, they transformed the street into a colorful open-air market.

A babble of voices in at least a dozen languages rose on every side. Two textile dealers, one Japanese and the other Prussian, were managing to communicate in a medley of

Portuguese and Dutch while striking a deal in Mexican piastres.

Nearby, a wizened Oriental gentleman gestured toward the display of fine porcelain outside his shop as he extolled its virtues in mingled English and French. His audience, consisting mainly of American buyers from California and New York, rapidly converted his asking price into their gold dollars.

The sale seemed about to be made, when a Canadian complicated the matter by offering to trade a scale model of a steam engine. As the jinrikisha turned a corner, Erin looked back to see the entire group locked in intense, multilingual bargaining.

"I could never have imagined such a place," she murmured dazedly. "Does anyone manage to do anything here besides conduct business?"

No sooner were the words out than it became eminently clear that the largely male population of Yokohama did find some opportunity for recreation. The jinrikisha sped past a row of buildings whose outer walls were made of translucent paper screens pushed aside to reveal gaudily painted women of all sizes and nationalities, who beckoned encouragingly to potential customers passing on the street.

Erin could not quite suppress a blush, which did not go unnoticed by the young lieutenant. He hastened to assure both her and Mrs. Gilhoully that the less reputable quarter of the city was being rapidly taken over by more respectable institutions. As an example, he cited the nearby cricket field, Masonic lodge, and the headquarters of the Chamber of Commerce.

"We hope to have a public garden quite soon," he added, "and possibly gaslighting for the major streets."

This evidence of progress was met with mixed feelings. Mrs. Gilhoully was all for it; Erin was less enthused. Much as she tried to keep her mind on the single goal of saving her family's business, she also hoped to discover something of the Japan beyond the foreign enclave of Yokohama. There simply had to be more to it than gentlemen in frock coats playing cricket in the shadow of the Masons.

According to Mr. C. P. Hodgson's absorbing book, Japan had existed as a national entity for thousands of years. It had a mysterious, complex, and, until recently, completely self-sufficient culture. Out there beyond the edges of the port and the swamp bordering it, there was an entire kingdom waiting to be discovered. To have come so far and not at least get a glimpse of it would be frustrating indeed.

But for the moment at least, she had to be content with far more restricted surroundings. The road they were traveling along became steadily broader and better paved as it moved away from the dock area. Trees painted with the vibrant oranges and reds of fall brightened the stolid stone edifices lining the avenue. On one side stood the Japanese government buildings—the customhouse, police headquarters and post office. On the other were arrayed the consular buildings of the Western nations.

The American consulate was smaller and less ornate than its British counterpart next door, but it was still a welcome sight. Erin glanced up at it, thinking about the man she was here to meet.

Early that morning, when fine curls of mist still clung to the pine-fringed hills surrounding the city, she had sent a note to Mr. Ned Carmody, a junior diplomatic official she had been informed might be of some assistance to her. He responded with an invitation to visit his office that afternoon to discuss her business in Yokohama.

Accepting Meg's announcement that she would remain outside to keep an eye on the luggage, Erin went in search of the man she hoped was going to make her journey worthwhile.

Mr. Carmody occupied a small cubicle toward the back of the consular building. He was sitting stooped over his desk when Erin entered. Autumn sunlight filtering in through the large windows shone on thinning blond hair, pale features and a somber black wool cutaway.

After waiting politely for several moments to have her presence recognized, she took a step forward. When Mr. Carmody still did not react, her suspicions were aroused. Only to be quickly confirmed as a healthy snore reached her. The junior consular official was fast asleep.

Biting her lip, Erin debated what to do. She had no wish to be impolite, but neither did she particularly want to wait until he chose to rejoin the living. The precarious pile of books and newspapers on the corner of his desk provided the solution. A brush of her hand was enough to topple them to the floor and startle Mr. Carmody back to consciousness.

"Whazza . . . ! Oh . . . blasted books . . ." He began to rise, only to become aware of the lovely vision standing before him. "*I say . . .*" Reddening slightly, he was nonetheless able to take command of himself with a speed that spoke well for his future as a diplomat, provided of course that he did not customarily sleep on the job. "I beg your pardon, miss. I must have nodded off. Excuse me just a moment while I tidy up this mess."

Erin felt it only right that she should help him. But Mr. Carmody would not hear of it. He quickly straightened the books and papers, assisted her into a chair, buttoned his jacket and sat down at his desk prepared to listen attentively to anything she might have to say.

But when she introduced herself, his professional composure wavered. *"You're* Miss Conroy? Whom I had the note from this morning? Forgive me, but I had no idea you were so young or so . . ." His Adam's apple bobbed as he swallowed hard. "What I mean is, I had presumed you were a lady of more advanced years."

"I rather think it is fortunate I am not," Erin said with just a hint of tartness, "since I have a difficult task ahead of me."

"Ah . . . yes . . . that's right, you did say something in your note about wanting to reclaim several ships belonging to your family."

"Belonging to me now. I inherited them from my uncle, who died last year. After the payment of his debts, they are all that is left of what was once a proud shipping line. I am determined to reclaim them." More softly she added, "If, that is, I can find out where they are."

"Oh, that's no problem. I know exactly where they are." He consulted a sheet of paper extracted from the pile in front of him. "Both the *Nantucket Moon* and the *Emerald Isle* are in dry dock not far from here, at Captain Davin's boatyard."

The relieved smile that had begun to light Erin's sapphire eyes vanished. She leaned forward slightly in her chair, her hands suddenly clenched in her lap. "Captain D-Davin . . . ?"

"That's right. Storm Davin. Late of the Confederate Navy. Not that I suppose it matters this far from home. He's holding them as collateral against debts incurred by the owner." Mr. Carmody frowned slightly. "I guess with your uncle gone, that means you."

Erin forced herself to take several deep breaths before responding. Every ounce of pride she possessed was concentrated on masking the shock Mr. Carmody had so unwittingly given her. "I don't understand . . . the last I had heard, the ships were in the possession of the Black Star Trading Company. There was no mention of a Captain Davin."

The young diplomat shrugged. "Storm Davin *is* the Black Star Trading Company. He started it upon his arrival in Japan a little more than a year ago. I understand he was practically penniless when he left the United States directly after the South's defeat." An envious sigh escaped him. "Of course, he's anything but that now. Black Star Trading controls a large portion of the Japanese market. Captain Davin has made himself a very wealthy and powerful man." Gallantly he added, "But I'm sure you'll have no difficulty with him. After all, who wouldn't wish to help a lovely young lady?"

Erin could think of at least one man who would not fall all over himself to do so; Storm Davin himself. But she resisted the urge to say so. Instead, she concentrated on marshaling her resources to face this new and potentially disastrous situation.

"Does the captain know of my arrival?"

"Why, yes, as a matter of fact he does. After I received your note this morning, I got in touch to tell him when you would be coming by the consulate." Mr. Carmody consulted his pocket watch. With no hint of the impact his words would have, he announced, "He should be here at any moment."

"*Here! But why*?" Erin jumped up, unable any longer to hide her dismay. "He must be a very busy man, and this can't be particularly important to him, so why would he . . . ?" She broke off, aware that her host was gazing at her in surprise.

"Miss Conroy . . . is there some reason you are concerned about meeting Captain Davin? I assure you there is no cause to be. Granted, he has a well-deserved reputation for being rather ruthless, but I'm certain you will get along famously."

Erin opened her mouth to try to make some reasonable response, only to be abruptly forestalled by a low, mocking drawl from the vicinity of the doorway.

"Oh, I'm certain we will, too. After all, Miss Conroy and I are . . . old friends."

No amount of self-discipline could prevent the ashen pall that spread over her cheeks. The voice was the same that had haunted her dreams for eight long years. She had only to close her eyes to see again every detail of the fateful night when a dashing Southern officer had dared to ask a beautiful but spoiled Yankee belle to forget the turmoil that was about to explode around them and become his wife.

The young girl who had so unfeelingly refused him was gone forever, and not at all lamented. But memories remained to tear at her heart and fill her mind with thoughts of what might have been.

Valiantly she told herself dreams had no place in the harsh reality confronting her. Taking a deep breath, she turned to face him.

In the first instant that their eyes met, she was struck by two things: he had changed a great deal and he had changed not at all.

Beneath thick chestnut hair just long enough to curl slightly, the broad planes and hollows of his face stood out in sharp relief. His pewter eyes were deepset under slanted brows. There was a certain grace about the long, aquiline shape of his nose and the mouth whose contained sensuality she had never before fully appreciated. His chin was broad and firm, free of the beard and mustache many men favored. To keep it that way, he had to shave at least twice a day. Although it was barely afternoon, bristly shadows lay against his burnished skin.

His big, hard body remained the epitome of male strength and virility. A perfectly tailored dark blue frock coat stretched tautly over his powerful shoulders and chest. Beneath it, she caught a glimpse of a white linen shirt open at the throat. Matching wool trousers hugged his narrow hips and sinewy thighs before disappearing into highly polished black leather boots.

At thirty-five, he was easily the most compellingly attractive man Erin had ever seen. But there was a cynical gleam in his thick-fringed eyes and a smattering of silver in his glistening hair that bespoke harsh lessons well learned.

An ache rose within her as she studied him. How many times in those violent years had she pictured him wounded or dying? How many times had she searched the columns of names released by the Northern prison camps, praying she would not find his? How many times had she dragged herself wearily out of bed after just a few hours' rest to return to the hospital where she worked in the hope that if he ever needed such care, it would be available?

After the war, she had made discreet inquiries about his whereabouts. In the back of her mind was the thought that she might sometime, somehow encounter him and have an opportunity to undo a small measure of her cruelty. But all she was able to discover was that after returning briefly to his Virginia plantation to find it completely destroyed and his entire family dead, he had vanished from sight.

Suddenly confronted by him, she had to struggle against the desire to go to him at once and offer her woman's softness as comfort for all he had endured.

The disparaging twist of his chiseled mouth made it clear how any such attempt would be received. "I almost failed to recognize you, Erin," he declared. "The last time we met, you were an enticingly pretty sixteen-year-old. But now . . ."

Despite herself, Erin winced. She didn't have to be told that her practical clothing, subdued hairstyle and sedate manner bore no resemblance to the beribboned coquette she had been. But neither was she about to apologize for her appearance. Not when it was the result of experiences that had made her a better person.

"You, on the other hand, look much the same, Captain," she murmured. "Japan seems to agree with you."

He frowned slightly at her formality, but did not attempt to override it. Instead, he sat down and nodded at the bemused Mr. Carmody before returning his attention to her. "I gather you have been apprised of the whereabouts of your ships?"

"Mr. Carmody explained that you are holding them in lieu of debts you claim against Conroy Shipping, but I—"

"Not *claim*," Storm interrupted firmly. "There is no doubt about the liability. Your uncle has had ample opportunity to honor his obligations. He simply has not chosen to. What he expects to gain by sending you on this errand, I hesitate to imagine."

Erin's back stiffened. There was no mistaking his implication. The speculative light in his eyes as he blatantly looked her over made it only too clear. Taking a deep breath, she said, "My uncle is dead, Captain Davin. The ships belong to me now, and I assure you, I have every intention of meeting all *proper* business obligations."

Did she imagine the faintly appreciative smile that vanished almost the instant it appeared? She must have, for there was no hint of approval in his tone. "Ah, yes, you were always one for propriety, weren't you, Erin?"

Refusing to be baited any more than she already had been, she contented herself with a glare. For long moments they stared at each other in uneasy silence.

It was left to Mr. Carmody to put an end to a situation he could not begin to understand but sensed was somehow dangerous.

"Ah . . . Miss Conroy . . . I'm sure you must be eager to get settled in Yokohama before pursuing your business any further. My wife and I would be delighted to have you stay with us."

As Erin began to protest that she could not take advantage of such generosity, he explained, "There really are no suitable accommodations for young ladies in the city, and besides, Elizabeth would never forgive me if I denied her such congenial company. Please say you will accept."

Realizing that it would be churlish to refuse such a sincere invitation, and grateful for the opportunity it afforded her to escape from Storm's unrelenting scrutiny, Erin graciously agreed.

But her relief was short-lived, for as they all rose, he took her hand in his and touched a light kiss to it that seared her even through her glove. "Then I will look forward to seeing you at supper tomorrow evening, Miss Conroy." Glancing over at Carmody, he asked, "That is, if the dinner party you were planning is still on?"

"Why, yes, of course," their host assured them. "Miss Conroy is undoubtedly eager to make the acquaintance of Yokohama society, and I'm sure everyone will be equally happy to meet her."

"Undoubtedly," Storm murmured, so softly that only Erin could hear him. "They have no idea what a treacherous creature you are. But I harbor no such illusions. Be assured, my dear, I will enjoy exacting payment for every cent of your debt!"

With that he was gone, leaving a confounded young woman to wonder how she was ever going to cope with the man whose love she had once so thoughtlessly spurned and who now saw her as an enemy to be crushed.

Chapter Two

"I'VE PRESSED THE ROYAL-BLUE SILK, MISS
Erin," Meg announced in that no-nonsense
tone that meant she was not prepared to tolerate disagreement. "And I've been able to secure several petticoat hoops from Miss Elizabeth's maid, so you have no excuse for not
being properly dressed this evening."

Erin sighed. She climbed reluctantly out of
the bath and wrapped herself in a large towel
before sitting down at the dressing table to
brush the tangles from her waist-length ebony
hair. The oval face that stared back at her
from the mirror was pale but composed. It
revealed little of the turmoil of her thoughts.
But she knew perfectly well that her apparent
composure didn't fool the sharp-eyed Irishwoman.

Meg was certainly aware that Storm's presence at the consulate had upset her young mistress and that she had conflicting feelings about seeing him again at that evening's dinner. Wisely she had decided to provide the best possible weapons to bolster Erin's flagging self-confidence and inspire her courage.

"That bath should have perked you up," she murmured soothingly. "It's been a long time since we've seen that much fresh water."

Erin nodded absently. She had enjoyed her leisurely soak in the privacy of her large bedroom in the Carmody house, but it had failed to ease much of her anxiety. Nor did the fact that much of the strangeness she naturally felt upon arrival in a new country was dispelled by Ned and Elizabeth, who already seemed like friends.

"Of course you will stay with us," the petite Mrs. Carmody had announced when Erin delicately suggested that if her arrival at all inconvenienced the household, she and Mrs. Gilhoully would be perfectly content to stay elsewhere. "I wouldn't dream of passing up the chance of becoming acquainted with one of the few other American ladies in Yokohama."

Elizabeth laughed warmly, belying the porcelain delicacy of her blond prettiness. "Or at least one of the few that I'm allowed to know about. I declare, Ned seems to think I have to be protected from the very air itself. Just because we've been married only a few weeks, he acts as though he expects me to vanish at any moment."

With her new understanding of what caused the young diplomat's fatigue, Erin took pains to give her host and hostess plenty of time alone. In turn, they seemed concerned that she recover from her journey before attempting to make any headway with the man Elizabeth described as "that very attractive but rather frightening Captain Davin."

Frightening indeed, Erin thought. The moment she imagined facing him again, doubts assailed her.

"Meg . . . do you think the blue silk is really right for this evening? After all, it is cut low on the shoulders and we can't be sure that the ladies here don't dress more modestly."

The motherly woman shook her head firmly. "Do you really think I'd let you wear anything that wasn't ladylike? Heavens, child, you favored more daring gowns when you were sixteen."

That was true. At sixteen she had been the closest thing to wild the staid Conroy family had ever seen. Pampered and indulged from the time she was born, she had taken it as a natural right that young men should flock about her, ready to do her slightest bidding. Other girls had struggled to hide their envy while striving for her friendship. Adults who might have known better forgave her anything simply because she was so lovely.

Until Storm Davin came along. He provoked her, challenged her, and set her afire with longings she had never experienced before. He shook her safe, privileged world to its foundations. She both loved and hated him with all the fervency of her unfledged spirit.

When he asked her to marry him on the eve of war, the hatred won. She had turned on him unrestrainedly, punishing him for all the doubts and insecurities he made her feel, for the sleepless nights she had lain in her bed dreaming of him, for the hot yearnings of her body that left her ashamed—for all that she now understood made her a woman instead of a callow child.

"Perhaps," she murmured, slipping behind the modesty screen. "But it's been so long since I wore the blue silk that I can't even remember how it looks. Are you sure it will do?"

"Absolutely. Besides, it's time you started dressing in something other than those serge skirts and cotton blouses. Now that we're off that leaky rowboat, you can start looking like a lady again."

Erin grinned at the description of the *Pacific Star* that would have made Captain Foster apoplectic. Dropping the towel, she slid a white linen chemise over her head. Trimmed with lace, the almost sheer garment skimmed lightly over her body.

Through it, the outline of her high, full

breasts was clearly visible, as were the velvet smoothness of her nipples, the narrow indentation of her waist, the ripe swell of her hips and the shadowy triangle of dark curls that lay between her long, tapered legs.

The chemise ended at mid-thigh and was tucked into lacy pantaloons tied beneath her knees. When she stepped out from behind the modesty screen, Meg was waiting with a whalebone corselet and a stern look.

"Into this, now, and no arguments. You can't wear the blue silk without it."

"Then I'll find something else. I'm not sitting through any dinner party unable to breathe properly."

She tried to dodge out of the way but was too slow. Before she could move, Meg had dropped the garment over her head and begun tightening the laces.

"Don't exaggerate," the Irishwoman ordered. "I'm only fastening it the least little bit."

"Then what do I need it for if you're only going to . . . *Ouch!* Not so tight!"

"You haven't been in one of these things for so long that you've forgotten what tight really is."

"I'm getting my memory refreshed in a hurry," Erin muttered as she felt her already small waist clinched in even further and her full breasts thrust upward. They swelled precipitously over the lacy top of her chemise.

"I'm going to pop right out of that dress, and it'll be all your fault."

Meg didn't deign to answer. She merely gave the laces a final tug, secured them in a double bow and dropped the petticoats supported by steel hoops over Erin's head.

Gathering up the gown, she waited while her young mistress grudgingly slipped her feet into delicate blue silk slippers, then cautioned, "Stand still. I declare, you wiggle more than you did when you were a little girl."

"And you're bossier. I don't know why I put up with you."

The older woman laughed, not at all fooled by her young mistress's tartness. "Because you like a challenge." Hesitating a moment, she took it upon herself to add, "That's why none of those men who came calling on you in Boston got very far, nor the dozen or so on this trip who would have liked to court you. You need someone who has as much spirit and gumption as you do, someone who won't make everything so easy for you that you end up bored."

Their eyes met in the mirror. Erin silently admitted the truth of what Meg said, but she couldn't resist a quiet demurral. "It hasn't always been easy."

Sharp black eyes softened. "I know, child. You've had a hard road these last few years. Few men could have taken on what you did, much less a young girl. But that's all the more reason to be thinking about finding someone to share your life with. Neither the good nor the bad is meant to be faced alone."

Erin could hardly deny the wisdom of that. Next to remorse over what she had done to Storm, loneliness was often the harshest burden she had to bear. What worried her most was that she was becoming accustomed to it. She feared she was losing not simply the need to open her life to another person, but perhaps also the capacity.

Seeing Storm again had brought home to her just how much she had missed in all the years since they were last together. Her cheeks grew pink as she caught herself wondering if there might still be a chance for the happiness he had once offered.

Meg mistook the faint blush for her reaction to the sight of herself in the gown. Cut low on her shoulders, the royal-blue silk highlighted the sapphire radiance of her eyes, the graceful curve of her throat and the alabaster purity of her skin at the swell of her full breasts.

It was a dress another woman would have felt compelled to wear with an elaborate necklace. Erin had long since sold all her jewelry, but she did not feel the lack. The bell-shaped sleeves, snug-fitting bodice, tapered waist and wide, graceful skirt were all the ornament she needed.

When Meg had fashioned her hair into a soft chignon, and handed her the shawl, fan and gloves that completed the outfit, the older woman pronounced herself satisfied. "I told you this was the right dress. You've never looked better."

Gazing at herself in the mirror, Erin couldn't doubt her. The restrained young woman Storm had seen in the consular office was gone. In her place stood a vibrant beauty whose glowing eyes, perfect skin, sensual mouth and slender but curvaceous body were undeniably provocative.

No outward sign hinted at her hard-won maturity. She looked utterly free and untroubled, as though she had never known a difficult moment in her life. Even as she regretted the impression she was bound to give, Erin was glad that her vulnerability was well hidden. She could not bear to let Storm see how greatly he affected her and how susceptible she would be to anything he might choose to do.

Giving Meg a quick peck on the cheek, she moved carefully from the room, mindful of the need to keep her voluminous skirt from wrinkling, and made her way downstairs.

The Carmody home, situated in the most genteel quarter of Yokohama, had nothing in common with the marvelous descriptions she had read of Japanese housing. It was, however, a very nice wood-and-brick row house of the type favored in Boston, New York and San Francisco.

The rooms were large and high-ceilinged, but rather overfurnished for Erin's taste. She realized she was out of step with fashion when she longed for open space and bare walls. Ned and Elizabeth clearly had no such desires. A full complement of fringed Oriental rugs, potted palms, ornately framed etchings, solid mahogany and oak tables, upholstered chairs and elaborately carved sofas graced each room.

The effect was a bit stifling but still comfortable. Erin was feeling more relaxed as she entered the parlor. Her host and hostess were already there preparing to meet their guests. They were seated so closely together on the couch that she felt reluctant to disturb them, but both rose the instant they caught sight of her.

"How lovely you look," Elizabeth exclaimed. No hint of envy marred the compliment, nor was there any reason why it should. The young Mrs. Carmody was a vision of dainty prettiness.

She was dressed in a gown of pale mauve satin trimmed with lace at the elbows and bodice. Her golden blond hair was swept up in a braided coil that gave her added height while emphasizing the purity of her delicate features.

Green eyes sparkled with happiness as she gazed up at her adoring husband, looking very elegant in a black cutaway, matching trousers and a sparkling white linen shirt lightly ruffled down the front.

"Indeed you do," Ned avowed. "You are only the second lady of my acquaintance to recover so quickly from such an arduous journey." Beaming a loving smile at his wife, he explained, "Elizabeth was the first."

"Your hospitality has a great deal to do with it," Erin assured them both. "I must thank you again for making me feel so much at home."

"I just hope you plan to stay a long time," her hostess said. "I'm so eager for all the news from the States."

Erin attempted to satisfy her curiosity as they settled down in the parlor. Both the Carmodys had left the United States before the end of the Civil War, Ned on his own to take up his present consular posting and Elizabeth to be with her parents, who were missionaries. They had naturally heard about the last days of the war and the murder of President Lincoln, but they knew little of what had happened afterward.

Briefly Erin described the progress of Reconstruction, which, despite what she considered to be Andrew Johnson's valiant effort to carry out the policies of his martyred predecessor, was being controlled by vengeful factions determined to strip the South of all remaining wealth.

As she did so, she was relieved to note that neither Carmody took it at all amiss that she should be interested in political events. Too many people she had met seemed to think a woman should have no thoughts in her head beyond how to set a gracious table and sew a fine seam.

But perhaps because of Ned's diplomatic calling and Elizabeth's upbringing by parents who struggled daily against the abuses of worldly power, both were every bit as eager for information as she herself.

As the rigorously correct Japanese houseman stepped into the parlor to announce that the first guests had arrived, they were forced to break off their discussion, but with promises to continue later.

Erin instantly found herself the center of attention as she was introduced to a Dutch couple involved in the silk trade, a British officer and his wife, who were with the local garrison, a beautiful Portuguese lady and her French husband, who owned a porcelain-exporting firm, and half a dozen others who helped form the small but growing international community that had sprung up over the last decade or so since Admiral Perry "persuaded" the shogun to end Japan's centuries of isolation.

But as absorbing as she found the fascinating men and women who had chosen to make their home in such an exotic corner of the world, her attention kept wandering. Over and over she caught herself glancing toward the door.

As she stood chatting with the French porcelain dealer, a sudden sense of unease swept over her. In the midst of laughing at his very amusing story, she stiffened instinctively.

Storm stood beneath the arch that separated the entry hall from the parlor. The houseman had just relieved him of his black silk cloak. Riveted to every detail of his appearance, Erin could not help but notice that he scorned the customary top hat. The thick pelt of his chestnut hair was left unencumbered. It glistened in the light from the gas-lamp chandelier as he glanced around at the assemblage.

She felt rather than saw his gaze settle on her. Refusing to look at him any more than she already had, Erin struggled to give all her attention to the charming Frenchman. But the image of Storm standing lean and hard in his perfectly tailored black evening clothes kept intruding on her thoughts.

When she had known him eight years before, his overwhelming strength and virility had affected even her immature sensibilities. But now she was deluged by emotions she could hardly credit. Even as she told herself she had the best possible reasons to be wary of him, she could not deny the compelling attraction he had for her.

Beneath the thin silk of her gown, her heart began to beat alarmingly. A spark flared deep within her, struck flame and spread almost instantly. Waves of warmth swept over her, making her legs feel weak and bringing a tremor to her hands.

"Mam'selle, are you all right?" Monsieur Chantail inquired solicitously. "Perhaps your journey was more tiring than you realize. Pray allow me to fetch you a *restoratif.*"

"I hardly think that's necessary," a deep voice interjected. "Miss Conroy looks as though a breath of fresh air would do her far more good."

The Frenchman frowned at the sudden interruption, but endeavored to maintain the facade of courtesy so essential to such gatherings. "Ah, of course, that is an excellent suggestion, Captain Davin." Holding out his arm, he smiled encouragingly. "If you would care to accompany me, my dear . . ."

She did not, but there seemed to be no way to refuse without being rude. As she reconciled herself to the need to accept, rescue came from an unexpected quarter.

"A word of caution, Chantail," Storm murmured. "Your lovely Rosalinda is looking this way, and doesn't appear at all pleased by what she sees."

The Frenchman paled. He found it prudent to avoid provoking his wife's ire. Besides being able to deliver a formidable tongue-lashing at the slightest hint that she did not possess his utter loyalty and devotion, she also controlled the purse strings.

Sighing regretfully, he bowed to Erin, nodded grudgingly at the tall, sardonic man beside her and departed.

The moment he was gone, Storm took her arm. His touch was light but unmistakably firm. It burned through her gown, searing the soft skin beneath. She tried to pull away, only to stop as his hold inexorbably tightened. Without hurting her in the least, he still made it clear that unless she wished to create a scene that would embarrass the Carmodys, she would do as he wished.

"I suggest we step into the garden. There are some plantings you really should see."

This last was said for the benefit of the sharp-eared matrons standing nearby. They smiled benignly as he ushered a silently fuming Erin through the tall French doors and into the walled enclosure behind the house.

Barely had they gotten a few yards along the gravel path than she yanked her arm free and turned to face him. "Your manners leave a great deal wanting, Captain. Perhaps you would be good enough to explain to me why you felt it necessary to intrude on my conversation with Monsieur Chantail?"

Storm didn't answer at once. He simply stared down at her from his foot or so advantage in height. His expression seemed compounded of equal amounts of amusement and annoyance, with a touch of something that looked remarkably like tenderness. But that couldn't be. She knew better than anyone that he didn't have the slightest reason to feel tenderly toward her, no matter what dreams she might cherish to the contrary.

"Chantail fancies himself a connoisseur of beautiful women. A certain sense of male camaraderie compelled me to stop him from wandering into your web, where you would undoubtedly have made short work of him."

Though she suspected she would greatly regret the question, Erin could not stop herself from asking, "What harm do you think I could possibly do him?"

"A great deal. Unless I gravely misunderstand the situation, you are in dire financial straits. Your privileged existence must be teetering on the edge of penury. Since you were willing to come all this way to try to prevent that disaster, I can only conclude you would not be averse to going a bit further."

He shrugged derisively. "But you really must select a more worthy target. The judicious use of your charms might well convince Chantail to give you the money you need. But that would do you no good, for his wife controls their finances."

Erin gasped, hardly believing that he would insult her in such a way. For all practical purposes, he had accused her of being willing to prostitute herself. The accusation was so unjustified as to border on unreality.

"What do you imagine gives you the right to

speak to me in such a vile way? You know nothing about me, yet you presume to judge me contemptibly."

Anger and hurt flushed her cheeks. Her sapphire eyes gleamed coldly. She knew she should walk away from him right then, seek the shelter of the house and do her best to stay out of his range of fire for the rest of the evening. But something kept her rooted to the spot.

Hard on the heels of her outrage came sadness. The gulf between them was even greater than she had thought. They might have been strangers for all the understanding between them.

Her head drooped slightly as she murmured, "I remember you as an honorable man, Storm. What happened to that sense of rightness that was once the keystone of your life?"

The moment the words were said, she thought she had gone too far. Beneath his rugged tan, he paled. His quicksilver eyes glowed with a molten light. A jagged pulse began to beat in the corded column of his bronzed throat.

"You are a strange one to speak of honor," he muttered. "I remember you had little. Your idea of what was right went no further than the indulgence of your every whim."

His mouth tightened as he took a step toward her. "Do you ever regret leading so shallow an existence, Erin? Have you ever felt the slightest desire to give something to the world, instead of merely taking?"

Burnished hands fastened on her arms beneath the bell-shaped sleeves. "Even the butterfly contributes more than sheer beauty. Nature has a use for her beyond the purely ornamental. And for you, too, though you may not have deigned to admit it yet."

Frightened by the implacable determination she sensed in him, Erin tried to take a step back. But he would not permit it. Slowly, inexorably, he drew her to him.

A piercing sensation—half fear, half longing —shot through her. Her lips parted on a soundless gasp.

That was all the invitation he needed. A rueful laugh escaped him, as though in acknowledgment of his own susceptibility, before his tall head swooped and his mouth claimed hers with completeness that drove the breath from her.

If she had allowed herself to wonder what it would be like to kiss him again, she would have expected roughness and complete disregard for her feelings in place of the erotic skill that had once so confused her. But Storm's touch was not at all like that. Even as he burned with long-denied hunger, he seemed determined she would acknowledge that her need was no less than his.

One big hand cupped the back of her head as the other slipped tantalizingly along the curve of her waist upward toward the swelling fullness of her breast. When he felt the tremor that ran through her, his mouth gentled. Light, teasing kisses nibbled at her lips, making her yearn for more.

No thought of resistance remained in her as his tongue coaxingly traced the sensitive inner flesh of her mouth before plunging with rapierlike swiftness past the barrier of her small white teeth to fully possess the moist cavern within.

A purely female moan sounded deep inside her as he provoked her to join in an erotic duel that made her limp with yearning. When his mouth left hers to trail feather-light kisses down the silken column of her throat, she could not resist the need to return the pleasure he was giving her.

Her hands stroked the wide, hard sweep of his shoulders, relishing how his powerful muscles tensed beneath her gentle touch. Gaining courage, she let her fingers caress the nape of his neck, where chestnut curls brushed the crisp collar of his shirt.

The essentially male scent of shaving soap, fine wool and tobacco filled her breath. She savored the faintly salty taste of his skin as her tongue darted out along the slight roughness of his jaw.

Years before when he kissed her, she had always sensed he was holding something back, as though understanding that she was not ready to know the full force of his masculinity. Now he felt no such restraint. His mouth left off its enticing torment of her throat and returned to close on hers with captivating ferocity.

Again his tongue plunged deeply, licking at the roof of her mouth and the delicate inner flesh of her cheeks until she writhed against him. A guttural sound of satisfaction rippled from him.

"You're like fire . . . sweet, entrancing fire. . . ."

The blaze threatened to consume them both. Only the steely strength of Storm's arms enabled her to stand upright. She was turning to shimmering light inside, all form and substance dissolving in the heat of desire more intense than she had ever imagined could exist.

Not until his hands slipped below her waist to urge her even closer did the impossibility of the situation reach them. The metal hoops blocked the contact they both so ardently wanted, while forcing them to recall their surroundings.

At any moment one of the other guests might stroll into the garden, or the houseman might come to announce dinner. Erin flushed as she thought how her reputation would be shredded if she was found in such compromising circumstances.

For herself, she did not particularly care. She had long since stopped living her life according to the dictates of others. But she was not about to subject Elizabeth and Ned to such embarrassment.

"Let me go, Storm." The breathless pleading of her voice made her sound as though she was asking for something quite different. But she could not help that. At all cost, she had to put some distance between them.

When he did not comply immediately, she raised her fists, pushing against the wall of his chest. The gesture was singularly futile. Though her active life and excellent health made her unusually strong for a woman, she could no more force him to move than she could shift a mountain.

Seizing both her hands in one of his, he compelled her to admit the uselessness of her effort. She resisted until she realized that he was carefully controlling his great strength to keep from hurting her. Somehow, his consideration made it possible for her to yield. When she once again stood quietly beneath his touch, he tipped back her chin and coaxed her into meeting his gaze.

His rugged features were oddly gentle as he murmured, "You can't escape me, Erin. What started between us eight years ago is going to be concluded before very much longer. Somehow, I always suspected it would be. . . ."

"H-how? You couldn't have known we would ever see each other again."

"I never thought about it one way or the

other. You were always meant to be mine, and now you can't run from that anymore."

The implacable determination she could feel coursing through him frightened her almost as much as the clamoring of her own body. A creature she had never sensed before was stirring to life within her. An ancient female being driven solely by the most primitive desires.

The clarity of her own needs shocked her. For the first time in her twenty-four years, she understood exactly what it meant to yearn for total physical union with a man. Not just any man. Only Storm. Only his possession could satisfy the burning need that raged within her.

But what for her would be the supreme act of love would be for him no more than a weapon for achieving vengeance. How could she look into his eyes afterward and see the callous satisfaction she was certain would be there?

As badly as she wanted to make up for what she had done to him, she was not willing to destroy herself in the process. And destruction would surely be the bitter fruit of their joining. A fruit she would need to taste only once to know the full venom of despair.

Unaware that the tear-filled glow of her eyes had made his throat tighten painfully, she yanked herself away from him. Caught unawares, he did not move quickly enough to hold her. A soft curse broke from him as her silk-shod feet darted along the gravel path back to the house.

Yet even as she fled, she sensed that he was right. There would be no escape.

Chapter Three

AFTER THE TUMULTUOUS SCENE IN THE GAR-
den, Erin seriously doubted she would be able
to face Storm at dinner. She retreated to her
room, grateful that Meg was elsewhere. Seated at the dressing table, she struggled to
restore some degree of order to hair tangled by
long, lean fingers.

The flushed cheeks, glowing eyes and pout-
ing lips she saw in her mirror made her
tremble. She looked like exactly what she
was—a woman who had been thoroughly
kissed and was ready for a great deal more.

Sighing, she dabbed on a bit of rice powder,
with little or no effect, and tried to regain her
composure sufficiently to go back downstairs.
Her absence was certain to be noted before
much longer.

Elizabeth would be bound to come looking

for her. She was far too conscientious a hostess not to try to find out what was wrong. Erin dreaded the thought of her questions even more than the knowing glances she was likely to receive from the other guests.

Years before, when working in the military hospital, she had learned to control her emotions under even the most trying circumstances. Then it had been a matter of ignoring the horror and grief she felt when confronted by the mutilated bodies of young men so that she might provide them with the calm, reasoned care on which their survival depended.

Now it was her own survival she suspected lay in doubt. She had fought long and hard to become the woman she was; she wasn't about to give herself up without an all-out struggle.

Resolved that if she was to have any hope of winning the battle Storm seemed determined to wage, she had to prevent him from discovering how easily he could hurt her, Erin took a firm grip on her courage.

Standing up, she smoothed the wrinkles from her skirt, cast a final glance in the mirror and left the room.

Downstairs, the party was in full swing. Several more guests had arrived, with the result that the parlor could no longer hold them all and they spilled out into the entryway. No one seemed to mind. True devotees of social convention did not last long in the cosmopolitan colony perched on the edge of an ancient, mysterious empire.

In one way or another, all the men and women gathered under the Carmodys' roof were adventurers. They were sufficiently brave or restless or desperate to cut loose from the secure world they had known and dare something vastly different. Yet they still carried the outward trappings of that world along with them, like some huge tortoise weighed down by potted palms and overstuffed chairs.

Erin smiled a bit wanly at the comparison. She wasn't traveling very lightly herself, not when she took into account the burden of her emotions. It might be wise to give some thought to strengthening her shell before it caved in under the load.

In the whirl of being introduced to the late arrivals and doing her best to satisfy their curiosity about recent events at home, she did not see Storm again until dinner was announced. Hoping that she would be able to avoid him in the crowd, she was dismayed when he appeared next to her.

Pride demanded that she meet his gaze unflinchingly. When she did so, Erin's eyes widened with surprise. Far from the contempt she had feared she would see, he was looking at her with an odd mixture of tenderness and contrition.

As he offered his arm, he smiled down at her wryly. "Shall we?"

Distracted by his sudden change of mood, Erin responded automatically. Her hand rested on the sleeve of his impeccably tailored frockcoat as they joined the couples streaming into the dining room.

In a single concession to their exotic surroundings, the long table covered by a snow-white linen cloth was set with fine porcelain in vivid blues and reds. Crystal wine and water glasses gleamed beneath gaslit chandeliers.

Japanese servants dressed in Western-style uniforms were carrying in tureens of soup, baskets of fresh fruit and rolls, platters of beef and vegetables, and numerous other courses. But it was on the array of knives, forks and spoons that Erin's attention focused. She could not restrain a soft gasp when she realized that despite the Carmodys' modest origins, they were all made of gold.

Beside her, Storm caught her surprise and explained, "Not too long ago, the exchange rate for precious metals was far lower here than anywhere in the West. Many Europeans and Americans made huge profits by importing silver and trading it for gold. No one will ever know for sure how much left the country, but when the Japanese realized how they were being taken advantage of, they clamped down on the practice. Not in time, however, to keep from losing a vast amount of their national wealth and inspiring more than a little bitterness against the foreign 'barbarians,' who, ever since, have been considered less than honorable."

"Does that mean they aren't all as eager to

trade with us as the merchants I saw in the streets yesterday?" Erin asked with some surprise. That possibility had not occurred to her.

With what she belatedly recognized as a subtle form of condescension, she had presumed the Japanese would all be delighted to finally be in contact with the more technologically advanced and enlightened West.

As he held out her chair, Storm nodded. "It certainly does. We face a great deal of opposition from some very powerful corners."

"That's putting it mildly," snorted the English naval officer on Erin's other side. "This whole blasted country's about to erupt over exactly that issue."

"You're exaggerating," Madame Chantail insisted. She shrugged her creamy white shoulders and smiled prettily. "All the Japanese I know are very happy to have us here."

"Then you have been most fortunate in your acquaintances," the Dutch silk merchant pointed out from across the table. "I had the bad luck to be on a ship in Yokohama harbor back in sixty-three when those Choshu fanatics attacked. None of us expected to escape with our lives."

"Choshu?" Erin echoed, her eyes wide with surprise. "What is that?"

"A fiefdom in western Japan," Storm said. "Its daimyo—in Europe I suppose he would be an earl or duke—was the first to object to the Western presence in Japan. But he is no longer alone. Since then, several other powerful lords have asked the shogun to get rid of us, or at least impose greater restrictions than we currently face."

"But I thought the Japanese nobility made a great deal of money from trade with the West," Erin said. "Why would they wish to stop it?"

The Dutchman set down his wineglass and sighed resignedly. "Like everything else in the world, it all comes down to greed. Those lords closest to the shogun do very well. Those he does not favor get nothing. So they are naturally resentful."

"Don't forget," interjected Monsieur Chantail, "that there are some Japanese who are opposed to dealing with us simply because they think their country should have been left to itself in the splendid isolation it enjoyed for centuries. They have not yet come to terms with the fact that your Admiral Perry forced them to accede to his demands by virtue of superior military strength."

"The treaty to open Japan wasn't forced on anyone," Ned objected, though only mildly. "It was negotiated to the mutual satisfaction of all parties."

Storm shook his head derisively. "'Negotiated' is a strange word to use for what went on in the shadow of Perry's cannons. Which, I might add, he took pains to show off to the Japanese before the talks ever began."

"Are you suggesting he should not have?" Madame Chantail twitted. "But then, none of us—including you, Mr. Davin—would be making so much marvelous money."

Inclining his head graciously, he sent the lady a smile which made Erin's stomach clench. "You are quite right, madame. We must never lose sight of exactly what we are doing here."

Raising a glass half-full of blood-red burgundy, he offered a toast. "To the Japan Trade. May it prove as profitable as the Triangle Trade that preceded it, but not, in the end, as costly."

"Should I conclude from that," the Dutchman inquired perceptively when the toast was drunk, "that you are a Southerner?"

"I was," Storm corrected quietly. "And I saw to my own misfortune how the search for profits can end in violence. The Northern shipowners were quite content to supply the vessels that hauled slaves and cotton, so long as their pockets were well-lined. Their conscience was conveniently quiet until they found easier ways to make money. Not until then did they discover their sense of outrage or their desire to stamp out the system they had helped to create."

"That is an enormous oversimplification of a very complex problem," Erin objected. Though her family had never dealt in the slave trade, she was still stung by the suggestion that their business was somehow founded on hypocrisy. "There was far more at stake than simply money."

"You think so?" Storm asked skeptically. "Oh, there was a smokescreen of morality thrown up around what was really a brutal effort to stamp out a way of life incompatible with what Northern industrialists visualize for the country's future. I suppose there might actually have been a few people who believed the dogma they spouted. But there's precious little evidence of them now."

"It's true Reconstruction has spawned enormous abuses," Erin admitted. "But that doesn't change the fact that there are well-meaning people on both sides who are trying to make things better."

"Spare me the wages of good intentions," he chided. "I'll take plain old selfishness and greed anytime."

Frustrated by his cynicism, she responded more sharply than she intended, "Yes, I'm sure you would. After all, if you claim people aren't really capable of anything other than self-interest, then you automatically excuse the same deficiency in yourself."

His slate-gray eyes narrowed slightly as he toyed with the beef on his plate. "Actually, I don't do anything of the sort. When a man reaches a certain level of achievement, he has no need for excuses. Other people will be more than happy to make them for him."

"Such cynicism!" Elizabeth protested, apparently not at all put out by a conversation that went far beyond the usual dinner-table chitchat. "You would have us believe you care for nothing but your profits, Mr. Davin. When in fact it is well known that you are one of the most outspoken proponents of fairer dealings with the Japanese. Unless I am very much mistaken, you have gone so far as to spend a large amount of money on housing for the workers at your boatyard, as well as a school and medical clinic that is open to everyone in Yokohama, most particularly all the Japanese not served by Western establishments."

Her emerald eyes twinkled as she observed the effect this revelation had. Storm looked decidedly put out at having his good works discussed. Erin was at once surprised and relieved. So the mask of cynicism was only that—a facade behind which the man she remembered might still exist.

Nothing could prevent the warm smile that curved her generous mouth. Storm returned it with a glare. In an attempt to undo the damage done by his overly knowledgeable hostess, he said, "It is simply a matter of good business. People who have decent shelter and medical care, and who don't have to worry about what their children are doing all day, tend to work more efficiently."

"Whatever the reason," the Dutchman muttered, "you aren't doing the rest of us any favors. That sort of coddling sets a bad example."

Erin tensed slightly, believing that Storm would respond angrily. But instead he merely brushed the comment aside. "I am perfectly content with both the manner in which I conduct my business and the profits it produces. Therefore, I see no reason to change."

"Not even when you know you are creating problems for your associates?" Monsieur Chantail asked waspishly.

"Associates? I have none. If you mean that I should feel some sense of fellowship with other Americans and Europeans simply by virtue of their presence here, I cannot agree. That would be a singularly narrow-minded approach to a highly complex situation."

Meeting Erin's eyes, he added, "I have already been accused of oversimplification once tonight. Pray do not attempt to lead me into the same trap again."

Heedless of curious looks from the other guests, who were hardly unaware of the tension rippling between the compellingly attractive pair, they gazed at each other silently for long moments. A world of communication passed between them, but it consisted solely of questions.

For Erin, there was a gathering sense of bewilderment. Who exactly was this alarming yet somehow vulnerable man? A man who had triumphed over tragedy beyond most people's comprehension, yet claimed to have learned nothing of mercy or compassion in the process. A man who showed none of the narrow-mindedness others exhibited, but who carried a legacy of hate he was not willing to relinquish. A man who could make her desire the most fundamental reaffirmation of life possible at the same time that he threatened her destruction.

Even as those thoughts and more whirled through her mind, Storm was fighting his own inner battle. He wanted to believe she was the same shallow, selfish girl he had foolishly loved eight years before, if only to justify his desire to punish her. But he could not ignore the unmistakable signs of great change.

Not only was she far lovelier in a somehow haunted, wistful way that made his heart ache, but she was also much more sensitive to other people than he would have thought possible. He was torn between the urge to strip away all her defenses and discover what lay beneath, and the need to protect her even from himself.

With the ruthless honesty that marked his life, he recognized the conflict he faced. But he also saw that time was on his side. She would have to come to him about the ships. He would see to it that she had no other alternative if she wanted to save her company. And when she did . . .

His thoughts trailed off, replaced by images that made him regret they were both seated at a dinner table surrounded by other people. A slight smile curved his hard mouth. Soon enough he would have her alone.

Beneath the quicksilver fire of his gaze, Erin shivered. She had a fairly good idea of what was going through his mind. She supposed she should be outraged. But much as she tried, she couldn't manage it. A growing sense of anticipation blocked out even the most basic instincts for survival.

Storm had spoken of a trap. She could almost feel the sharp teeth of it about to close on her.

Chapter Four

"THE BOATYARD?" MEG REPEATED DISBELIEV-
ingly. She sat bolt upright in the bed, resisting
Erin's efforts to calm her. "You're not seriously planning to go there alone? What will people think?"

"I'm afraid I can't be too concerned about
that. For three days now I've tried to convince
Captain Davin to meet with me here or at the
consulate. He insists he will speak to me
about the ships only if I go to his office."

Erin saw no reason to mention that Storm
had suggested an alternative to the boatyard,
namely his home on the outskirts of Yokohama. The amusement her vehement refusal
had provoked still rankled.

"If you could only wait a bit," Meg suggested, "until this blasted ankle is better. Then I
could go with you."

"You know perfectly well the doctor said you mustn't try to get around for at least a few weeks. That was a bad fall you took."

"My own darned foolishness. If I'd been looking where I was going . . ."

"Anyone can have an accident," Erin reminded her gently. The memory of finding Meg crumpled at the bottom of the stairs still made her tremble. She could hardly bear to think of how close her dearly loved friend had come to something truly serious.

With deliberate lightness she added, "Heaven knows, you saw me through more than a few bumps and scrapes. The least I can do is make sure you follow the doctor's instructions and stay in bed."

"I don't suppose a bit of rest would hurt me," Meg allowed grudgingly. "But I'm sure to be up and about in a couple of days."

Erin was privately certain that would not be the case, but she wasn't about to say so. Instead, she pointed out, "The easier you take things, the faster you'll get better."

"I suppose. . . ." Gazing at her worriedly, Meg asked, "Do you really have to go see him now?"

"I'm afraid so. There's no reason to think Captain Davin will become more reasonable over time. In fact, the contrary is more likely. But besides that, I can't simply sit here twiddling my thumbs and waiting for someone else to solve my problems."

A rueful smile lit the Irishwoman's black

eyes. "No, that wouldn't be like you. You were always a great one for taking the bull by the horns."

"This is more a matter of bearding the lion in his den."

Meg chuckled, but her tone was serious as she asked, "Couldn't you ask Miss Elizabeth to go along with you?"

"I don't think that would be a good idea. Our hostess has been looking a bit green in the mornings and has taken to skipping breakfast."

"You mean . . . ?"

"I suspect so."

An envious sigh escaped Meg. "It wouldn't do you any harm to take a lesson from her."

With some effort, Erin managed a look of pained shock. "Meg Gilhoully, I'm surprised at you. Suggesting such a thing to an unmarried lady."

"Get away with you! You know perfectly well what I'm saying. It's time you settled down."

"I have one or two things to do first. Getting my ships back, for a start, and then building the Conroy line up again. That's going to take all my time and energy for quite a while."

Meg didn't appear impressed. "The finest shipping line in the world won't keep you warm at night or fill your arms with children. You'd do well to remember that."

Erin did, but she wasn't about to admit it. Instead, she talked awhile longer with the older woman, to be certain she was calmed down enough not to try to leap out of bed and go chasing after her. Meg had dozed off by the time she let herself out of the room and made her way quietly downstairs.

Ned and Elizabeth had thoughtfully put a carriage at her disposal. The groom who hitched up the horses for her looked doubtful when he realized she intended to drive herself, but his concern faded at the sight of her able hands on the reins.

The soft gray-blue cashmere day dress she wore beneath a white fringed shawl was warm enough for the pleasantly cool fall day. Its high collar and long sleeves were secured by rows of tiny buttons that matched the fabric's delicate shade. The tapered bodice and narrow waist did not disguise the perfection of her figure, but neither did they unduly emphasize it.

The silken mass of her ebony hair was caught up in a loose coil on the crown of her head. Feathery wisps caressed her smooth brow and slender throat. As usual, she had eschewed a bonnet, preferring to feel the sun and wind against her skin.

Despite the seriousness of the task ahead of her, she could not deny a sense of pleasure in the day. It stemmed in part from the sparkling perfection of the cobalt sky reflected in the tranquil water lapping at the shore, the vibrant colors of the goods on display in the market, the exotic scents and sounds that reached her as she carefully maneuvered the phaeton through the crowd of shoppers and browsers.

But her enjoyment also came in large measure from the knowledge that she was doing something to improve her situation. As she had told Meg, action of any kind was better than waiting.

Drawing up in front of the headquarters of the Black Star Trading Company, she sat for a moment absorbing the sheer size and scope of Storm's business. Besides the boatyard itself, with wharves and dry docks that could hold at least four times the half-dozen ships then in port, there were also several large warehouses, the quarters for workers that Elizabeth had spoken of, and a mess hall.

At the center of it all stood a two-story wooden building with a sloping roof covered in red tile. Above its door was the discreet sign "S. Davin, Offices" with what she presumed to be its equivalent written below in Japanese.

Gathering up her skirts, Erin stepped lightly from the carriage. In the process she exposed several inches of black high-button boots covering trim ankles and the white lace fringe of her petticoat. Several seamen working nearby whistled appreciatively.

Ignoring them, she secured the horses to a post in front of the building and went quickly inside. The entire first floor was taken up by a single large room housing innumerable bookkeepers' desks, stools and wooden filing cabinets. The walls were covered by maps of the world with the sea lanes marked and charts indicating the approximate positions of various ships, notations about the cargo they carried, and their anticipated arrival dates. Sturdy brass and copper gas lamps were positioned at intervals around the room. Several more hung from the rafters. In each corner, a potbellied stove stood ready for use as soon as the weather turned truly cold.

It was all very orderly and impressive, hinting at far-flung activities generating considerable amounts of capital. Storm had obviously accomplished a great deal since he arrived in Japan. But then, with nothing to return to, he must have been driven beyond all limits to create a new life for himself or perish in the attempt.

Erin's crystal blue eyes darkened. This was not the time to be thinking of what he had suffered. Reminding herself that she was here for only one purpose, to get her ships back, she looked around for someone who could direct her to him.

A slightly built Japanese man wearing a dark blue kimono and a green eyeshade glanced up from the wooden frame strung with beads on which he appeared to be counting. "You wish something, miss?"

"Yes, I would like to see Captain Davin. Is he here?"

"Upstairs, miss. Does he expect you?"

"I think so. He . . . suggested I should come here."

The man nodded, apparently finding nothing odd in the idea that an unaccompanied young woman would call on his employer at his place of business. With the quiet courtesy that was an innate part of the Japanese character, he said, "I will take you up, if you like."

Though she appreciated the offer, Erin shook her head. The pile of papers, ink pots and pens on his desk made it clear he was very busy. "Thank you, but I'm sure I can find the way."

As she climbed the steep steps to the second floor, the seriousness of what she was doing engulfed her. If she failed to convince Storm to return the ships, the entire purpose of her trip to Japan would be for naught.

But even beyond that, she realized that she had never quite managed to give up the dream that someday their love might have another chance. What happened in the next few days would show whether or not that dream had any basis in reality.

She took a deep breath, trying to still the painful racing of her heart. Her palms were damp against the railing and she trembled slightly. Anxiety rippled through her as she reached the head of the stairs and came face to face with Storm.

He stood in front of a large table spread

with documents. Sunlight streaming in the window behind him turned his hair to burnished gold and softened the harsh lines of his face.

The white silk shirt he wore was open at the collar to reveal the beginnings of a thick mat of hair covering his powerful chest. Snug black pants tapered from his narrow hips down long, sinewy legs. His feet were planted slightly apart, his arms braced on either side of the paper he was studying.

Another Japanese man, apparently his assistant, was jotting down instructions in a notebook. The flow of orders broke off abruptly when she appeared.

Storm glanced up, catching sight of her at the head of the stairs. A light flared in his quicksilver eyes, only to disappear instantly as his gaze became hooded.

The impact of his presence made Erin forget her resolve to be cool and calm. Her shoulders tensed and a soft flutter spread outward from her stomach. Anything she might have said vanished from her mind. It was all she could do to take the last step up to him.

"That will be all for right now, Ito. We'll finish later." His voice was low and matter-of-fact. Erin envied his composure. She concentrated even more on hiding the effect he had on her.

The Japanese bowed and left. She was hardly aware of his departure. All her attention was focused on Storm. It took her a moment to realize he meant for her to sit down in the chair he had just pulled out.

Her soft wool skirt brushed against him. The contact, slight as it was, startled them both. He moved away quickly, taking a seat across the table from her.

Leaning back in the big chair, he studied her over the bridge of his lean fingers pressed together. "You surprise me. I didn't think you would come here."

More calmly than she would have thought possible, Erin asked, "What choice did I have?"

His eyes narrowed slightly at her matter-of-factness. "None. But I thought it would take you a while longer to acknowledge that."

"There is no point in delaying what we both know has to be faced. You are holding my ships. I want them back."

A lock of hair fell across his forehead. He brushed it away impatiently. "You don't believe in wasting any time, do you?"

"I have none to waste. Unless I can outfit the ships soon and take a cargo back to the States, my family's business will cease to exist."

A sardonic smile curved the mouth she could still feel against her own. "Would that be so terrible?"

"Not to you, certainly. But I'm proud of the

heritage passed down to me by generations of Conroys. I don't want to lose it all simply because my uncle was a profligate wastrel."

"That would be Uncle Bates, wouldn't it? I seem to remember him. He drank quite a bit."

Erin inclined her head slightly. She hoped that her silence would discourage him from pursuing recollections of their earlier acquaintance. It did not.

"How did Bates end up running the line? Your father was in charge when the war began."

"Papa . . . died in a carriage accident shortly after Bull Run. My mother was with him. She was . . . killed also."

The shock that registered on his tanned features was followed instantly by a softening of his expression. He straightened in the chair, studying her intently. "I'm sorry, Erin. I know you loved them both."

Inexplicably, those simple words were enough to make her throat tighten with unshed tears. The rigorous self-discipline she had imposed on herself ever since her parents' death abruptly threatened to crack. She looked away hastily. "Thank you. But that was a long time ago. I would prefer to speak of more immediate concerns."

Storm was not fooled by her apparent coolness. Though he was tempted in view of her obvious unease to let the topic drop, he found that he could not. The urge to know more about her life during the years they were apart was irresistible.

His gaze settled on her slender, ringless hands folded neatly in her lap. On impulse, he asked, "How is it you have not married?"

He hardly expected her to admit what he now believed to be the truth, namely that she had cared for him too much to be attracted to another man. But neither was he quite prepared for her emotionless explanation. "I've been very busy."

Storm laughed. "At what? The war put a halt to the social round. How did you manage to keep so thoroughly occupied that you had no time for your admirers? And don't try to tell me there weren't any," he insisted when she tried to interrupt. "I'll wager more than a few of Boston's upstanding young men tried to convince you to marry them before they went off to battle the traitorous rebs."

Erin's eyes darkened to the consistency of a storm-tossed sea. His mocking tone pierced her fragile defenses, making her acutely aware of her vulnerability. Holding her head up proudly, she said, "You forget, I was in mourning."

He flushed slightly at what should have been an unnecessary reminder, but did not relent. "Even so, there must have been some who tried to convince you to overlook the usual proprieties because of the war."

Unwelcome recollections flowed through her. He was right about that. A few of the young men who had flocked around her were genuinely concerned about her being left alone at such a time, with her family led by a drunkard uncle. Most of them simply desired her and hoped to take advantage of a particularly susceptible time in her life.

She had dealt gently with the first group and sent the second packing without a second thought. Her refusal to take shelter from her grief in the arms of a husband was the first true sign of her maturity.

But it was also at least in part a recognition of the fact that Storm still stood between her and any other man. Beside him, everyone else faded into insignificance.

In an attempt to cut short what was rapidly becoming a very difficult conversation, she said, "Does it matter whether or not I received proposals? We have already determined that I never married."

"I suppose not. But I can't help but be curious. You are the last woman I would ever have thought of as a candidate for spinsterhood."

The word stung, as it was no doubt intended to. Erin bit her lip, determined not to let him provoke her into a confrontation that she had little chance of winning.

Instead, she said, "And you are the last man I would have suspected of trying to evade an issue. Or is there some reason you don't want me to discover what has happened to my ships while in your care?"

The pewter sheen of his gaze warned her she was treading perilously close to the edge. He was not a man to tolerate any questioning of his honor. With difficulty he controlled what she did not doubt would have been a scathing retort.

"Your ships have been as well-cared-for as my own. But I think you should see that for yourself."

Standing, he held out his hand. Erin hesitated before taking it. His skin was pleasantly warm against hers, his fingers strong and firm. She remembered the way they felt tangling in her hair, caressing the nape of her neck, sliding along her shoulders and arms to the curve of her waist.

The staircase was so narrow that only one of them could go down it at a time. She used that as an excuse to break the contact between them. When they reached the bottom, both her hands were occupied holding her skirt above the sawdust-strewn floor.

Storm did not miss her unease. He smiled sardonically before saying a few words in Japanese to the employee who stepped forward to open the door for them. The man looked surprised, or at least as close to it as rigorous courtesy allowed.

Erin was tempted to ask him what he had

said, but she wasn't sure she would appreciate the answer. Resolutely silent, she accompanied him along the wooden-plank sidewalk laid over the dirt-packed roads that ran between the docks and warehouses.

The sailors who had greeted her when she arrived stepped aside to let them pass. There were no further comments about her beauty and desirability. Instead, their eyes were kept rigorously averted and their mouths firmly closed. More than one looked appalled at the thought that they might have offended a woman in whom their employer had a proprietary interest.

The dry docks in which ships were stored and repaired lay off to the side beyond the wharves. Erin had no difficulty picking out the *Nantucket Moon* and *Emerald Isle*.

Both clipper ships sat well out of the water, their hulls scraped free of barnacles, the seams sealed with waterproof tar. The decks gleamed with fresh varnish, and all brass and copper implements shone in the sunlight. Even the wheelhouses were newly whitewashed, as though awaiting the arrival of their captains.

The ships' fluid lines, proud masts and graceful prows fairly begged to slide back into the sea and feel the wind once more fill their sails.

Storm's claim was correct: they had clearly received meticulous care. Turning to him, she could not deny her appreciation. "I had no hope of finding them in such good condition. Please forgive me for doubting you."

Embarrassed by her gratitude, he attempted to shrug it off. "There's no need for that. I understand you were worried." Sternly he added, "As you should be. Just because they're in good shape doesn't mean you're going to sail them out of here anytime soon. There's still the matter of your uncle's debt to settle."

"I realize that," Erin murmured, her elation fading as the truth of what he said reached her. She raised her head, facing him squarely. "You have yet to convince me there is a debt."

"Is that so? Then how do you account for the shipments your firm received from here last year? If you paid any attention at all to the business, and I am beginning to suspect that you did, you must know your funds were exhausted. Without borrowed money, you couldn't have financed the cargoes."

Erin didn't attempt to repudiate that, but neither did she accept it as proof of his right. "But you didn't lend us any funds. If you had, I would have found some record. Even failing that, if we had borrowed from you, you would certainly have been aware that my uncle was running the company, yet you admitted yourself you didn't know that. So I don't see how you can claim to hold a lien on my ships."

"Not even if I tell you that the company your uncle did borrow from went bankrupt a few months ago, leaving among its debts a substantial liability to the Black Star Trading Company? I agreed to take control of property it was holding in lieu of the payments."

Erin stared up at him bleakly. What he said had the ring of truth. It explained why she had not known the fate of the ships, and why he had indirectly become involved in the affairs of the company run by a family he must despise.

Worse yet, it was a sufficiently complicated legal tangle to leave little hope of her being able to regain the ships anytime soon. At least not without Storm's approval.

"I see. . . . That does make it clearer."

"I'm so glad you think so."

"There is no reason to be disdainful. I simply wanted to understand how you came into this."

As he looked down at her from his great height, a hint of gentleness softened his features. "And now you do?"

Erin nodded mutely. The heady impact of his nearness made it difficult for her to speak. For a moment she was struck by the absurdity of their situation. Why were they standing on a dock surrounded by other people, locked in a discussion of business, when all they both wanted was to be alone together to revel in the passions that threatened to break free at any moment?

She retreated from that thought as she

might from an inferno threatening to engulf her. Sternly she lectured herself on the importance of establishing realistic objectives and sticking to them.

Not for her the dreamy-eyed visions of a handsome prince on a white charger who would whisk her away to eternal happiness. She was an intelligent, sensible woman prepared to make her own way in the world. *If she could get her ships back.*

Taking a deep breath, she managed to keep her voice steady. "I would like to know the extent of the debt so that I can arrange to repay you."

Storm studied her for a moment before apparently deciding not to delay any longer in letting her know the full magnitude of the problem she faced. Quietly he said, "Twelve thousand dollars."

Erin gasped. All the color fled from her face. Her small hands clenched at her sides, the knuckles white. *"T-twelve thousand . . . ?"*

He might have said a million, so far beyond her reach did it appear. Once, long ago, when she had no comprehension of what it took to earn even a single dollar, she would not have been more than mildly impressed by such a sum.

But now that she had an all-too-acute understanding of the sheer toil that went into acquiring so much money, she felt stunned.

The meager resources she had managed to protect from her uncle's profligate spending would not stretch to cover half the debt.

There seemed only one course left open to her. As calmly as she could, she said, "I will have to ask you to wait for payment until I can get cargoes back to the States and sell them. From what I have learned, a single voyage by the *Nantucket Moon* and *Emerald Isle* should yield profits to more than cover the amount owed to you."

Masking her apprehension, she glanced up at him. His reaction was not encouraging. A frown darkened the eyes that a few moments before had looked as bright as a moon-washed sea.

"Do you have any idea of the enormity of what you are proposing to do? The wiliest traders in the world are flocking to Japan. They snap up all the best products for distribution through well-oiled networks of middlemen and merchants. Compared to them, you are a rank amateur. Yet you seriously believe you can secure not one cargo, but two, get them safely back to the United States and sell them profitably? All while I wait patiently for my money? That is a risk I see no reason to run. Not when I can outfit the ships myself much more easily."

His doubt in her abilities was hardly surprising, but it still hurt. As did his presumption that she was so gullible as to believe everything he had just said.

"If you can make use of the ships, why haven't you already done so instead of letting them sit in dry dock?"

A glimmer of respect flitted across his features, only to be instantly quenched. "Because I didn't take possession of them until a few weeks ago and they needed extensive repairs. I will admit that if you chose to make an issue of whether or not I have a right to use the ships, you could delay my doing so. However, I honestly see no alternative."

"But there is. Let me carry out my original plan. That way we will both benefit."

"Erin, you don't know what you are saying. It is much too difficult."

"For whom?" she demanded, unable to contain her anger any longer. "For the simple-minded child you choose to think me? I have done many things in the last few years which you undoubtedly would not have believed possible. And I will do this as well, with or without your help."

Her vehemence provoked his own ire. For reasons he did not care to explore, the idea of her being completely independent and self-sufficient troubled him.

Driven by the purely male urge to take her down a peg or two, he deliberately taunted her, "Will you? I rather doubt it. However, it will be amusing to watch you try. Just don't look to me for help when you inevitably run into trouble."

Erin bit her lip against the angry retort she

was tempted to hurl at him. Instead, she contented herself with a dignified dismissal. "You are the last man I would ever look to for assistance. But that is beside the point, because I will not need any. Just make sure you continue to care for my ships as well as you have so far, because I intend to sail them out of here before the month is done!"

Without giving him a chance to reply, she turned on her heel and marched down the dock toward her carriage. Storm stared after her in mingled perplexity and admiration.

Never had he encountered such a spirited combination of beauty and intelligence wrapped up in a delightfully feminine package that provoked him to the most unbusinesslike thoughts possible.

Part of him wanted to ruthlessly bend her will to his and force her to yield pliantly to anything he desired. But another, gentler part yearned to protect her from a world he suspected was harsher than she yet realized.

Running a hand through his thick chestnut hair, he sighed deeply. Try though he did, he could not begin to guess which side of him would win.

Chapter Five

"THE DRAFT FROM YOUR BANK IN BOSTON IS perfectly acceptable here," Ned explained, "so you shouldn't have any difficulty doing business." He hesitated a moment before adding, "If you are quite sure that is what you want to do."

"I am," Erin assured him firmly. "I've come ten thousand miles to save my family's ships. No man will stop me now. The sooner I get started, the sooner Mr. Davin will realize that."

Her host cast a worried look at his wife seated beside him on the couch. Elizabeth took the hint and spoke up. "I understand why you are concerned about securing the best possible cargoes, but it might be a good idea to acquire the services of an intermediary to actually do the work for you. Otherwise, you'll have to go through the markets yourself, negotiate with the traders, check out the merchandise, and all sorts of other things."

Erin smiled slightly at her concern. Elizabeth was too polite to say that what she proposed to do was unwomanly, but it was clear her thoughts were tending in that direction. Gently she reminded her, "I won't be doing anything all that different from what you do when you buy goods for your household. Just on a larger scale."

"I suppose . . . but the only people who buy from the same shops as me are other housewives. Not crafty merchants who aren't too particular about how they get the best possible deals."

That was true, Erin admitted silently. She was well aware that her competition would be formidable. Unless she was very careful, she would either miss out on the truly top-quality goods or be forced to pay exorbitant prices that would leave no margin for profit.

"Nonetheless, I must try, for the reasons I have explained."

Both Carmodys were still doubtful, but they made no further effort to dissuade her. Each understood that there was simply too much at stake for her to turn back. ·

With Meg still grudgingly nursing her broken ankle and Elizabeth in the throes of early pregnancy, a fact Ned had shyly announced at dinner the previous night, Erin opted to go to market alone. In the last few days, she had become quite accustomed to making her way around Yokohama without an escort. So long as she stayed on the main streets and took care not to be out after dark, she felt perfectly safe.

Accordingly, she left the house later that morning, with the intention of stopping at the cloth merchants' first. If she was to have any hope of her goods selling well in the States, silk had to be one of her top concerns. The demand for it seemed to be insatiable, provided the quality was there.

After turning her horse and buggy over to one of the street urchins who for a modest fee promised to keep both safe, she took a few minutes to stroll up and down the street dominated by fabric shops. Several she dismissed immediately as lacking a sufficient selection of goods. Two more were crossed off her mental list because the quality of the fabric on display was clearly inferior. That left half a dozen to choose from, which she thought must certainly be an ample number to afford her the best possible buys.

That confidence was shaken almost the moment she entered the first shop and smiled courteously at the owner. The small, kimono-clad gentleman returned her greeting but did not hide his dismay when she explained the purpose of her visit. Instead of being pleased by a potential customer, he frowned sharply.

"I am not sure I understand. You wish to purchase a large quantity of silk to send back to America?"

"That's right. I am buying cargoes for my two ships and I expect silk to be an important part of them."

"You are buying . . . ?" The somber-faced man shook his head in bewilderment. "*You* own ships?"

Erin stifled a sigh. She had expected some surprise at a woman involved in a business usually reserved to men. But the silk merchant's shock made her wonder if she had underestimated the magnitude of what she was attempting. Summoning patience she did not truly feel, she explained, "Yes, I own two clipper ships which are presently in Yokohama. I want them to return soon to America, with cargoes. So I would like to see the goods you have to offer to determine whether or not I am interested in buying them."

Instead of accepting her quiet request with the eagerness a merchant might be expected to demonstrate, the man continued to stare at her stubbornly. "You have money?"

"Of course I do. I would hardly be trying to buy goods without it."

"You show me."

That was going too far. Did he truly believe she had wandered into the store simply to waste his time? "I will do no such thing, at least until I am certain you have something I wish to buy."

To her astonishment, the man shook his head. "Not good enough. If you wish to see my silks, you must show me money first. Then I will consider doing business with you. But," he cautioned sternly, "I will not bargain with a woman. I will say price, you say yes or no. Nothing else."

"But that's absurd! You can't expect me to take the first price you offer, when everyone bargains."

"Not with a woman. I would lose face."

"Face? What is that?"

The man sighed exaggeratedly, coming as close to outright rudeness as anyone Erin had yet encountered in a land which seemed devoted to rigorous courtesy. "Pride," he explained grudgingly. "Honor. Women do not know of such things, but they are all-important to men. I will not lose face just to do business with you."

"I see . . ." Erin said slowly, although she most certainly did not. "Perhaps it would be better if I took my business elsewhere." To add emphasis to her words, she turned in the direction of the door.

She had thought the merchant would relent when he realized she intended to leave, but instead he merely shrugged. "Go, then, but do not expect to find any difference elsewhere. Face the same for every man."

Surely he wasn't right, Erin thought after she had stifled the angry retort that sprang to her lips and let herself out of the shop. Just because one silk dealer was doing so well that he could turn away business did not mean that others were equally arrogant.

Or did it? At the next shop, no request was made to see her money. She was merely told in no uncertain terms that the owner would not do business with women and was ushered out. Her next stop was equally unrewarding. There she was simply ignored until she finally gave up and left.

Back outside on the narrow wood-plank walkway, Erin struggled to keep her temper in check. Getting angry would serve no purpose. She needed all her wits to confront this unexpected problem. How could she hope to secure cargoes for the *Nantucket Moon* and the *Emerald Isle* if no one would sell her goods? It didn't seem to matter that she had the money to pay for them. The Japanese she had spoken with so far that morning were adamant in their refusal to deal with a woman on anything approaching equitable terms. And her pride—not to mention her pocketbook—made it impossible for her to accept anything less.

Aware that she was becoming the subject of unwanted attention by standing alone outside the row of stores, Erin looked around for some place where she might sit down for a few minutes to think over her predicament. A small, not particularly clean tearoom across the street seemed her only alternative. Lifting her skirt clear of the mud, she crossed the road in between heavily loaded wagons, speedy carriages and riders on horseback who seemed disinclined to give way to anyone.

A soft groan of disappointment escaped her when she realized upon closer inspection that it would not be wise for her to enter the tearoom after all. It was jammed with large, boisterous men who clearly preferred the fast-flowing whiskey to any milder beverage. Several turned as she peered in the door. Their reception left no doubt that were she so foolish as to venture inside, she would be caught in a situation from which there might well be no escape.

Backing out hastily, Erin continued to make her way along the street. Her feet were beginning to hurt and she could no longer deny that she was feeling decidedly discouraged. But determination stiffened her spine. She would hardly be worthy of her seafaring forebears if she let just a few disappointments throw her off course.

Perhaps the silk merchants would not do business with her, perhaps she would have to spend some of her small cache of funds to hire an intermediary to deal with them. But there were other shops along the street selling other types of goods. Perhaps she would have better luck in some of them.

It did not turn out that way. By afternoon, Erin was forced to admit that no Japanese merchant she could find was willing to negotiate with a woman. In store after store, the response was the same. Either they would not talk with her at all or they would simply quote an outrageous price for their goods and leave it to her to decline.

Frustration gave way to anger and finally to deadening weariness. But she could not afford to relax. Like the men in the tearoom, too many of those she passed on the narrow walkways made it clear they would like to know her better. Though she prided herself on being neither fainthearted nor prissy, some of the suggestions they made caused her face to flame. Despite her fatigue, she walked faster while debating whether or not she should give up for the day and return to the Carmodys'.

The decision was not yet made when a disturbance up ahead brought her to a sudden stop. At first, she had difficulty determining what she was seeing. In the midst of the genial chaos that was a normal feature of the bustling market, the sight of men arguing did not immediately spell danger.

Only when she realized that their fierce demeanor, bulky armor of interwoven leather and steel strips, horned helmets, and the double swords they wore buckled around their waists marked them as samurai did she feel the first stirrings of concern. In the back of her mind, she remembered hearing that such men followed a rigorous code of honor and discipline. They rarely gave the slightest evidence of their feelings, but when they did, the repercussions were likely to be severe.

Certainly the other people in the marketplace thought so. In the space of seconds, the packed street emptied. Shop owners rushed to yank merchandise from the outside display tables and slam down heavy shutters over doors and windows. Wagons and buggies vanished around corners at top speed, their drivers heedless of the bundles that went flying off them. Top-hatted shipowners, kimono-clad merchants, bewhiskered sailors, all fled. Only the samurai remained, now clearly divided into two sides, with each hurling taunts at the other.

Erin instinctively pressed back against the nearest wall. She had no idea what was happening or how grave the danger might truly be. But she could not ignore the all-pervasive sense of fear that swept the street from one end to the other.

Frozen by mingled terror and bewilderment, she stood without moving until the sudden clang of steel and the shouts of men intent on battle woke her to the full extent of her peril. By then it was too late. All the shop doors were securely bolted, the windows barred. There was no place to hide, nowhere to run. She could do nothing but shrink farther back against the wall, praying she would not be seen.

At first, it seemed that her prayer would be answered. The warriors were too intent on each other to notice her. Hideous shouts reverberated off the walls of the surrounding buildings as razor-sharp weapons slashed through the air. The men moved in what almost appeared to be a choreographed dance of death. The steps were slower and more formalized than the way she imagined Westerners might fight, but the results were the same.

If the wounded hoped for any mercy, they did not show it. A scream caught in Erin's throat as she saw a young samurai, bleeding heavily from the chest, laugh disdainfully at his opponent before hurling himself directly onto his blade. That the man appeared to die instantly was slight consolation. Her stomach whirled sickly as she turned away, pressing her face into the rough wooden wall.

Even that small motion was a mistake. While she stood perfectly still, her brown linen skirt and jacket blended into her surroundings just enough to make her unnoticeable to the struggling warriors. But when she moved, sunlight caught the pearly opalescence of her skin and the rich ebony sheen of her hair.

Without taking his attention from the man he was about to kill, a blood-spattered samurai noted the presence of one of the hated foreigners who had come to defile his nation. The fact that she was a woman daring to be in the streets alone only increased his rage. A savage smile twisted his lean mouth between the draped ends of his narrow mustache. Abruptly dispatching his opponent, he moved toward her.

Erin saw him coming. She recognized the implacable intent stamped on his lean features. His dark, seething eyes held not even the faintest suggestion of humanity or compassion. Whatever tenderness he might be capable of in different circumstances was burned out of him by sheer blood lust. Not for an instant did she harbor the hope that he would spare her.

Throughout the long, bitter years of the Civil War, she had faced death many times, but never directly. Always before, she had fought to keep others alive. Now, abruptly confronted by her own mortality, she had no idea of what to do.

Only one thing seemed clear—the desperate need to escape. She turned to run, only to realize at once that there was no place to go. Both ends of the street were blocked off by fighting samurai. Already several shops were on fire, acrid smoke from the blazes spreading like a living stain against the cobalt sky. Bodies of both Japanese and Westerners unlucky enough to be caught by the murdering band littered the muddy road. A few were still moaning, but most did not move at all.

Far off in the distance she could hear the trumpet blast of the British cavalry unit which formed the major part of the Western enclave's defense. But she nurtured no hope that they would reach her in time. Long before they arrived, the samurai's deadly blade would have claimed her life.

But not without a struggle. Perhaps his code of honor called for people to submit to death stoically, but hers did not. She would do everything possible to stay alive, no matter how futile the effort might seem.

Lifting her skirts, she attempted to dart past him, only to have her path effectively blocked by a slight motion of his sword arm. His sardonic laugh and the gleam of white teeth against his sallow skin made it clear what he thought of her efforts. Again the blade hissed through the air, almost but not quite touching her body.

He's playing with me, like a great cat with a helpless mouse. I'm not even human to him.

That knowledge seared away her terror, replacing it with sheer, unmitigated rage. Mindlessly angry at such callous brutality that affronted her most fundamental sense of decency, she lost all thought for her own safety. The rage she had heard soldiers speak of but had never really credited swept over her in full force, enabling her to act with speed and strength far beyond her normal capacities.

Again she tried to dart past the samurai, and this time she almost succeeded. Despite the hampering weight of her clothes and the shaking of her limbs, she might have made it were it not for his superbly conditioned reflexes. As his blade rose once more to stop her, she thought she caught the faintest gleam of admiration in his hooded eyes.

The look was gone the instant it appeared. He muttered something harsh in his own language and took several purposeful steps toward her. Erin needed no translation to understand that he was tired of the game. Other, more worthy foes awaited his attention. He would dispatch her quickly and be done with it.

A sob tore from her throat, a desperate acknowledgment of what she could no longer deny. She stood absolutely still in the bright sunlight, watching the downward slash of the blade, thinking of Storm and all the stupid things that had kept them apart.

What a strange place to die, on a cluttered street ten thousand miles from home, killed by a man whose motivations she would never know. There was so much she regretted, so much she still wanted to do. No time left. No time. . . .

The world narrowed down to a single heartbeat. The rush of blood through her body blocked out all other sounds. The air, sour with the smell of smoke, seemed to have turned into a heavy curtain through which everything moved in excruciatingly slow motion.

Far in the back of her mind, someone screamed. The cry of lament and outrage went on and on, until she thought it must surely split her skull. She felt herself drawing inward, tighter and tighter, into a coiled spring ready to launch itself forth the moment the way was open.

With almost objective calm, she saw the instrument of her death come closer and closer, cleaving the air as easily as it would her body. She could feel the downward rush of wind before it as though the sword itself was breathing. The man who held it faded into insignificance. There was only the burnished metal reflecting the golden sunlight, the last breath filling her lungs, the final gathering in of everything she was and had hoped to be.

Her eyes snapped shut, seeking the darkness in the instant before it became eternal. Frozen in a second torn out of time, she waited . . . waited . . . Someone screamed. Not her. A harsh, guttural sound raw with surprise. The iron stench of blood filled her breath. So much blood.

Her eyelids trembled, opened gingerly, only to close again at once. She swayed weakly, overcome by the sight before her. The samurai was sprawled on the ground, his arms and legs thrown out, his sword still grasped in one hand. Several feet of muddy roadway lay between the bleeding stump of his neck and his head. His helmet was still in place, shielding sightless eyes that stared up at the sky in silent astonishment.

Bile burned the back of her throat. She put a hand to her mouth and bent forward, but not before her horror-dazed mind registered the identity of the man standing before her.

Storm. And yet not Storm. Stripped of the veneer of civilization she had always sensed was little more than skin deep, he stood there the epitome of male strength and ferocity. A sword much like the dead samurai's own was grasped in his right hand. Another, shorter blade remained strapped around his taut waist.

Soot and blood streaked the rugged features beneath glossy chestnut hair. His eyes glowed like molten silver afire with forces Erin could not begin to imagine. Black trousers clung to long, sinewy legs. A billowing white shirt was open almost to the waist, exposing his massive chest covered by a thick pelt of dark curls glowing with perspiration.

He might have been a marauding pirate bent on plunder instead of the rescuer who had saved her from certain death. As she took a shaky step toward him, her eyes wide with unconscious entreaty, he growled, "You little idiot! What the hell are you doing here?"

Erin opened her mouth to answer him, but no sound emerged. She swallowed painfully and tried again. Still nothing. As the full impact of what she had witnessed, and what had almost happened to her, sank in, she began to tremble. Her body was swept by alternating waves of heat and cold. What little color had remained in her delicate features vanished completely. Against the milky whiteness of her skin, her eyes were huge terror-filled pools. All the blood seemed to rush out of her arms and legs, leaving her barely able to stand.

Without realizing that she did so, she reached out a hand to Storm. He was fading away, becoming less and less distinct with each moment. Or was she the one disappearing? Falling into a whirling vortex of darkness splintered by shards of darting light. Tumbling down a spinning chute to nowhere.

Someone called her name, but Erin did not hear. Merciful unconsciousness seized her as she slipped like a broken flower to the ground at Storm's feet.

Chapter Six

STORM'S FIRST REACTION WAS ASTONISHMENT, plain and simple. Erin Conroy faint? It couldn't happen. Even in her most flirtatious coquette days she had never shown the slightest susceptibility to the vapors. Yet there she lay, white-faced and helpless before him.

Hard on the heels of surprise came outrage at himself. How unfeelingly stupid could he be? She had damn near been killed! Cut in two by that bastard samurai. If it had taken him a moment longer to force his way through the churning mob and reach her . . .

Unable to think of that, Storm took a quick glance around to confirm what he had already suspected: the battle was over. It was safe to give her the attention she needed without further endangering them both.

Sheathing his sword, he lifted her easily.

With Erin cradled tenderly in his arms, he stepped over the body of the man he had slain moments before and strode toward the end of the street where the shattered survivors of the melee were pouring out their stories to horrified cavalrymen who had arrived too late to do more than gather up the dead and succor the injured.

His eyes glittered dangerously as he thought of the army's failure to reach the battle scene in time. But his anger died as he silently acknowledged that the samurai had struck so suddenly there was no opportunity for anyone to truly challenge them.

Settling Erin across the saddle of his big ebony stallion, which was far too well-trained to have made any effort to flee the terrifying scene, he glanced up and down the street.

Most of the bodies were those of merchants unfortunate enough to be caught outside or of the shogun's samurai who were sworn to defend the foreign enclave. But a few, including the man who had attacked Erin, wore the insignialess armor of ronin, renegade samurai without land or leader.

They were among those most bitterly opposed to the "Westernization" of Japan. Several times in the past, ronin had risen up to try to expel the foreigners and return the country to what they believed was a more virtuous past. Each time, the shogun, ruling in the name of the emperor, had managed to throw them off. But this time, Storm wondered if he might not confront more than was immediately apparent.

Perhaps he was being unduly suspicious, but it did not seem impossible that factions who wanted to destroy the shogun himself might make use of the ronin to stir up civil unrest and create a climate of violence in which anything could happen.

Shaking his head, he reminded himself that this was hardly the time for political ruminations. Erin was still unconscious, her slender body pressed against his so intimately that he could not deny its effect. Gazing down at the pale face surrounded by a silken fall of midnight-black hair, he cursed silently.

God, how he wanted her! More than eight years ago when she had rejected him so coldly. More than when he kissed her in the garden during the Carmodys' party and thought his desire might snap all bounds. More even than when she had come to see him at the boatyard and he had caught himself struggling against the almost overwhelming need to help and protect her.

And now he was doing just that. But under circumstances that made it possible to accept what he might otherwise have regarded as weakness on his part.

After all, he could hardly have left her to the samurai, or, having saved her, abandoned her unconscious in the street. The fact that he was taking her to his home meant nothing beyond a simple act of humaneness.

As he reflected on the near-fatal danger she had passed through, his arms tightened around her achingly. Surely she was the most stubborn woman on earth. It wasn't enough that she had braved the perils of a journey that taxed the strength of the most robust man; she had to go on proving herself against challenges she should have never even considered confronting.

This nonsense about outfitting the *Nantucket Moon* and *Emerald Isle* was a case in point. Not for a moment had he believed she meant to go through with it. Her presence in the market indicated just how wrong he could be.

Shaking his head ruefully, Storm urged the stallion to a faster pace. He was becoming more concerned with each passing moment that did not restore her to consciousness. If she had suffered a blow to the head or any other injuries, he wanted to find out about them as quickly as possible.

Reining in before his home some slight distance from the center of Yokohama, he was relieved to see that the serene Japanese-style structure was undamaged.

The high wooden palisade completely surrounding the residence was intact and the barred gate firmly locked. Beyond it lay a meticulously maintained garden set off by scarlet and gold maple trees, softly babbling brooks, lotus-strewn ponds and nests of wild herons and ducks.

In the midst of the bucolic enclave stood the house itself. Two stories tall with polished wood walls and a red tile roof, it nestled harmoniously into its surroundings as though nature itself were responsible for its presence. A large veranda protected by bamboo shades gave way to sliding panels which allowed direct entrance to any of the rooms on the first floor.

Settling Erin on a low wooden bench before the main vestibule, he slipped off her shoes and his own boots, then scooped her up again and headed inside. For once, the spacious, austerely beautiful interior failed to relax him. He was oblivious of the graceful symmetry of paper screen walls, golden mats covering the floors, airy ceilings, natural wood supports and unobtrusive recesses discreetly furnished with choice pieces of artwork.

Entering a chamber he had learned to think of as a bedroom but which bore no resemblance to its Western equivalent, he set Erin down carefully on a straw mat and went over to a low, carved chest hidden away in an alcove. From it he took a thick, fluffy mattress, several blankets and a pillow. When they were spread out on the sleeping platform, they made a more-than-respectable bed.

Erin moaned softly as he lowered her onto it. Her face was as pale as ever and her breathing seemed shallow. Becoming more concerned by the moment, he hurried out of the room to find cool water and towels.

The silence in the rest of the house informed him that his servants were nowhere about. Their absence did not surprise him. Knowing them as well as he did, he understood they must have hurried into town to help the injured. He could only hope none of them were among the victims of the ronin's rampage.

The kitchen was as deserted as the rest of the house. A large, open area surrounded the wood-fired range made of tiles and topped off by a metal funnel that guided the smoke outside. Nearby was the indoor well, a vital part of the facilities, since meticulous cleanliness was maintained at all times. Adjacent to it stood a sink comprising a large water jar and dipper.

Storm used it to fill a porcelain bowl, then grabbed a towel off one of the bamboo racks that held various utensils. Returning to the bedroom, he knelt beside Erin and studied her worriedly.

She didn't seem to have moved since being laid down. When he touched a coolly damp towel to her forehead, she made no response. Lifting the silken fall of her hair out of the way, he gently bathed her face, throat and hands, noting as he did so that she had suffered several scratches and bruises in her effort to escape from the samurai.

Quelling a moment's hesitation, he began to undo the long row of tiny buttons down the front of her dress. Her modesty would have to be sacrificed if he was to discover the extent of her injuries.

Easing the garment from her, he made a determined effort to ignore the pearly opalescence of her skin, the soft swell of her breasts, and the tapered slimness of her waist and hips. Struggling for a physician's objectivity, without a glimmer of success, he drew off her heavy petticoat and stockings, leaving her in only a thin cotton camisole and pantaloons that did little to hide the beauty of her form.

A sheen of perspiration broke out on his broad forehead as he gazed on her loveliness. His impassioned scrutiny missed nothing of the velvety darkness of her nipples showing through the delicate fabric, the slender line of her ribs leading inexorably to the indentation of her navel, the flat plane of her belly, and the shadowed delta beyond.

Cursing softly under his breath, he forced himself to search for injuries without regard to the havoc the touch of her body beneath his hands wreaked on his already fevered senses.

There were several more bruises and abrasions caused by contact with the rough wooden wall against which she had sheltered. But her head, which he checked with special care, showed no bumps or cuts.

Hoping that this meant her faint was merely the result of the terrifying experience she had passed through, he made her as comfortable as possible before settling down to wait for her to return to consciousness.

His vigil did not last long. Barely had he settled on the mat next to her than Erin's eyelids fluttered and she moaned softly. Recollection flowed back into her mind, bringing with it terrifying images of the street littered with bodies, the samurai, the raised sword . . .

She sat up abruptly, her eyes wide with fear. Her gaze locked on Storm, already moving to soothe her. She felt no surprise at his presence, nothing but overwhelming gladness and the need to communicate her relief in the clearest way possible.

Without pausing to think, guided only by instinct, she reached out to him as her soft, moist lips shaped his name.

"Storm . . ."

Steely arms closed around her with infinite gentleness. Cradled against his massive chest, Erin luxuriated in the exquisite sense of safety and care. Enveloped in warmth and strength, she breathed in deeply, savoring the intrinsically male scent of burnished skin, crisp linen and tobacco.

She almost purred with contentment as his big hand tangled in her hair, tilting her head back so that she was forced to meet his quicksilver gaze.

"You gave me a hell of a scare," he muttered thickly, his breath warm against the delicate curve of her cheek.

Incredibly after the terrifying events of barely an hour past, she managed to laugh softly. "I didn't do myself a whole lot of good, either."

"What was Carmody thinking of, to let you go to the market alone?"

"He didn't know there would be trouble. How could he?"

"It's his job to know," Storm insisted. When he calmed down a bit, he might be willing to admit that no member of the diplomatic community could have anticipated the ronin's attack. Even with all his own contacts among the Japanese, Storm himself had not had any hint that it was coming.

But just then he knew only that Erin had been gravely endangered. The knowledge of how close he had come to losing her forever ripped through him. With a low growl, he bent his head, claiming her mouth with fierce demand.

Far from being dismayed by his kiss, she met it with desire every bit as intense as his own. The nearness of death had brought home to her once and for all how much she loved him. All thought of caution, propriety and doubt vanished before the sheer force of her need.

Her lips parted willingly to admit the rousing strokes of his tongue. Arching even closer to him, she teased the silken chestnut curls at the nape of his neck with her fingers as her breasts and hips moved against him heatedly.

"God, Erin, do you know what you're doing to me?"

Not completely, but she wasn't about to admit how innocent she still was. Instead, she gave herself up to a delicious sense of her own womanly power. Dazzled by her ability to move him, she held nothing back. What began simply as a kiss quickly became an erotic duel which neither could lose.

Her breath was coming in ragged pants that matched his own before Storm at last reluctantly raised his head.

"Much more of this," he growled, "and I will be tempted to forget the matter of your debt." Without really intending to do so, but driven by forces he could not begin to understand, he added ominously, "Or perhaps that is what you hoped."

Stung by the utterly unjust accusation, Erin yanked herself out of his arms. Very deliberately she wiped her hand across her mouth in an effort to blot out the lingering taste of him.

Storm scowled at the motion. It was oddly childlike in a way that made him feel more than a bit uncomfortable. Reluctantly he was forced to remember a certain conversation with Meg the night of the Carmody's party when, after having witnessed his encounter with Erin in the garden, the Irishwoman took it upon herself to inform him in no uncertain terms that her young mistress was utterly without experience in such matters.

"She may seem worldly-wise," Meg had warned, "but it's just a pose she's had to adopt to keep people from trying to take advantage of her. Don't be fooled by it, Captain Davin, else you'll be making the biggest mistake of your life. For eight years, that girl's held your memory in her heart. She's been blind to all others. Don't you dare treat her like some . . . some lightskirt!"

He could no longer doubt that Meg's words were true. Erin's passionately innocent response to him had made that clear. His tormenting visions of her with other men were utterly false, as was his belief that she had never really cared for him. Something rare and precious had taken root eight years before. Far from being destroyed over time, it had grown stronger and more vibrant, even as Erin herself had.

The knowledge that she had never betrayed him brought intense relief and delight. But he was also embarassed at not having treated her as he knew he should, and uneasy with his own vulnerability. For the moment, his anxiousness won and he took refuge in scorn.

"Drop the outraged pose, my dear," he advised coldly. "I'm immune to it. You'll have to do quite a bit better if you hope to work your way out of your present predicament."

"What do you mean?" Erin demanded, striving to match his seeming imperviousness.

Storm settled back more comfortably on the mattress, a humorless smile curving the hard mouth that still vividly recalled the yielding touch of her lips.

"I mean that this fiasco in the market today should be enough to convince you of the futility of your efforts to outfit the *Nantucket Moon* and *Emerald Isle*. We can expect normal trade to be upset for some time, at least until the shogun finds out who was responsible and exacts punishment. In the meanwhile, how do you propose to keep me from seizing your ships?"

Erin had no answer. Even without the added complication of violence from some as-yet-unknown source, she had to face the fact that none of the merchants she had approached was willing to do business with her. Without an intermediary, which she really could not afford, she was stymied.

"I don't know . . ." she said slowly, hating herself for having to make that admission. Grief at the thought of losing the ships that were all that remained of her once-proud heritage washed out what little color had returned to her face.

She bent her head, unwilling to see him witness the proof of her defeat. Her hands picked absently at the soft blankets as she waited to hear him gloat.

But whatever pleasure he might feel at her helplessness was never voiced. Instead, after long, seemingly endless moments, he said quietly, "I have an alternative to suggest to you. A way to pay what you owe me at the same time you secure my help in outfitting the ships."

Erin's head snapped back, her eyes widening as she took in his words. Nothing in his manner suggested he was merely toying with her. Rather he looked absolutely serious and almost frighteningly determined.

"How . . . how could I do that?"

His smile widened, the gleam of white teeth against his bronzed skin making him appear almost predatory. Eyes with a hard pewter sheen that revealed nothing roamed over her slowly. He laughed softly at her unavoidable blush, his big hand going out to catch her chin, forcing her to meet his gaze.

"It's very simple, my sweet. All you have to do is agree to live with me."

Chapter Seven

ERIN STARED AT MEG OPENMOUTHED. SHE could hardly credit what she was hearing. Having just finished explaining, with much trepidation, what Storm wanted her to do, she steeled herself for an explosion of righteous outrage. Instead, the older woman merely nodded calmly, her plump face bobbing serenely beneath her ruffled bed cap.

"Yes, dear, I understand. Perhaps that might be for the best."

Erin shook her head dazedly. The terrifying experiences of the day before must have distorted her senses. "B-best . . . ?"

"Of course. Not only will Mr. Davin be able to assist you with your business, but he is also more than capable of assuring your safety. I'll rest much easier at night knowing that you're in such good hands."

Swallowing hastily to keep from choking on her own astonishment, Erin bit back the urge to point out that while Meg might rest easier, she most certainly would not.

The mere thought of what her nights would be like if she accepted his scandalous offer made her tremble with the heady mixture of fear and excitement. There was no room left over for the shame she knew she should be feeling but oddly enough did not.

A true lady, such as she was supposed to be, would never have even considered agreeing to his terms. She would have wrapped herself in the cloak of moral indignation and taken herself off in a huff. So what if the result was the destruction of all her hopes and dreams? At least she would still have had her honor.

Whereas now she would have . . . What? Her expectations were hazy at best. Not for an instant did she doubt that Storm meant to make her his mistress. As innocent as she was, it was impossible to mistake the unrelenting power of his desire for her.

Yet he had somehow managed to convince not only Meg but the Carmodys as well that he and Erin had nothing more than a business relationship which could be best facilitated by her living under his roof.

She longed to know what he had said to them after escorting her home the previous day. Her experiences in the market and afterward had left her weak and shaking, enough so that she could be bullied into going upstairs to lie down.

Almost an hour passed before she heard Storm departing on his big ebony stallion. By then Ned, Elizabeth and Meg herself were all soundly convinced that what they would ordinarily have viewed with shock and dismay was instead an eminently good idea.

Driven to try to discover exactly what he had said to them, she studied Meg carefully. "Are you certain you think this is a good idea?"

The older woman nodded firmly. "Absolutely, especially since I'm finally reconciled to the fact that I won't be able to get around anytime soon. Otherwise, you can be sure I'd insist on looking after you myself."

Meg's sudden willingness to admit the restrictions resulting from her fall was puzzling in itself. But her matter-of-fact acceptance of their impending separation baffled Erin. "You really don't mind staying here without me?"

"Of course I do, but it's still for the best. You'll be busy with your work and I'll be able to give Elizabeth some help getting ready for the baby."

Listening to her, Erin was filled with contradictory feelings. On the one hand, she had to admit to a certain pleasure at the possibility of being out from under the older woman's protective eye. Yet she also felt a bit abandoned, almost as though Meg had inexplicably lost all interest in her and transferred her loyalty to Elizabeth instead.

Telling herself that was nothing short of childish, she went off to consider her predicament in private. Caught up in her thoughts, she missed the tender look in Meg's eyes and the faintly knowing smile that curved the older woman's usually stern mouth.

Seated in the bay window of her room with a view of the formal gardens below, Erin puzzled over why she was on the verge of agreeing to a course of action that barely a few days before would have been unthinkable.

Reluctant though she was to admit it, the answer was all too obvious. She loved Storm. Not even the moral teachings of a lifetime could stand up against that pure, radiant truth. Yet powerful though it was, her love did not blind her to the realities of her situation.

He might well desire her as a woman, but he also meant to prove to them both that he was strong enough to force her to act in a manner that revealed what he believed to be certain less-than-flattering truths about her character.

Eight years before, Storm had decided she was a shallow, selfish girl with no thought for anything but her material comforts. Now he seemed determined to make her admit the correctness of that judgment through her own actions.

Far from despising him for his intentions, she could not deny a certain eagerness to accept the challenge of proving him wrong. Saving the *Nantucket Moon* and the *Emerald Isle* had become merely a side benefit in a far more vital struggle to win, once and for all, the man she could no longer deny held the key to her heart and soul.

Without giving herself any further opportunity to debate the matter, she penned a short message to Ned and Elizabeth. Rationalizing that there was no need for lengthy farewells when they were likely to see each other frequently, she thanked them for their hospitality and their care of Meg. Before her emotions could run away with her, she signed the note and propped it up against the gas lamp on her dressing table.

Going over to the closet, she pulled out her trunk and began quickly to pack. Half an hour later a wide-eyed houseman was loading her luggage into the carriage while she straightened her cloak and tried hard to control the frantic beating of her heart.

The boatyard swarmed with activity. Two new ships were in dock, their cargo being off-loaded onto wagons. A long line of crewmen snaked around one of the warehouses as the sailors waited impatiently for their pay, talking loudly of the exotic Oriental delights they intended to sample as soon as they had money in their pockets.

Their ribald suggestions did not penetrate

the haze of Erin's preoccupation as she maneuvered the buggy through the crowd to the main building. Spotting Storm's Japanese assistant out in front, she slipped quickly from the seat and went over to inquire as to his whereabouts.

"Captain Davin is on the wharf, miss. One of the ships that just came in was damaged in a storm last night. He is inspecting it."

Erin hesitated a moment, wondering if she shouldn't simply wait for him in his office. Unsure of how much longer her courage would last, she rejected the idea. If her sudden arrival angered him, so be it. Compared to the risks she was already running, that seemed little enough to worry about.

Oblivious of the sailors' curious looks, she strode purposefully toward the docks, her long skirt swirling around her slender body and her glorious ebony hair gleaming in the sunlight.

When she caught sight of Storm, she stopped, the determination that had propelled her thus far abruptly draining out of her. He had just pulled himself up onto the dock after diving to check on the damage beneath the ship's waterline.

Stripped to the waist, his buckskin trousers clinging to his big, muscular body, he looked like a magnificent bronze sculpture come to life. Diamond droplets shone against his massive shoulders and hair-roughened chest. As he spoke with an older man, he tossed his head back, sending a shower of water from his thick, sun-streaked hair.

Erin took a ragged breath. Panic flared on the edge of her mind. What on earth was she doing? How could she consider agreeing to his demands when she knew she had no defenses against him? To allow him to get any closer to her than he already had would be the height of folly. His uncompromising maleness was an iron-hard wall against which her softness would be battered unmercifully.

She turned shakily, torn between the need to go and the almost intolerable desire to stay. But the decision proved not to be her own. Storm caught sight of her and reacted instantly. He took a quick step forward, his hand lashing out to seize her arm in an implacable grip.

"What a pleasant surprise, Erin. Surely you didn't intend to go off without seeing me after having taken all the trouble to come out here?"

His mocking tone stung her. Lifting her head proudly, she glared at him. "I would hardly wish to be accused of disturbing you when you are so obviously busy."

A rueful grin touched his hard mouth. "You always disturb me. I've given up trying to deny it."

The admission of her ability to unsettle him surprised her. But not the swiftness with which he recovered his equanimity. "Dare I hope that your presence here means you have decided to accept my offer?"

"It might be better termed a demand," Erin said stiffly.

Storm shrugged, his gaze wandering over her so intently that it took all her willpower not to turn away. "Call it what you like. The terms stand. If you have come to try to negotiate a different arrangement, you are wasting your time."

"It never occurred to me to attempt anything so futile. You made your requirements quite clear. However, I do wish to be sure you understand mine."

A quizzical glance prompted her to continue. "If I agree to . . . live with you, you will return my ships to me and facilitate the purchase of cargoes for them. Is that correct?"

"It is."

"When those cargoes are ready, you will make no attempt to prevent either the ships or me from leaving Japan?"

Picking up his shirt, Storm pulled it on before answering. "If that is what you want. You understand, however, that it will take several weeks to purchase the goods you want?"

"Yes, I just wanted to be certain that you would not attempt to keep me here any longer."

"Do you rate your charms so highly?"

"Of course not! I only meant . . ." Biting her

lip, Erin broke off. If she was to have any chance of coming through the next few weeks in one piece, she had to stop letting him provoke her.

As coolly as she could, she said, "I gather that we understand each other. However, I have one other point to add. If I agree to your terms, I want your word that you will be as discreet as possible about our situation. I don't want Meg or the Carmodys hurt."

There was some small measure of satisfaction in the knowledge that she had managed to surprise him. Storm looked down at her narrowly. "You actually seem concerned about them."

Erin let her silence speak for itself. After a long moment, he appeared to realize that she meant what she said. "I have no need to advertise our arrangement, if indeed we have one. It can be kept as quiet as you wish."

With her last objection removed, the moment she had dreaded was upon her. Averting her eyes to keep him from seeing the contradictory emotions warring within her, she asked, "When would you expect me to move in?"

Storm's response was unequivocal. "At once. There is hardly any purpose in delay."

"No, I suppose not." Taking a deep breath, Erin squared her shoulders. So softly that he had to strain to hear her, she said, "My trunk is in the carriage."

If she had been watching Storm at that moment, she would have seen the surprised look that flitted across his rugged features as he realized she had just agreed to his outrageous proposal. When he had made the offer, he had envisioned a long campaign of resistance before she finally admitted the inevitability of her plight. Instead, she was giving in after only the most token objections. He couldn't begin to understand why his victory caused him such conflicting feelings.

Without taking his gaze from the slender, straight-backed young woman before him, he moved toward her. The faint shadows beneath her eyes and the tightness of her mouth hinted at emotions she was struggling to hide.

For a moment, it was all he could do not to reach out to her, to soothe away her fears and promise everything would be all right. Guilt at what he was putting her through threatened to make him forget the wrong she had done him.

Only the memory of her body, warm and pliant in his arms, strengthened his resolve. It would do her no harm to find out that she could not trample on a man's heart and still expect him to remain bedazzled by her charms.

Accompanying her back to the carriage, he spoke briefly with his assistant. As he did so, Erin climbed back up onto the buckboard. She sat with her eyes downcast and her hands tightly folded in her lap. When Storm settled into the seat next to her and picked up the reins, she did not look at him.

"I'll arrange to have this returned to the Carmodys' later today," he said as he urged the horses to a brisk trot.

Erin merely nodded. Out of the corner of her eye she was aware of him glancing into the back, where her small trunk lay.

"Don't you have any other luggage?"

She shook her head. "I find that quite enough." If he thought her wardrobe less than adequate for the role he was thrusting on her, too bad. With the single exception of the dress she had worn to the Carmodys' dinner party, her clothes had little to recommend them beyond being clean, comfortable and well-suited to her active life. She was not about to give them up in favor of the cumbersome garments weighed down with lace and ribbons that she had once worn.

Storm shrugged, making it clear that her clothes were hardly his prime concern. The appraising look in his eyes seemed to see right through her modest cloak and neat skirt and blouse to the satiny skin beneath.

A pulse beat in his lean jaw, and the rugged lines of his face were drawn even more harshly than usual. If she didn't know better, she would have sworn he was a man wrestling with his conscience.

From some hidden wellspring of courage

she found the nerve to ask, "Are you certain this is what you want? It isn't too late to change your mind."

The moment the words were said, she knew she had made a mistake. Lightning flashed in his quicksilver eyes. A wave of anger, almost smothering in its intensity, reached out to engulf her. The smile that curved his hard mouth held nothing of humor. He might have been a wild predator baring his teeth to attack.

"Don't credit me with principles I gave up a long time ago, Erin. I know exactly what I want and I intend to have it. Nothing you can say or do will convince me otherwise."

She had no choice but to believe him. But it still surprised her to discover how much pain his words could cause. They might have been swords, so brutally did they pierce her illusions.

Why should the knowledge that he was unencumbered by scruples cause her such dismay? Was it because she remembered him as he once was, a young, idealistic man ready to lay down his life for his beliefs? Now he seemed interested only in accumulating so much wealth and power that nothing would ever again be able to threaten him.

All his finer, gentler feelings appeared to have been blown away by the searing wind of tragedy. The tender compassion she thought she had seen in him the day before must have been nothing more than her imagination trying to give reality to her most cherished memories of him.

She would do well to remember that, Erin told herself as she sat stiffly beside him in the buggy. Her situation was bad enough without worsening it through indulgence in romantic fantasies that could never come true.

The jolting motion of the matched pair of bay horses pulling the vehicle knocked her against him. She pulled back instantly, as though burned. Storm shot her a sardonic glance. "You'll have to get used to that, you know."

Momentarily confused, she forgot her resolve to remain unaffected by anything he might do or say. Her voice shook slightly as she asked, "Get used to what?"

"To my touching you, of course. You do understand that's part of our . . . arrangement?"

The wave of color that stained her face was inspired as much by anger as by embarrassment. Was it really necessary for him to rub her nose in it? "I have no difficulty understanding business deals," she informed him frostily. "But even if I did, your terms were unmistakably clear."

She turned away too quickly to see the corner of his mouth twitch in what looked suspiciously like a grin. "I'm glad to hear it. That makes everything so much simpler, don't you agree?"

Erin shrugged, refusing to answer him. She stared out at the passing street, pretending great interest in the new protective measures being rushed into place by the shogun.

Already the shops damaged by the rampaging attackers were being quickly repaired, the burned merchandise was hauled away, and the bloodstains were scrubbed from the wood-plank walkways. New bamboo awnings were being lifted into place above the display windows, new signs were being carefully painted, and the usual bustle of the market was slowly resuming.

But none of that detracted from the wariness evident in the watchful eyes of heavily armed samurai, the guarded behavior of Western visitors, all of whom now had handguns strapped to their sides, and the nervousness of the Japanese merchants caught in a vise which threatened to destroy everything they had worked more than two decades to build.

"Have the men responsible for the attack been caught yet?" Erin asked. Her need to know what lay behind her own brush with death was so overwhelming that she was even willing to turn to Storm for information.

From Ned she had been able to gather only that the entire city was in an uproar, the diplomatic community stunned, and no one with any clear idea of what might happen next. She could hardly blame the young consular officer for being dazed by the assault, but she was willing to bet that at least a few people had a much firmer grasp of what had happened, and that Storm would be among them.

He did not disappoint her. Waiting until the buggy was out of earshot of any curious passersby, he said, "Unfortunately, the few attackers who didn't manage to flee the area couldn't be questioned. Before there was any chance to take them alive, they committed suicide."

"*Suicide*? But that's horrible. Why would they do that?"

"It's a Japanese tradition. All fighting men follow the code of Bushido, which translates roughly to 'the way of honor.' The greatest dishonor possible is to be defeated in battle. That failing goes far beyond what a Westerner might consider the worst sin. It is so bad that the only possible response to it is to leave this life as quickly as possible, namely by one's own hand."

His explanation only worsened Erin's dismay. Her vivid memories of the many young men she had seen die despite their desperate struggles to hold on to life made suicide seem a particularly obscene act. She could not hide her repugnance as she said, "You sound as though you approve of men killing themselves."

"No, I do not. But if I have learned anything in Japan, it is that making too swift value judgments about other people's way of life is usually an expression of bigotry. Bushido has worked well for hundreds, perhaps thousands of years. It is well worth trying to understand."

His obvious sincerity softened her outrage. More gently she asked, "But isn't it also extremely difficult to ever reach past the surface and achieve even the slightest grasp of what is really going on underneath? I've been in Japan only a few days, yet already I feel as though I could easily spend the rest of my life trying to get to know these people."

Storm shot her an assessing glance. "Are you saying you would consider staying here?"

"Why, no . . . that is, I can't stay, even if I did want to. My business is in the States."

"I thought all that was left were your two ships?"

"Yes, but once I get them back, I'll need to set up an office somewhere, perhaps in San Francisco." Aware that he might easily belittle her aspirations, she said stiffly, "You may as well know that I intend to stay in the Japan trade. Whatever the difficulties, it provides the best opportunity for me."

"I don't dispute that," Storm informed her mildly. "But why do you automatically presume you have to be based somewhere like San Francisco? You can run such a venture just as successfully from this end. I do."

"It's different for you." Unwilling to admit

the problems she had encountered with the merchants, she saw no reason to elaborate. But Storm understood her all too clearly.

"Perhaps I should have warned you about how Japanese men regard doing business with a woman. But I was sure you wouldn't believe me. It seemed to be a lesson you had to learn on your own."

The knowledge that he was fully aware of her predicament strained Erin's already over-burdened temper. Angrily she snapped, "Dare I hope there is nothing more you believe I need to be taught?"

"That depends," he muttered, his bronzed hands tightening on the reins.

Erin's eyes were drawn to them irresistibly. All too clearly she remembered how they felt moving over her body. Hardly aware that she did so, she asked, "On what?"

His mouth thinned to a sardonic line. "On how well you please me, of course." As she turned away quickly to hide her embarrass-ment, he continued remorselessly, "I may as well warn you right now that you are up against considerable competition. Japanese women are raised from birth to serve men in all possible ways."

Against her better judgment, Erin snapped, "I suppose that is one custom you do not hesitate to approve?"

"Hardly. What could be more delightful than for a man to find himself in a country where every female is devoted to fulfilling his slightest whim? Frankly, my dear, you couldn't have landed in a better place. From what I can see, your education in that area has been sadly lacking."

Long years of self-discipline enabled her to bite back the sharp retort that trembled on the tip of her tongue. But it could not wipe out her increasing nervousness as they neared Storm's home. The full implications of what she was doing were only just beginning to sink in.

Once she entered that house, she would be subject to anything he might choose to demand. Her ignorance about precisely what went on between a man and a woman behind bedroom doors did not prevent her from realizing that she could be badly hurt. Not only her body, but her heart and spirit could suffer enormously.

Her throat tightened painfully as she fought against an almost overwhelming upsurge of fear. Faith in her own instincts made her believe that Storm was not truly capable of harming her. But what if she were wrong? What if the romantic fantasies she had already resolved to disregard were affecting her more than she thought?

Glancing up at him, she was surprised to find his eyes focused on her narrowly. "It's a bit late to have second thoughts."

"I wasn't. . . ."

He laughed mockingly. "Of course you were. Whatever else you may be, you are hardly stupid. However, just to be sure there are no misunderstandings between us, let me spell out the situation. Once you step inside my home, I will take that to mean that you are in full agreement with our arrangement and I will behave accordingly. You will have no opportunity to change your mind or to try to back out."

As Erin tried to interrupt to insist she had no such intention of doing either, he ignored her and went on relentlessly, "Nor will there be anyone to rescue you. If you have any ideas about appealing to Ned for help, forget them. He is far too aware of the need to maintain good relations with the business community to risk my anger. Besides, by coming here of your own free will, you have provided him and anyone else you might appeal to with a built-in excuse for refusing you aid."

His gaze swept over her lingeringly, taking in every delicate line and gentle curve of her slender body. "The prideful belle of Boston is about to become a fallen woman. I wonder how you will react to the experience."

Prideful? Was that how he thought of her? Perhaps he was right. Certainly it was pride that enabled her to face him expressionlessly, all her fears hidden behind a frozen mask.

"I daresay I will react as well as I have to other grim experiences in recent years. Nothing you can do can be worse than the sight of a young man bleeding to death from severed limbs, or the stench of decay so thick as to be suffocating, or the sounds of dozens of soldiers screaming in agony until their throats were raw."

She hadn't meant to reveal so much of what her life had been like during the war, but when she had done so, she was glad. Whatever else she might have accomplished, she had at least managed to silence Storm. Beneath his tan, his skin was oddly gray. She did not dare look at him closely enough to try to read the expression in his eyes, but she suspected his callous bravado was at least dented. He did not attempt to provoke her further as they completed the journey through Yokohama and arrived in front of his home.

Chapter Eight

ERIN STUDIED THE HOUSE CURIOUSLY. THE day before, she had been too upset to take in much about it. Now she made up for that with a careful appraisal that missed little of the subtle interworkings of nature and craftsmanship. Once past the perimeter wall, it was immediately apparent that what appeared bare and uninviting from the roadway was in fact a refuge of remarkable beauty and comfort.

Given as she was to preferring uncluttered spaces and simple designs, Erin had no difficulty appreciating the clean lines and discreet ornamentation of the house. It did not disturb her that two of the four outside walls were nothing more than sliding screens built around a dark wood frame. The idea of being able to open the entire residence to the sun and air delighted her. Nor did the unpainted plank walls of the remaining two sides look unappealing. She recognized how the subtle weathering of the wood had created patterns no artist could ever duplicate.

Small, enchanting details were revealed wherever she chose to look. The lintel above the entrance was made from a twisted, bleached piece of driftwood. Its austere lines were echoed in the brush strokes of a water-color decorating the sliding door of an alcove just off the vestibule.

On a low lacquer table, an earthenware jug held a single sprig of maple leaves, their glowing russet tone adding warmth to the paleness of the straw mats covering the floor and the oiled paper squares set in the ceiling to form a skylight.

The disparaging comments of Westerners who found Japanese architecture uncomfortably austere came back to her as she marveled at her own response. Far from being put off by the almost total absence of furniture or other ornamentation, she found the house soothing and peaceful. It was a refuge from the cluttered morass of day-to-day existence. No wonder Storm had chosen to live here rather than in the crowded Western enclave.

She was about to say as much when the sudden appearance of a woman hurrying from the back of the house cut her off. Erin watched with growing dismay as the kimono-clad beauty smiled shyly before bowing first to Storm and then to her.

In softly accented English, she said, "I am so sorry I was not here to receive you. Please forgive me."

"That's quite all right," Storm assured her, his voice gentle as he eyed the woman's bent head. "Odetsu, this is Erin Conroy. She will be staying here."

Turning to Erin, he said, "Odetsu is my housekeeper and easily the most valued member of my staff. She never raises her voice above a whisper, but she could give any master sergeant lessons on getting things done."

Though he spoke humorously, his manner made it clear that he held the young Japanese woman in high esteem. Erin could hardly blame him. With her delicate features set off by huge almond-shaped eyes, high cheekbones and a full mouth, her honeyed skin and her sleek black hair coiled at the nape of her slender neck, Odetsu was breathtakingly beautiful.

Her ivory kimono embroidered with cloud, wave and shell motifs and secured by a scarlet sash emphasized the perfection of her slender form. Every motion she made was graceful, as though she were a flawless blossom blown gently by the wind. Her air of deference and self-effacement was unmistakable, as was her genuine concern that her employer might be put out by her failure to be at the door waiting to greet him.

"Please," she murmured as she bowed yet again, "allow me to welcome your guest." Addressing Erin directly for the first time, she added softly, "If you like, I will show you to your room now."

"I'm sure Miss Conroy is anxious to get settled," Storm said mockingly. "I will leave her in your capable hands. See to it that she is ready to dine with me tonight."

Without another look at his outraged guest, who was having a more-than-difficult time coping with such blatantly male pomposity, he strode off. The deep-throated chuckle that floated behind him only added to her disgust. Erin's hands were tightly clenched and her sky-blue eyes glittered dangerously as she snapped, "It isn't necessary for you to see to anything, Odetsu. Just tell me where my room is and I will take care of myself."

If she had struck the girl, she could not have provoked a more shocked response. Odetsu's vermilion-hued mouth trembled as her eyes took on the look of a wounded doe's.

"Please," she whispered, "I have done something to give offense?"

Baffled by such an extreme reaction, Erin shook her head. "No, of course not. I only meant that there is no need for you to worry about me, when I'm sure you have plenty to do elsewhere."

"That does not matter," Odetsu said with gentle firmness. "Davin-san said to look after you. Therefore, I will do so."

Erin eyed her uncomfortably, suspecting that if *Davin-san* told her to walk through fire, she would promptly immolate herself. Such slavish devotion was disconcerting under the best of circumstances. When it came from an undeniably beautiful woman and was directed toward a man whom Erin could not help but want for herself, she was hard pressed to deal with it.

"I really don't need any help," she began tentatively, "but if you insist . . ."

Odetsu did. Beneath her gentle, serene demeanor lurked a streak of stubbornness not even Erin could overcome. Within minutes she had guided her to the spacious chamber she would occupy, seen to the unpacking of her trunk, ordered a bath prepared and sent a bashful serving girl for a tray of green tea and rice cakes.

Delighted by her room, which like the rest of the house was classically Japanese in style, Erin would have been perfectly content to be left alone to get acquainted with her new surroundings. But that was not to be the case. To her dismay, Odetsu gently but firmly insisted on helping her off with her clothes.

As she did so, she kept up a soothing stream of questions about Western fashion, which had the effect of distracting Erin so thoroughly that she barely had time to note that every scrap of covering was removed from her before she was wrapped in an exquisitely soft silk robe and led over to a low table on which the tray of refreshments had been set.

Following Odetsu's lead, she settled down on her knees before it, finding the position uncomfortable but tolerable. As she sipped the tea and nibbled politely at a cake, the Japanese woman took down her hair and gently brushed it free of tangles.

"How beautiful," Odetsu said with apparent sincerity. "I have never seen hair like this. It is almost as dark as mine, but it catches the light in a different way." She studied it for a moment before declaring, "Davin-san is right. You should wear it down so that it flows over your skin like silk."

Erin swallowed the sip of tea she had just taken too hastily and coughed. She did not doubt for a moment that Storm was perfectly capable of speaking of her in such intimate terms. But the thought of what else he might have said to his housekeeper made her flush.

Was Odetsu aware of her true reason for being in his home? If so, it was difficult to understand why she was being so friendly and kind. Even the best-trained Western housekeeper would look down her nose at a woman in Erin's position.

But if Odetsu saw anything the least untoward about it, she hid it well. Against her will,

Erin found herself relaxing as the tensions of the last few days slid away. When her bath was ready, she went into it unhesitantly.

The separate room paneled in aromatic cedar planks and dominated by a huge, steaming tub was only one more delightful discovery in a house that seemed to possess an endless supply of them.

Guided by Odetsu, Erin washed thoroughly before entering the water. The extremely high temperature made her gasp, but she found herself quickly adjusting to it. Muscles she hadn't even realized were clenched relaxed and became fluid as she leaned back against the rim of the tub, letting her body float languidly. Breathing deeply, she savored the fragrance of jasmine incense burning nearby.

She was dimly aware of Odetsu moving about the chamber, keeping a close eye on her to make sure she didn't remain too long in the extremely hot water. But the sounds she made were carefully muted and did not intrude on Erin's thoughts. Reluctant though she was to do anything to disturb her unexpected serenity, she could not help but consider what lay ahead in the next few hours.

The contradictory feelings Storm never failed to set off in her were once again at work. The mere thought of being made a woman by him was enough to make her tremble with excitement even as she had to fight against the sense of panic that threatened to rob her of all courage.

Briefly she wondered if it would do any good to ask him for more time. Everything she knew about him convinced her it would not. Once set on a course, he was not likely to be deterred for any reason. Nor could she honestly claim to want any delay. Each slowly passing moment was enough of a torment without wishing to extend them further.

At last Odetsu came to fetch her from the tub, gently toweling her dry as she exclaimed with concern over the bruises and abrasions left from her encounter with the ronin. At her insistence, Erin allowed a soothing salve to be rubbed into her limbs before she was dressed.

As she stood naked in the center of the room, giggling servant girls appeared with a magnificent silk robe in shades of violet darkening to mauve at the hem. The color brought out the delicate rose hue of her complexion and gave an added sparkle to crystal blue eyes already bright with emotions she did not care to identify.

Although she had long ago given up the habit of lacing, she was still a bit dismayed to realize that the robe was meant to be slipped on without benefit of undergarments. Yet despite this, it proved a perfect fit.

The scoop neckline revealed the high curve of her breasts, but was not so low-cut as to make her uncomfortable. The wide sleeves fell gracefully down her slender arms to conceal her hands. A broad sash emphasized the narrow span of her waist and the ripe curve of her hips.

It was only when she moved that Erin recognized the full attraction of the garment. Slit up the front, it opened with each step, revealing a creamy expanse of slender legs clear to her thighs.

Unable to still her protest, she said, "I'd prefer to wear something else. Some of my own clothes, or perhaps a kimono like yours."

Odetsu shook her head firmly. "Davin-san does not like Western styles in his home, and my clothes would not be comfortable for you."

Erin could hardly argue with that. Though Odetsu's garments were beautifully made, they so tightly restricted her movements as to leave her all but hobbled. Having heard of the Chinese custom of binding women's feet, she had to give the Japanese credit for going one better and tethering the entire body.

The sash Odetsu called an *obi* was so wide that it encased almost her entire torso in a rigid tube of material. As though that were not enough, the folds of the kimono itself were pulled so snugly that they would not open above the knees.

When she moved, she looked for all the world as though her legs were bound together, as in effect they were. Even her soft white socks that took the place of shoes in the house looked uncomfortable, with the toes rigidly separated in a way nature had surely not intended.

By comparison, Erin's robe left her utterly unfettered and free. She could not help but note the contrast and wonder what, if anything, it was meant to convey.

Storm had praised Japanese women, yet he seemed to have no wish to force her into their mold. She could only hope he would continue to be as tolerant as the last barriers between them vanished and the emotions shaped by eight tumultuous years were finally released.

Chapter Nine

ERIN HAD NEVER BEFORE CONSIDERED IT AN act of courage to walk down a hallway and enter a room. But as she followed Odetsu through the house to where Storm awaited her, she needed all her determination to put one foot in front of the other.

She wasn't helped by the fact that her robe kept gapping open with each step, until she was driven to hold it shut with a tightly clenched hand. Even then the thinness of the fabric and the way it clung to her curves added to her spiraling nervousness.

By the time Odetsu slid open a screen partition and beckoned her to enter, Erin was trembling. Nothing she had ever imagined had prepared her for this moment.

Vainly she wished she had paid more attention to the giggling confidences of young girls exchanging what little information they could ferret out about the mysteries of love. However much of it might have been inaccurate, she would at least feel better prepared to deal with whatever lay ahead. Instead, she felt for all the world as though she were jumping off a cliff.

Pride stiffened her spine and held her head erect as she stepped into a room much like the one she herself occupied, but larger and more elaborately furnished. A low lacquer table set against a wall held papers and maps. Beside it, shelves built into a recess were crowded with books.

Across the room, a raised platform was covered by a mattress and quilts. Nearby, another table was surrounded by silk cushions and set with stoneware dishes and a charcoal brazier. The dining area faced a grouping of indoor plants placed on polished stones. A tiny waterfall sent glistening droplets of light and sound down among the verdant setting.

Her spirit responded intuitively to the harmonious surroundings, so much so that for a moment she began to relax. Until she saw the man standing in the shadows at the far end of the room. As Storm turned to her, all her apprehension returned tenfold.

He was dressed in an ankle-length robe of heavy black silk loosely belted at his narrow waist. Against the richly dark material, the burnished skin of his hair-roughened chest shone clearly. He looked even bigger and more threatening than he had when he killed the samurai, only now it was on her that his attention focused.

The heat of his gaze taking in every detail of her appearance made her flush. She knew full well that he missed nothing, from the top of her shining hair falling in a silken tumult down her back, to the tips of her slipper-shod feet peeking out from beneath her robe.

What he saw must have pleased him, for he smiled sardonically. "I see my instructions were carried out, Odetsu. You have done very well."

The Japanese woman bowed, obviously relieved by her employer's praise. Modestly she said, "Miss Conroy is very beautiful, Davin-san. It was necessary to do very little."

Erin's chagrined look did not go unnoticed by Storm. He laughed softly as he came toward her. "No matter how annoyed you try to appear, you will not be able to convince me that you didn't enjoy Odetsu's pampering." Perceptively, he added, "I would guess it's been a long time since you were so well cared for."

That was true. Erin's busy life had left little time or energy to coddle herself, and Meg's advancing age made her spare the older woman all possible effort. She had forgotten how good it could feel to be looked after. Reluctant though she was to admit as much, she couldn't deny the truth of what he said.

Turning to Odetsu, she smiled gently. "Thank you for your help. But you really mustn't be concerned about looking after me while I'm here. I'm sure you have quite enough to do as it is."

Surprised by such consideration, the Japanese woman was flustered for a moment. But she quickly recovered and returned Erin's smile before hurrying away to check on dinner.

"I suppose you will soon have all my servants on your side," Storm grumbled as he led her over to the low table. "Whatever else you've done in the last few years, you haven't forgotten how to be charming."

"It's a simple matter of courtesy," Erin said, settling herself carefully on one of the cushions. She still wasn't comfortable kneeling with her legs tucked under her and her weight on the heels of her feet, as Odetsu had shown her, but given what she was wearing, it seemed the safest posture.

Storm folded himself agilely beside her, cross-legged so that his robe fell open to reveal the muscular expanse of powerful calves covered with thick, dark curls. At Erin's startled look, he laughed.

"Don't try to tell me you've never seen a man's legs before. That I won't believe."

She hadn't been about to claim any such thing, but the difference between the shattered bodies she had cared for during the war and the compellingly male physique beside her was painfully obvious. The contrast with her own far smaller and softer form enthralled her. Even as she wondered at the wanton direction of her thoughts, she was helpless to hide her response to him.

In a futile effort to appear unmoved, she murmured, "I'm just not accustomed to such . . . informality."

Storm grinned appreciatively. He gave her top marks for spirit. Any other woman of her background would be frozen with horror at the impropriety of her situation. But then, Erin was never one to let circumstances get the better of her. She possessed a degree of resiliency he could not help but admire.

Driven by an irrepressible masculine urge to test the limits of her composure, he said, "This is hardly the height of abandon. We have quite a way to go before we reach there."

Erin blanched, but managed to answer him coolly. "Since you are undoubtedly an expert in such matters, I will defer to your far greater knowledge. Otherwise I might be tempted to say something rude about the wages of licentiousness."

"That would be foolish."

Accepting the quietly voiced warning, Erin fell silent. She occupied herself by looking around the room, taking in the subtly elegant appointments and the attention to detail that suggested Storm meant to stay in this house for a long time to come. Tempted to ask if he gave any thought to returning to the States, she did not do so for fear of arousing memories that could only worsen his mood.

When Odetsu returned carrying a lacquer tray with a small porcelain bottle and tiny cups, she almost sighed in relief. Several young serving maids followed, struggling to contain their wide-eyed stares as they laid out the ingredients for the meal which was apparently going to be cooked over the charcoal brazier before them.

The thin slices of beef, mushrooms, radishes and other vegetables Erin could not identify were undeniably appetizing. But she doubted she would be able to swallow a mouthful, given her nervousness. Her hope that Odetsu's presence might afford some slight reprieve from Storm's attentions proved misplaced.

As soon as the various foods began cooking in a covered dish full of steaming broth, he said, "There's no need for you to stay. I'm sure Miss Conroy can manage the rest."

That earned a soft smile from Odetsu and a glare from Erin, who watched in dismay as the servants bowed themselves out and the sliding panel was pushed shut behind them.

When she and Storm were once again alone, he gestured toward the stone bottle and cups. "In Japan, women do all the serving of food and drink."

"How interesting."

"That was not a rhetorical statement."

"If you expect to be waited on, you should have asked your servants to stay."

"Oh, no, that would have been far too easy. I prefer to get some idea of just how good a . . . house guest you will make." His eyes hardened as he said, "Pour the wine, Erin. Save your resistance for something more important."

Gritting her teeth, she silently acknowledged the wisdom of his advice. Already, she knew her small store of courage and strength was being strained. It would do no good to exhaust herself before the true battle began.

Lifting the bottle, she filled both cups, noting as she did so that each held barely a single swallow of the clear wine. As Storm raised his in a mocking salute, she forced herself to lift her own, but she barely touched the rim to her lips before setting it back down again.

Noting that, he laughed. "You're already more Japanese than you know. Here the women hardly ever drink sake, preferring to leave it to the men to get sore heads."

"If they like to drink it so much, why don't they have bigger cups?"

"And make less work for the women? Never. A Japanese man believes that the more his wife or concubine has to do, the better. That way, she's less likely to get into mischief and cause him to lose face."

Stifling her disapproval, Erin refilled his

cup, but left her own as it was. "I've heard a little about face, but not much. What is it?"

"Pride, honor, the respect of the community. It's considered absolutely vital to existence. People will go to incredible lengths to keep from being shamed in any way."

Erin glanced up at him sharply. Was he suggesting that she should have refused his demands, no matter what the cost? There was nothing in his expression to suggest his words were aimed at her directly, but she still felt compelled to say, "Some of us have different priorities. Pride can become a luxury when the simple necessities of life are in doubt."

"That depends on your definition of necessity. For instance, there was a time when you thought satin gowns and rare jewels were essential to your happiness. Yet now you seem perfectly content in the simplest clothes."

"I don't think I was ever quite as dependent on such things as you believe. They were a symbol of sorts for the security I was afraid to do without."

Storm emptied his cup again in a single swallow. Watching the play of muscles along his corded throat, Erin momentarily forgot her unease. So absorbed was she in the heady aura of his nearness that she was only distantly aware of what she had just revealed to him.

Not until she saw his assessing look did she feel driven to explain, "When I put on beautiful dresses and went to parties, I was like a child playing at being grown-up. I had been so overprotected and indulged that I never gave much thought to the consequences of my actions until it was too late."

"I've wondered sometimes if that might not have been the problem," Storm admitted reluctantly. "I was so acutely aware of you as a woman that it seemed impossible you didn't realize your own impact. But now I can see how that could have been the case."

Surprised by his understanding, Erin smiled. "Fortunately, I grew out of it. At least for me, the war accomplished some good. By the time it ended, I had become a very different person."

"Earlier today you said something about your experiences with wounded soldiers. Did you work in a hospital?"

"Several of them. There were never enough nurses. After I was sufficiently well trained, I was moved around wherever the need was greatest." Hesitating, she added, "Toward the end of the war, I worked in a camp for Southern prisoners. When the authorities realized the men were going to have to be released soon, they decided to try to improve their situation a little. It wasn't until then that I fully understood the level of brutality people were capable of."

She didn't add that throughout her time working in the prison camp, she was plagued by nightmares in which she suddenly discovered Storm among the starved, abused captives. Such dreams always ended with the sound of her own sobs driving her back to consciousness.

"Didn't anyone in your family object to what you were doing?"

Erin shook her head. After her parents' death, she was left with drunken Uncle Bates, two maiden aunts and a cluster of cousins, all of whom were much too busy with their own lives to give a thought to hers.

Their blatant disinterest had hurt, until she recognized it as a blessing in disguise. Because of it, she was able to grow into a truly strong, independent woman instead of being condemned to the shallow, frivolous existence that might otherwise have been her fate.

"Meg said you were hell on wheels to try to control," Storm muttered. "I can see now that she's had her work cut out for her."

"What else did Meg tell you?" Erin demanded. "For that matter, what did you say to her? She hardly batted an eyelash when I told her I was thinking of living here."

Storm shrugged, as though the answer were obvious. "I just assured both her and the Carmodys that we had a great deal of business to take care of and that it would be facilitated by your being close at hand."

"Is that all you said?"

"Pretty much."

Erin didn't believe him. She knew Meg far too well to think the older woman would docilely accept such a story, nor did she buy the idea that the Carmodys could be as easily fooled.

Storm must have offered some far more convincing explanation of why it was not a breach of propriety for her to be living with him, but she couldn't begin to imagine what he might have told them. Nor did he seem inclined to discuss the matter further.

Lifting the lid of the steaming bowl, he said, "I believe dinner is ready. Do you know how to use chopsticks?"

Erin was tempted to proclaim her ignorance, if only because that would make it very difficult for her to serve the meal. But she wasn't sure he wouldn't insist that she do so anyway.

"I learned during the voyage over here." Deftly wielding the slender sticks of polished wood, she filled two smaller bowls with choice pieces of beef and vegetables. The aroma was so appetizing that her stomach growled.

Having skipped both breakfast and lunch that day, she was ravenous. Her concern that she would be too nervous to eat vanished as she took her first bite. It got very quiet as both she and Storm did full justice to the meal.

When the bowls were being refilled for the third time, he grinned at her teasingly. "How do you manage to eat like this and still stay so slender?"

"I get a lot of exercise," Erin murmured, wondering if he thought her too slim. The look in his quicksilver eyes convinced her otherwise. A hot flush stained her cheeks as she stalwartly refused to think of what would happen after dinner.

Drawing out the meal as long as she could, she was still unprepared for its end. All too soon, Odetsu and the serving girls returned to carry away the dishes, pour glasses of plum wine, and vanish again into the nether reaches of the house.

When they were gone, Storm rose and stretched luxuriously. His big, hard body seemed to fill the room. The sense of latent strength and virility flowing from him was almost overwhelming in intensity.

Erin's breath caught in her throat as she looked at him. The yearnings he had set off in her eight years before were as nothing compared to what she was now feeling. Long-denied feminine instincts were stirring within her. Her carefully constructed defenses were crumbling even as the very core of her being seemed to glow with hidden fires.

When Storm glanced down at her a moment later, his mouth quirked. She seemed enthralled by the surface of the table and refused to meet his eyes. Reaching out a hand, he touched her shoulder gently. When she jumped, he laughed. "Here, let me help you up. You may be a bit stiff."

More than a bit, she thought grudgingly.

After being sat on for more than an hour, her legs were almost numb. As she tried to stand, they gave way under her. Instinctively she grabbed for Storm's hand, only to be saved from falling by his arms closing gently but implacably around her.

Lifting her easily, he cradled her against his hard chest. For a moment he hesitated, as though struggling with a temptation that swiftly proved irresistible. Before she could open her mouth to protest, he strode across the room and laid her down on the low platform bed.

The touch of soft fabric beneath her back sent lightning bolts of panic through Erin. Everything was happening much too quickly. She wasn't ready for such sudden intimacy. A very natural fear of the unknown threatened to smother her.

Frantically, she tried to twist free of him, only to realize swiftly that her struggles were worsening the situation. The movement of her slender body against his aroused Storm to a point where he could not deny the urge to bend her to his will.

A big hand on her shoulder pushed her farther into the soft mattress. He loomed above her, his bronzed features taut with need. The molten glitter of his eyes warned her of what he meant to do in the instant before his mouth claimed hers with compelling intensity.

At the touch of his lips against hers, Erin

moaned. The fierceness of her own response stunned her. A shimmering flame of desire flared within her, quickly raging out of control.

His mouth was cool, liquid flame, burning away the last remnants of fear and doubt. His long, hard body pressed to hers was the only security in a world tilting out of control.

Work-roughened fingers gently stroked down along the delicate curve of her cheek to the smooth line of her throat and the vulnerable hollow between her collarbones, making her yearn for closer contact. His deep voice rumbled in her ear, whispering words of tenderness and reassurance she could not quite catch but whose meaning was still unmistakable.

No thought of resistance remained in her when his tongue gently demanded entrance to the moist secrets of her mouth. She gave it willingly, arching against him in unbridled response.

The groan that rumbled from him was her reward. Delighted by the knowledge that she could so move him, she thrilled to the touch of his big hands cupping her breasts through the thin silk of her robe. As his callused thumbs rubbed rhythmically over her straining nipples, a low whimper broke from her. Her head tossed wildly back and forth across the down-filled mattress as undulating waves of pleasure claimed every cell of her being.

Without even being aware that she did so, Erin reached out to him. Driven by the desperate need to give pleasure as well as receive it, she stroked the massive breadth of his shoulders and arms before yielding to the urge to touch the hair-roughened expanse of his chest.

Drowning in sensation, she savored the enthralling differences between them, loving what her fingers discovered about the bulging strength of his muscles, the fiery heat of his rough-textured skin, the shudders of pleasure that followed the path of her gentle touch.

The harsh intake of his breath thrilled her, as did the racing beat of his heart beneath her hand. When his mouth slipped down to nuzzle the sensitive line of her throat, she could not help but respond in kind. Her tongue darted out to taste the faintly salty flavor of his skin, lapping at him like a kitten at a dish of cream.

"So beautiful," he moaned huskily, his fingers trembling as they swiftly undid the tie of her robe, pushing open the delicate fabric to reveal the lovely body beneath.

The flickering light of oil lamps shone on the opalescent perfection of her skin. Her breasts swelled at his touch, the velvet tips hard and taut. His hands easily spanned the narrowness of her waist, brushing down across her flat abdomen toward the dark tangle of curls between her thighs.

Slowly, almost reverently, he bent his head,

tracing the curve of her breast with his lips, coming ever closer to the straining peak that begged for his touch. As he drew her gently into his mouth, Erin gasped. It had never occurred to her that a man might suckle her, much less that the effect would be so devastating.

Undulating waves of rapture rippled through her. Behind her closed eyelids, pinpoint sparks of light exploded riotously. Blood pounded in her ears like the rush of an ancient wind blowing away the last fragments of resistance.

Stretched out beneath him on the bed, her arms twined around his massive chest and her body arched against his sinewy length, she knew only that she wanted to belong to him in the most elemental way possible.

When he abruptly stopped his dizzying caresses, frustration stabbed through her.

"Storm . . . please . . ."

He didn't answer. Instead, he sat up shakily, running a hand through his unruly hair. *My God, what am I doing?*

Erin stared at him in dismay. Even with all her inexperience, it seemed perfectly obvious what was happening. What she couldn't understand was why he had stopped, just when they seemed on the edge of a glorious revelation she could not bear to be denied.

A cry of protest rose in her throat, only to be cut off by his sudden movement. Seizing the edges of her robe, he yanked them together over her body, as though he could not bear the sight of her nakedness.

Jumping up, he pulled her to her feet and, without a word of explanation, marched her back to her own room, where he left her dazed, bewildered and more frustrated than she had ever been in her life.

Chapter Ten

RAIN SPLATTERING AGAINST THE TILE ROOF woke Erin from an uneasy sleep. She turned over gingerly, reluctant to give up her dreams. The damp smell of dying foliage mingled with the cozy aroma of the charcoal brazier that had burned all night to help keep her warm. In the distance, she could hear the sounds of the household beginning to stir.

The kitchen would already be busy with preparations for the day's meals. Sleepy-eyed serving girls would be rinsing rice kernels, slicing vegetables, and pounding soybeans under the watchful gaze of the cook.

In the stables, grooms would be cleaning out the stalls that housed Storm's half-dozen horses and filling the troughs with clean water. Gardeners would be raking up the scarlet and gold leaves that had fallen from the almost bare trees. They would be put carefully away in the compost shed to help form fertilizer for the next year's flowers.

Odetsu would be up and dressed, overseeing the household with her usual calm efficiency. There would be no slacking off just because her employer happened to be away.

Erin sat up slowly, stifling a sigh. In the three weeks she had lived in Storm's home, she had grown more and more puzzled by his behavior. Since that first night, when he had so unexpectedly broken off their lovemaking, he had scrupulously avoided touching her. Though they shared most meals and spent hours in each other's company, he seemed content for her to be no more than a friend and business associate.

Certainly he had never again suggested by word or deed that he wanted her to be his mistress. At a loss to understand his behavior, Erin finally concluded that she must lack some essential quality he required in a bedmate. While he seemed willing enough to keep his promise regarding the purchase of cargo for her ships, he appeared to want nothing in return other than companionship.

That left Erin singularly unsatisfied. The strain of being in his presence without revealing the vast love she felt for him was almost unbearable. She could not deny a certain relief when he had announced a few days before that he had to take a trip down the coast on some unspecified business.

While he was gone, she was making a sincere effort to come to terms with her complex emotions, in the hope that when he returned she might be able to confront him openly about their situation.

Distracted by a soft knocking at the door, she got out of bed and padded quickly across the smooth wood floor to admit Odetsu. The Japanese woman's cheery spring-green kimono embroidered with white and pink plum blossoms made Erin smile. Odetsu had confided to her that she loathed cold weather and viewed the advent of each winter with dismay. Her choice of garments declared her unwillingness to accept the gray dankness of the season.

"Ah, you are awake," she said, standing aside to admit two little serving girls carrying a basin, towels and a tray of tea and cakes. "That is good. It is much too nice a morning to sleep away."

"Nice, but chilly," Erin said, eyeing the steaming water appreciatively. "I expect to see frost any day now."

"Soon enough," Odetsu agreed. "The chrysanthemums we collected yesterday will be the last for a long time. Perhaps later you would like to help me arrange them."

Splashing the sleep from her eyes, Erin nodded. "I've enjoyed the flower-arranging lessons you've given me, as well as the instruction in playing the samisen and performing the tea ceremony. But I don't want you to think you have to keep me occupied."

Odetsu laughed as she held out a quilted cotton kimono for Erin to slip on. The ready friendship that had sprung up between them allowed her to indulge in a little gentle teasing.

"Are you saying you don't regret not being able to go to the boatyard or into town? When Davin-san gave instructions for you to remain here during his absence, he said you were liable to chafe at such restrictions. Was that not correct?"

"I suppose," Erin admitted. "It's a good thing I understood the reasons behind his orders, or you can be sure I would have objected to them strenuously."

"Ever since that attack in the marketplace, it is not safe for anyone to go about without an escort. Yokohama looks calm enough on the surface, but I fear we have only begun to see the trouble that is coming."

Brushing the tangles from her hair, Erin nodded somberly. Unable to hide the worry in her voice, she asked, "Do you think Davin-san will be home soon?"

Odetsu smiled gently. She did not ascribe to the widely held believe that Westerners were artlessly transparent. But she had to admit that Erin's feelings were hardly mysterious.

From the first moment she had seen her

employer and his lovely guest together, she recognized the intense currents of passion running between them. What she had difficulty understanding was why two people who were so obviously meant to be together seemed intent on staying apart.

"Yes," she said reassuringly. "I had a message early this morning. If all goes well, he should be back tonight."

"Goes well? Does that mean there is some danger in what he is doing?"

Odetsu hesitated. She did not want to worry Erin, but on the other hand she thought it might be beneficial for her young friend to know the truth of the situation.

"Davin-san has gone to meet with several leaders of the movement to overthrow the shogun. He is in sympathy with their objectives and they accept him as one of the few Westerners who can be trusted. The main purpose of this trip is to bring one of the leaders into Yokohama without the shogun's guards discovering his presence."

"But that sounds very dangerous," Erin exclaimed. "What would happen if they are found out?"

"They will not be," Odetsu assured her gently. "Davin-san has much experience with such matters, and the man he is bringing back, Satsuma Takamori, is very clever."

Something in the way she spoke the other man's name alerted Erin to the fact that he and Odetsu were not strangers. Glancing at her, she saw that her friend's almond-shaped eyes were unusually soft and pensive, as though focused on some inner vision. She seemed suddenly very far away, caught up in her private thoughts.

Curious about the man who could have that effect on such a calm, self-possessed woman, Erin nonetheless did not pursue the matter. She had learned enough about the intensely private Japanese character to know that any questions she might ask would be the height of discourtesy. Besides, she would be able to see what was happening for herself when Takamori and Storm arrived.

If they arrived. Despite Odetsu's assurances, Erin had no doubts that the mission was extremely dangerous. The shogun's guards were everywhere, manning every watchtower and gateway. Since the attack in the market, they were more vigilant than ever. A shiver of fear ran through her as she considered what would happen to Storm if he were caught.

Hard upon it came anguish at the thought of all the time she had wasted. How could she bear it if they were parted forever without her ever telling him how she felt? The pride and doubt that had prevented her from speaking up now seemed singularly unimportant. What did they matter when compared with the overwhelming love she could no longer deny?

But what if, far from returning her love,

Storm genuinely no longer even desired her? Erin shivered at that thought. Should she discover that to be the case, all the joy and promise of her life would be gone.

Driven by an almost intolerable need for reassurance, she murmured, "Do you think . . . that is, from what you've seen, does it appear to you that Davin-san . . . wants me to remain here?"

Struck by a very un-Japanese desire to laugh, Odetsu had to take a deep breath before answering. "Of course he does. Why else would he spend so much time with you? I cannot pretend to understand all the ways of Westerners, but some things are the same for men and women everywhere. It is very clear that Davin-san cares for you." Deliberately she added, "Just as it is obvious that you care for him."

"I do," Erin admitted huskily. She glanced down at her hands, twisting in her lap. "So much that sometimes it actually hurts. I just don't know what to do about it."

A gracefully curved eyebrow arched eloquently. "When a man and woman desire each other, there is only one thing to do. Westerners must already know this. How else could there be so many of you?"

Erin smiled faintly, but could not prevent a slight blush. "It's different for us. Here in Japan, you seem to be very matter-of-fact about . . . physical matters. Where I come from, it is all shrouded in mystery. Unless a woman has actually been married, she very often doesn't know much about these things."

Odetsu frowned slightly. "Are you saying that you have not been taught how to please a man, and how he can please you?"

Erin's blush deepened. "We don't speak of such matters."

"But why not? They are one of the great joys of life."

"I know, or at least I'm willing to believe they are. But people back home think that it's improper, even immoral, to bring them out in the open and talk about them. So even though I'm twenty-four years old and I've worked as a nurse, I feel very ignorant."

"So you desire Davin-san but you do not know how to encourage him to feel the same way about you?"

"That's only part of the problem. Even if I did know, I can't imagine what good it would be. If I made any . . . overtures to him, he would think I was being unbearably forward."

Odetsu shook her head in astonishment. She had difficulty believing that any people could create such complications in what was essentially a very simple matter. Yet Erin was obviously sincere. She had not considered making the first move toward Storm, despite the fact that his own sense of morality hindered him from following through on what they both so clearly wanted.

Smothering a sigh, she marveled at the quandary two apparently intelligent people could get themselves into. How fortunate that there was a Japanese on hand to help them out. She hesitated barely an instant before deciding it was up to her to end the stalemate between her honored employer and his beautiful guest.

Very quietly, so that Erin had to lean forward to hear her, she asked, "Have you thought that perhaps there is some reason for Storm's behavior which you are overlooking? Something that prevents him from making love to you?"

Erin swallowed hard. Far from being distressed by Odetsu's frankness, she was grateful for it. At last there was someone she could turn to for help and advice.

"No . . . I hadn't considered that. Except, of course, to wonder if he just doesn't desire me."

"His behavior has made it clear such is not the case. But are you aware that sometimes it is not enough for a man to simply desire a woman?"

"Not enough? I don't understand."

Odetsu smothered a sigh. Such ignorance was truly remarkable. But in this case, at least, it just might be for the best. "Davin-san fought in your Civil War, did he not? Men in battle are very vulnerable. Are you certain he was not injured in some way?"

"He may have been. But there's no sign of any lasting wound."

"Isn't there? Sometimes when a man has been through a terrible experience, he needs a very loving, caring woman to help him believe he is still truly a man. Otherwise, certain physical acts become extremely difficult."

As the full meaning of her words sank in, Erin's eyes grew saucer-wide. She turned bright red, but only for an instant. All the color drained from her features, leaving her ghostly white. "Are you saying . . . ?"

"I am not saying anything," Odetsu corrected quickly. "I would never presume to discuss such an intimate matter about my employer. All I mean is that if you were to throw off your modesty and let yourself be guided by your heart, I do not believe either of you would be disappointed."

Erin had considerable time to think that over as the day passed slowly. She helped Odetsu in the kitchens, where a special meal was being prepared. But her interest in the exotic dishes was hardly enough to deter her thoughts.

It was difficult to believe that a man as compellingly virile as Storm could have the slightest problem with a woman. But given the terrible wounds she had seen in the hospitals where she worked during the war, she had to admit that anything was possible.

What if Odetsu's hints were correct? Erin's

throat tightened at the thought of the anguish and frustration he must be enduring.

No wonder he had broken off their lovemaking weeks before. What confidence could he have that a young, untried girl would be able to cope with any such problem? Especially when she had once before proved herself incapable of thinking about anyone other than herself.

He had no way of knowing that the vast, all-encompassing love she felt for him made it possible for her to contemplate behavior that would ordinarily have been unimaginable. Innocent though she was, there was nothing wrong with her instincts. They were in sufficiently good order to make her relish the challenge he presented, even as her compassionate nature drove her to do everything she could to help him.

It was well after dark when an excited servant ran in to announce that Storm and his guest were approaching the house. By then her mind was made up. The relief she felt at knowing he was safe only served to confirm what she had already decided. The barriers of social convention had come between them for the last time. Whatever the consequences, she was going to make it crystal clear to Storm that she loved and desired him.

But first there was the seemingly endless evening to get through. Satsuma Takamori's arrival was the occasion for an outpouring of respectful awe. As he dismounted from the stallion next to Storm's, the tall, leanly built man was the recipient of repeated deep bows from all the servants.

In observance of the rigid hierarchy of such demonstrations, Odetsu's own welcome was more restrained. But the tender warmth of her eyes and her tremulous smile made it clear how delighted she was to see him.

Only Erin spared barely a glance for their visitor. She was too busy drinking in the sight of Storm. Clad in dusty trousers and a frock coat, with his hair mussed and his rugged features stained by the grime of the road, he was the most beautiful vision she had ever seen. Her eyes swept over him hungrily, missing nothing of the powerful sweep of his shoulders and chest, the tapered slimness of his hips or the strength of his long, sinewy legs.

As he glanced up, their eyes met, the expression in his sending a quiver of longing through her. He held out a hand, and without hesitation she went to him.

"Takamori, may I present Miss Erin Conroy, my guest and business associate."

The young Japanese bowed gravely. If he found anything unusual in the idea that Storm shared professional interests with a lowly woman, he hid it well. Erin was instantly won over when he smiled with unexpected openness and said, "Now I can see why my friend was so anxious to get home. And here I believed he was merely concerned about our safety."

"I never gave it a thought," Storm claimed good-humoredly. "With you along, I figured no one would dare to attack."

Takamori laughed, but Erin guessed the words were only half in jest. Storm by himself would make a formidable opponent for anyone, but with the Japanese warrior beside him, she could well believe even the shogun's finest soldiers would have been hard pressed to stop them.

Although the samurai lord was simply dressed in a plain homespun kimono instead of the usual ornate armor, he exuded an unmistakable sense of confidence and strength that was a match for Storm's own. He was far taller and broader than most Japanese men she had seen, and his aquiline features and keen black eyes spoke of a powerful will equaled by keen intelligence. It was easy to understand why Odetsu was so taken with him.

Despite Erin's preoccupation with Storm, she could not ignore the change in the lovely Japanese woman since Takamori's arrival. All her deeply suppressed tension and anxiety had fled, leaving her more relaxed and at ease than Erin had ever seen her. Her high-boned cheeks were becomingly flushed and her eyes glowed warmly as she ushered the men inside.

"It is good to see you again," Takamori told her softly. "Are you well?"

Odetsu nodded shyly.

"And Saido? He must be growing fast."

Odetsu laughed gently at the mention of her little son. "It is hard for me to believe he was a baby only three years ago."

"A great deal has happened since then. Saido is lucky to have a mother who has kept him so safe."

Odetsu looked taken aback by such praise. She lowered her eyes, seemingly uncertain as to what to say or do next. Storm wasted no time solving the problem for her.

"Why don't you show Takamori to his quarters and let him get reacquainted with Saido. We can all meet for dinner in about an hour."

The grateful glances they shot him made it clear his suggestion was very welcome. Moments later, Erin and Storm found themselves alone in the corridor. Neither spoke. With her newfound awareness of his vulnerability, she was too self-conscious to think of anything to say, and he seemed content merely to look her over.

Although he had always found her almost unbelievably beautiful, several weeks of good care and rest had made her lovelier than ever. "I don't have to ask how you are," he said at length. "It's obvious you haven't missed me at all."

Erin's head darted up, a quick denial on her lips. She bit it back as she met his teasing gaze. Shrugging, she said, "Oh, I don't know about that. Once or twice I noticed you weren't around."

"How gratifying," he muttered dryly, taking her arm and guiding her toward his room. "You can tell me all about it while I change. Half of Japan seems to be clinging to me."

Although she went along without protest, Erin could not help but be struck by his casual attitude toward her. They might have been an old married couple, for all the concern he showed for propriety. Not that she minded. It was far too good just to be near him again to object to anything he might do.

Or so she thought until, having dismissed the little serving girls who brought him hot water and towels, Storm matter-of-factly stripped off his jacket and shirt and began vigorously to scrub himself.

Erin could not tear her eyes from him. The burnished expanse of his heavily muscled torso fascinated her. She could almost feel the silken roughness of chestnut hair covering his chest and tapering down his lean abdomen to disappear beneath the belt of his trousers.

Her hands clenched spasmodically as she fought against the almost irresistible urge to touch him. Everything in her longed for the feel of his warm skin against hers, to know again the strength of his arms holding her close and the latent power of his body pressed to hers.

"Something wrong?" Storm asked, eyeing

her above the towel he was using to dry himself. His sardonic look made it clear he had a good idea what was going through her mind.

At any other time, Erin would have been embarrassed by the obviousness of her feelings. But thanks to her conversation with Odetsu, she was better able to overcome her own inhibitions.

Meeting his eyes calmly, she said, "Not that I can see. You're easily the best-looking man I've ever encountered."

Storm's response was as gratifying as it was amusing. His mouth dropped open and a dull flush stained his chiseled cheekbones. For a long moment he could do no more than stare at her.

Just when he thought he had finally begun to understand her delightfully complex character, she did something totally unexpected. Was this the same young girl he had watched teetering on the brink of womanhood, unaware of the full power of her sensuality and uncertain of her feelings? She seemed suddenly more than confident about both.

"Uh . . . I'm glad you think so." His pewter gaze softened as he watched her bite her delectable lower lip. She glanced away, unconsciously trailing a small foot across the floor. Storm laughed gently. "Do you realize that's the first time you've ever paid me a compliment?"

"Oh, no, it can't be."

"I assure you, it is. Does this mean you no

longer find me an unredeemable black-guard?"

"I never thought that," Erin protested softly.

"Which? That I was unredeemable or a blackguard?"

Spurred by his teasing tone, she faced him saucily. "I confess there were times when I considered you a bit of a rogue, but not once have I thought you were beyond redemption."

"Oh, Lord," Storm groaned, "don't tell me you harbor hopes of reforming me?"

Erin shook her head firmly. "Not at all. I just think sometimes you have tried to appear harder and more ruthless than you really are."

In the act of pulling on a fresh shirt, Storm paused. Though he tried hard to glare at her, he could manage only a semblance of a frown as he said, "I warned you once before about attributing motives to me that I do not possess."

"Yes, you did. But it seems to me that you have also gone out of your way to make me feel comfortable and happy here, without receiving much, if anything, in return. That is hardly the act of a ruthless man."

"How do you know I'm not simply lulling you into a false sense of security before taking advantage of your faith in me?"

Erin shrugged, unperturbed by the implied threat. "Are you?"

"If I am, I'd hardly tell you now."

"And if you aren't, which is far more likely, you'd die before admitting it. No, I'm afraid you will just have to put up with my high opinion of you, since you seem disinclined to do anything to change it."

Storm frowned, unsure of how he should take that. On the one hand, he was delighted that Erin thought so well of him. But on the other, it left him in more of a quandary than ever. His restraint of the last few weeks was beginning to tell. He didn't share her absolute confidence in his fortitude, yet he was loath to disappoint her.

"Just don't go around telling everyone what a nice person I am," he muttered gruffly. "My reputation couldn't stand it."

Erin laughed softly. As he buttoned his shirt and tucked it into his trousers, she picked up the clean jacket laid out on the bed and held it for him. The service, offered instinctively, was received just as matter-of-factly. Only as Storm slid his powerful arms into the sleeves did both suddenly realize what they were doing.

Their eyes met in silent acknowledgment of the new, companionable intimacy enriching the sensual tension that had existed between them from the beginning. When the jacket was in place, Storm turned to her. A big bronzed hand reached out, the knuckles gently brushing the curve of her cheek.

Erin trembled beneath his touch, but made

no effort to move away. Her breath became shallower as ripples of pleasure darted through her. The feather-light caress moved her more than she would have believed possible. Without even knowing that she did so, she swayed toward him.

Storm hesitated only an instant. His self-control was precarious at best, yet he could not deny himself some small relief for his raging hunger. All the weeks of pent-up desire came together in a burning firestorm of need that threatened to consume him.

His hand slipped to the nape of her neck beneath the silken fall of her ebony hair. Drawing her closer, he breathed her name like a whisper on the cool night air.

"Erin . . . do you really understand what you're doing?"

Beyond speech, she could only nod. The luminescent glow of her indigo eyes told him more eloquently than any words how much she wanted him. A low sigh of thankfulness escaped him as he brought her tenderly to him.

Erin nestled against him, infinitely secure and content in his embrace. Her head rested just below his broad shoulder; her arms were wrapped snugly around his taut waist beneath the soft wool of his frock coat. She could feel the rapid beat of his heart under her cheek and knew it matched her own.

Storm savored the feel of her in his arms. She was so delicately formed, yet lacked nothing of a woman's attributes. Her body might have been made for his, so perfectly did they fit together. He was struck by an overwhelming desire to cherish and protect her, even as he yearned to plunder her beauty without restraint.

The urge to lay her down on the bed where he had come so close to taking her just short weeks before was almost irresistible. Only his concern for her innocence, and for how she would feel afterward, stopped him. Ruefully he acknowledged that he was putting her well-being above his own. Scruples he hadn't known he possessed were in firm control.

For all his thoughts about wanting revenge for the hurt she had done him eight years before, he was incapable of harming her. What happened then seemed singularly unimportant. All that mattered was the woman he held in his arms, who he was at last willing to admit bore no resemblance at all to the shallow girl he remembered.

Tilting her head back, Storm touched a gentle kiss to her lips. Erin's eyes were closed, so that she could not see the sweeping tenderness of his expression. But she felt it in his touch, and knew it signaled a turning point in their relationship. Whatever doubts she still had about her own course of action vanished at that moment.

A radiant smile curved her mouth as her eyelids fluttered open. Gazing into quicksilver depths, she murmured, "You don't have to go away again soon, do you?"

Storm shook his head a bit dazedly. "No . . . I don't think so."

"Good, because even though Odetsu did her best to keep me occupied, I was very lonely while you were gone."

"I thought you didn't miss me."

"No, you didn't. You knew I was fibbing."

He laughed softly, delighted by her candor. "Maybe I hoped a little."

Unwilling to let her go completely, he kept an arm around her shoulders as they left the room and walked down the hallway to the enclosed veranda where dinner would be served. As they did so, Erin glanced up at him, her eyes sparkling. "Did you miss me?"

Storm hesitated. He was tempted to tell her the truth—that he had ached for her every hour that they were apart, that the journey had been made in record time not just because of safety considerations but because he couldn't stand to be away from her a moment longer than necessary, that he had lain awake every night thinking of her and longing for the feel of her next to him.

But he was concerned that the full revelation of his passion might frighten her, so he said only, "It's a good thing Takamori is such a good friend. Otherwise he would never have been able to put up with my impatience and eagerness to get home."

Erin was content with that. She was still smiling as they entered the room overlooking a garden of gnarled pines beside a slowly winding stream spanned by a latticed bridge. Odetsu and Takamori were already seated before the low lacquer table. They broke off their conversation when the other couple arrived, but it was clear from their tender expressions that whatever had been said was satisfying to them both.

"You look much more cheerful, my friend," Takamori said. "Should I attribute that to the serene atmosphere of your home, which banishes all care?"

"Attribute it to whatever you like," Storm advised good-humoredly. "But don't belabor the point or I will feel compelled to point out that you look rather more relaxed and content yourself."

Erin watched in fascination as the rugged samurai warrior blushed. He cast a hurried look at Odetsu, who was struggling to hide a smile. Wryly Takamori shook his head. "I regret to say that we are not very good examples of the inscrutable Oriental. For myself, I can at least claim the years I spent at school in California are to blame. But Odetsu has no such excuse."

"Why do I need one?" she parried teasingly. "If I must hide my thoughts from Davin-san and Erin, I will have no energy left for anything else. Besides," she admitted guilelessly, "it would do no good to try."

Storm laughed as they all took their places around the table. Eyeing Takamori, he asked, "Did you really think I came after you just because our politics happen to agree? The truth is, I knew that Odetsu would never forgive me if you ran into trouble and I wasn't around to help get you out. I faced a lifetime of cold tea, stale rice and lumpy beds. Compared to the havoc this gentle lady could wreak in my house, the shogun's warriors pose no threat at all."

They were still chuckling over that as the serving girls entered with bottles of sake, ceramic cups and a wicker basket full of small steaming towels, which they set in the center of the table.

As Odetsu handed the towels around, she explained to Erin, "These are called *oshibori*. They are scented with eucalyptus and are intended to refresh the weary traveler."

When each had been used to clean hands and faces, they were returned to the basket and quickly whisked away by an attentive maid. Moments later, small dishes of soy sauce, chopsticks and tiny ceramic bars for holding the sticks were placed before each of them. The soothing music of a samisen, the three-stringed instrument played by geishas, picked up in the background as the sake cups were filled and the first course arrived.

Although Erin had helped to prepare the meal, she was still surprised by its complexity and elegance. Bamboo mats held a tempting selection of appetizers, including shrimp wrapped in seaweed, chestnuts cooked in green tea, slices of steamed duck, and marinated asparagus.

Black-and-gold lacquer bowls were filled with a clear soup flavored with bits of sea bass and garnished with thin slices of lime. Next came wooden trays decorated with rice kernels and seaweed to resemble a miniature seashore suited to the paper-thin slices of raw fish arranged like the petals of a white-and-red flower.

Erin had at first balked at eating uncooked fish, but she quickly learned why *sashimi* was so popular. Accompanied by the potent green horseradish aptly called *wasabi,* or tears, it made a delicacy she could not resist.

By mutual agreement, a brief respite was taken before the next course.

As lovely dancing girls appeared from behind a screen at the far end of the room and began to perform their slow, ritualistic movements to the accompaniment of the samisen, Takamori said quietly, "It has been a long time since I was able to relax like this. I had almost forgotten how good it could feel."

Storm nodded somberly. "Perhaps soon your efforts will be rewarded. From what I can see, the shogun's power is beginning to crumble."

"I hope you are right. This new spirit that is abroad in our land will not be contained much longer. If it is not soon released in positive action, we may be in for an orgy of violence that will surpass anything that has gone before."

At Erin's dismayed look, he smiled gently. "I don't really believe there will be great bloodletting. Some, certainly, but not the sort of civil upheaval your own country endured. We in Japan learned much from that."

"I'm glad you did," Storm murmured. "I doubt if anyone else can say the same."

"You are understandably bitter," Odetsu interjected softly. "But there must be some consolation in the knowledge that you are working to prevent a similar tragedy here."

"There is," he admitted, "but that isn't the only reason for my involvement. I believe in what the reformers hope to achieve—a new form of government which will encourage development of the entire country instead of just lining the coffers of a chosen few."

Takamori nodded firmly. "Otherwise, Japan will never be able to make the advances we need to become truly equal with the Western powers. We will evolve into little more than an international colony."

"How can anyone object to changes that will make you stronger?" Erin asked. "Surely the shogun would approve of that?"

"Unfortunately not," Odetsu said. "He sees any change as a threat to his power, and really he is right about that. Much of the nobility wants to do away with the shogunate entirely and build a new government around the emperor."

"Does the emperor support this?"

Storm nodded to the serving girl who waited to bring the next course before he answered. "Who knows? He is little more than a child and he has been trained from birth to defer to the shogun, who is the true ruler. But I think that perhaps, with the proper encouragement, he could be made to see the importance of reform."

As lacquer trays of batter-dipped shrimp and vegetables were placed before them, Erin remembered something Odetsu had mentioned to her several days before. Dipping one of the deep-fried morsels into a bowl of sauce set beside it, she said, "I understand that Takamori's family is one of those in the forefront of the reform effort. But isn't there another, the Choshu, who also wish to defeat the shogun?"

Takamori and Storm glanced at each other worriedly as Odetsu's soft black eyes clouded over with sadness. Very softly she said, "Yes, the Choshu are working secretly toward that end."

"If their efforts are secret, how do you know about them?"

Odetsu hesitated. She put down the *tempura* she had been about to taste. Her gaze went to Takamori, who reached out and gently covered her hand with his. His touch gave her the encouragement she needed to go on.

"I know because I am Choshu. So was my late husband, who was also my distant cousin. Three years ago, he and a group of other well-meaning but hotheaded young men were accused of plotting against the shogun. It is true that there had been some conversations about the need for change, but it had not gone beyond that. Nonetheless, my husband and the others were ordered to commit *seppuku*."

At Erin's puzzled look, she explained softly, "That is the ritual form of suicide. There was no choice but to obey. To refuse would have disgraced our entire family and given the shogun even more reason to be suspicious of us. So my husband died, but that was not enough. The shogun was so enraged that he also ordered all wives and children to die as well."

Erin's eyes widened in horror. The image of her friend's little boy, Saido, who was a joy to everyone in the household, sprang into her mind. Odetsu must have been pregnant with him at the time. It was inhuman to think that anyone would have expected her to take her own life. "Surely your family refused to let you be harmed?"

Odetsu shook her head sadly. "Like many Japanese men, my father and brothers place their honor above all. They felt my husband's precipitate action had brought shame to them, so they wanted all reminders of it blotted out. They also realized that by obeying the shogun in this matter, they could lull him into a false sense of security. Therefore, I was ordered to comply."

Her throat tight with horror, Erin asked, "How did you get away?"

"With help from Takamori and Davin-san. They had known my husband and when they heard what was happening, they offered their assistance. Not only did they rescue me, but Davin-san also gave me shelter in his home so that I could bring up my son safely."

The extraordinary level of devotion Odetsu showed toward Storm was now explained. With Erin's new understanding of the situation also came embarrassment. For a few days after she realized Storm did not intend for her to be his mistress, she had wondered if that position might not already be occupied by the beautiful woman he called his housekeeper.

Such an arrangement was certainly not impossible, especially in a country where the will of men was supreme and women were expected to be accommodating. But even before she learned the truth of how Odetsu came to be in his home, Erin had realized that Storm was far too decent a man to ever take advantage of a woman who was dependent on him. She herself was living proof of that, much to her exasperation.

Now that she had met Takamori, she also understood that the lovely Japanese noblewoman's affections were firmly engaged elsewhere. There was no doubt that only his unwillingness to expose her to further dangers kept him from publicly returning her esteem.

Erin was certain that as soon as the political crisis was ended, Odetsu and Takamori planned to marry. Even as she wished them well, she could not help but hope that her own relationship with Storm could be settled as happily.

Glancing out at the tranquil garden, Erin drew her courage around her. Silently she resolved that before the night was over she would know once and for all whether she had any real chance of undoing the damage done by eight sorrow-filled years and winning the heart of the man who held the key to hers.

Chapter Eleven

"GOOD NIGHT, ERIN. SLEEP WELL." ODETSU smiled as she spoke, her knowing glance making it clear she was well aware that her friend had other plans. The men had gone off to talk and the servants were clearing up the remnants of dinner. In a short time, the household would be settling down for the night. The hours of darkness were the perfect time for soft murmurs and languorous sighs.

Erin nodded absently. She was too busy thinking about how she could contrive to be alone with Storm to really hear what Odetsu was saying. But her next words brought her up short.

"Don't be disturbed if you hear sounds from the bathing room. Takamori and I used it earlier, but I believe Davin-san will want to wash away the grime of the road before retiring. I heard him tell one of the servants to be sure the water was especially hot."

With a soft smile and what sounded suspiciously like a chuckle, she was gone, leaving Erin to stare after her in bemusement. Several moments passed before she was able to collect herself enough to act. Hurrying to her room, she took off the padded kimono she wore and exchanged it for a thin robe in black silk embroidered with tiny mauve blossoms.

The robe had appeared in her wardrobe several weeks before, yet another gift from Storm, who insisted on showering her with all manner of comforts. Its wide sleeves and flowing lines were reminiscent of Japanese styles, but far more sensuous. The almost sheer fabric rested low on her shoulders to reveal the creamy curve of her breast. Light from the oil lamps shone through it, making it little more than a tantalizing veil over her slender body.

Brushing her hair vigorously, she left it to flow down her back, just touching the curve of her small, firm buttocks. Drops of precious attar of roses were placed at the pulse points of her throat and wrists, and in the cleft between her breasts.

As she gazed at herself in the framed mirror above her dressing table, Erin could not help but note that her nipples were hard and thrusting through the fragile silk. Telling herself that was only because she was cold, she slid the door open carefully and peered outside.

The corridor was empty. The only sounds that reached her were the soft rustle of wind in the pine trees outside and the distant splash of water from the bathing chamber. Taking a deep breath, she walked quickly toward it.

Having sent the last servants off to bed, Storm glanced around the small wood-paneled room. As always, it was meticulously clean and well-ordered, with fresh towels and a clean kimono laid out on the bench, rinsing buckets at hand, and the soaking tub full of steaming water.

Not yet accustomed to the Japanese custom of being bathed by young girls, he preferred to see to the task himself. Stripping off his shirt and trousers, he rubbed the back of his neck wearily.

The journey to find Takamori and bring him safely to Yokohama had been more trying than he liked to admit. Several times they had come close to discovery by the shogun's men. More than once, it would have been prudent to hide out for a day or two before continuing.

But his longing for Erin kept intruding on his common sense. He had pressed on, grateful for the fact that Takamori was every bit as anxious to see Odetsu and therefore did not object.

Picking up a bar of sandalwood soap, he

dipped his hands into one of the buckets and worked up a lather. Preoccupied with his thoughts, he was oblivious of the perfection of his rock-hard form. Powerfully contoured muscles defined every inch of his huge body, from his sculptured shoulders down across his immense chest to the sinewy thighs and calves lightly covered with hair. Dark curls of hair covered his torso, tapering down his flat abdomen to thicken again at his groin. His taut back and firm buttocks were burnished by the flickering lamplight as he turned to lift the rinse bucket.

Stepping over the wood-slat drain, he poured the water over himself, letting it flow from the thick pelt of his chestnut mane down over his massive length. Shaking his head, he sent a shower of droplets across the room before he slipped easily into the piercingly hot water.

His arms were stretched out along the side of the tub, his head tilted back and his eyes closed. More relaxed than he had been in days, he did not notice the sudden rush of cooler air as the door behind him slid open. Nor did he hear Erin's soft intake of breath as she beheld the magnificently naked male before her.

Nothing had prepared her for the sheer beauty of his body. Its impact was overwhelming, filling her with desire so intense as to block out all rational thought. A hot core of inner fire licked at her, making her tremble inwardly. Her eyes darkened to the stormy hue of a thunder-filled sky. The rush of blood to her cheeks gave her a becoming flush.

For long moments she could only stare at him. What she had seen of his body clothed and felt when he held her in his arms did not begin to approach the compelling splendor at last revealed to her. How had she managed to live twenty-four years without being aware that such wonders existed?

Even as she asked herself that, Erin knew the answer. Never before had she been ready to accept a man in all his glory, to delight in his unbridled maleness even as she discovered the full promise of her womanhood.

But she was ready now. There was no doubt of that. Her hardened nipples grew even tauter, straining against the sheer black silk of her robe. Her breasts swelled, threatening to spill out of the deeply low-cut neckline. In the secret place where she longed to receive him, she grew hot and moist.

When he turned suddenly, alerted by her soft moan, she met his stunned gaze unhesitantly.

E-Erin . . . ?

Storm doubted the evidence of his own eyes. He must be dreaming. The glorious vision before him could not be real. Never, even in his wildest fantasies, had he imagined Erin coming to him in this way. She was too reticent, too inexperienced.

Who, then, was the ravishingly beautiful

creature clad only in a gossamar-thin robe that hid little of her ripely curved body? She looked like Erin, or at least as he had always fantasized her. But the voluptuous gleam of her indigo eyes, the ripe fullness of her mouth and the unmistakable appreciation of her gaze were hardly in keeping with the woman he thought he knew.

Distracted by the rapid rise and fall of her barely concealed breasts, he did not at once realize that her small hands were sliding the garment from her. He was unable to tear his eyes away as beauty beyond any he had ever envisioned was revealed to him.

Erin swallowed hard in a futile effort to control her nervousness. She was risking everything on a desperate attempt to convince Storm that she loved him enough to overcome whatever problems might lie between them. If he rejected her, or sent her away pityingly, she would be crushed beyond any hope of recovery.

From some hidden well of courage, she found the strength to speak lightly. "I hope you don't mind my sharing your bath? Odetsu told me it's perfectly all right in Japan for men and women to bathe together."

He didn't answer; indeed the very capacity to speak seemed to have deserted him. All his attention was focused on the slender perfection of her alabaster form touched by wisps of sandalwood-scented mist. The fiery intensity of his gaze increased her shyness almost beyond endurance. But Erin was determined to persevere.

Despite the trembling weakness of her limbs, she managed to refill the buckets beside the tub and pick up the discarded bar of soap. The handful of hairpins she had thought to bring with her served to hold up the silken mass of her hair.

Repeating his motions of only a short time before, she lathered herself thoroughly, from the slender curve of her shoulders down across her high-pointed breasts to her tiny waist and slender hips. Propping a small foot up on the bench, she scrubbed each leg in turn before pouring the rinse water over herself.

Storm watched every graceful movement with fascination. Never had he seen anything so overwhelmingly, yet unconsciously sensual. Her poignant innocence enthralled him, as did her vulnerability. What on earth was she thinking of to let him see her like this? Did she truly have no understanding of what a man in the throes of uncontrollable passion might do?

Even as he marveled at her actions, he shifted uncomfortably in the tub. Fragrances tossed into the water gave it a deep blue stain, enough so that by sinking as far down as possible, he could conceal that part of himself believed to be most shocking to innocent maidens. Taking a deep breath, he schooled himself to endure the torment of her nearness.

Erin glanced at him out of the corner of her eye as she approached the tub. He was staring at the ceiling, as though the arrangement of wooden slats somehow fascinated him. Deeply chagrined, she dipped a toe into the water, only to jerk it out at once.

"It's hot!"

Storm laughed indulgently, giving up the brief battle to keep his eyes from her. A soft sheen of dampness shone iridescent against her pearly skin. The dusky velvet of her nipples beckoned his touch, and it was all he could do not to thrust himself out of the tub and pull her into his arms.

"It's supposed to be hot."

"Not that much. How can you stand it?"

"You get used to it. You'll see. After the first moment or two, you'll love it." Holding out a hand, he managed to control his surging need enough to gently encourage her. "Come on, now. It's too cold to stand out there."

Erin complied gingerly. The water burned her skin, making every pore throb. She bit her lip to hold back a gasp as slowly, hesitantly, she lowered herself into the tub.

Rather to her surprise, within seconds her body began to relax. Clenched muscles eased. Stiffened tendons and taut nerves slackened. She even forgot to be self-conscious, but only for a moment.

As she became aware of Storm still holding her hand, heat of a very different sort swept over her. It was all she could do not to throw herself into his arms and beg him to relieve the aching need pulsating within her.

If Odetsu was right, that was probably the worst thing she could do. As little as she knew about men, she was still sensible enough to understand that pressure of that sort would only heighten whatever problem might exist. To succeed with her plan, she had to go slowly and convince Storm that she truly cared at least as much for his pleasure as for her own.

That resolve served to take her mind off her own feelings and direct it firmly on him. With daring that would have been unthinkable even the day before, she leaned back against the rim of the tub and smiled enticingly.

"No wonder the Japanese spend so much time in these things. This is marvelous."

"Hmmm," Storm murmured, preoccupied with the ripe swell of her breasts visible above the indigo water. For a slender girl, she could hardly claim not to be well-endowed. He longed to fill his hands with those ivory mounds, to run his thumbs over the erect nipples and let his tongue taste once again her satiny sweetness.

Recollecting himself only through a massive effort of will, he said, "You certainly seem to be adjusting to life here. Or has mixed bathing become the norm in the States?"

Erin laughed softly, gladdened by the teasing gleam in his eye. If he was going to send her away, surely he would have done so by now? "Hardly. The penchant some ladies have developed recently for taking dips in the ocean while copiously swathed in cotton gowns is considered quite scandalous enough. I can't imagine what my Boston neighbors would say if they could see me now."

"The men would undoubtedly approve," Storm muttered. "It cannot have escaped your notice that you are a remarkably beautiful woman."

The tightness of his voice surprised Erin. She glanced at him warily. "You said the first day I arrived here that I was pretty at sixteen, but had changed a great deal. I took that to mean you found me less attractive."

Storm could not suppress a start of surprise. He stared at her for long moments before deciding she was sincere. She actually had no idea of her impact, far beyond what any flirtatious girl could ever achieve.

Grudgingly he said, "You misunderstood. The years have served you well. You are far lovelier now than you ever were."

Erin's eyes lowered, hidden by thick fringes as dark as her midnight-black hair. Relieved though she was to know that he found her attractive, she could not help but think that this only confirmed Odetsu's hints. Surely he would have done something about his desire for her by now, unless he was prevented by physical impairment.

Driven by curiosity she could not contain, she allowed her gaze to wander down along the hard, muscular plane of his chest as far as the dark swirls of hair around his navel. She could make out no sign of injury, but neither could she see any further. The water effectively blocked her view and heightened her frustration.

Storm shifted uneasily beneath her gaze. It was difficult enough to believe that such an incredible encounter was actually happening. When he tried to decide what he should do about it, he ran up against a stone wall of conflicting emotion.

Silently he conceded that he was acting completely out of character. He desperately wanted to touch and hold her, to let nature take its course regardless of the consequences. The strain of holding himself away from her was becoming intolerable. Driven by forces as fundamental as life itself, he reached out to caress the fragile nape of her neck.

Erin quivered under his touch. Her cheek rubbed against his hand, as though she were a small cat in need of petting. The low groan that escaped from him delighted her. She rightly judged it a sign of his weakening control. Confirmation came a moment later when a heavily muscled arm lashed out to close around her slender waist and draw her hard against him.

"My God, Erin," he rasped against the curve of her throat, "I'd have to be made of steel to resist you. You know that, don't you? Tell me that's why you came here."

"It is," she whispered breathlessly, stroking the massive expanse of his torso, her fingers rediscovering each entrancing muscle and sinew. "I can't deny it anymore, Storm. I want to give you everything possible. Please believe me. Let me show you how much I love you."

Hardly daring to credit what he heard, Storm shook his head dazedly. "You don't understand what you're saying. Just touching you like this isn't enough. I want all of you, in the most intimate way a man can have a woman."

"That's what I want, too," she murmured, her lips tracing the hard bulge of muscles along his arm. Beneath the water, their legs entwined, his steely thighs brushing against her softness. Erin moaned helplessly. Flames were raging out of control within her. She could no more deny her need for him than she could stop the beat of her heart.

Storm fought a brief, losing battle with his conscience. Honor demanded that he put her firmly from him. Survival required far different behavior. Growling deep in his throat, he lifted her chin, awed by the soft perfection of her mouth as it parted for him.

Their lips touched gently, tasting each other with delicate strokes until the sudden upsurge of passion beyond even what they had already experienced drove them to cling to each other, their tongues meeting in an erotic duel that sent starlight sparks of desire shimmering through both.

Erin clung as closely as possible to him, compelled by the most primitive hunger to feel him fill her body. Her hands stroked the broad expanse of his back, luxuriating in the discovery of taut muscles reaching from his shoulder blades down to his tapered waist and beyond to his sculptured buttocks.

The touch of his hair-roughened thighs against her softness dazed her. She was engulfed in male strength and power, drowning in desperate need for him, swept up in a raging fire that threatened to burn away her very soul and leave her transformed into a creature she could not yet imagine.

Inflamed by passion as great as her own, Storm could no longer resist his rampaging hunger. Sweeping her high against his chest, he rose from the tub. Water ran off them both in crystalline streams reflecting the flames of stone lanterns set around the small secluded room.

Laying her tenderly on the mats, he came down beside her, his arms cording with latent strength as he held his big body above her far smaller form. Slowly, so as not to frighten her, he let his mouth trail down the silken column of her throat to nestle in the scented hollow between her breasts.

"Erin," he groaned thickly, "if you're going to stop me, it has to be now."

A tiny dart of puzzlement raced through

her. That didn't sound like something a man who was concerned about his virility would say. But she could hardly quarrel with it, since his response was beyond anything she had even dared to hope for.

"I don't want you to stop. Please . . . don't leave me. I couldn't bear it."

Erin swallowed hard when she heard her own words. She hadn't meant to say anything that might put pressure on him. Hastily she amended, "Whatever you want, Storm, tell me. I want so much to please you. . . . It doesn't matter if everything doesn't happen, if we don't . . ." She broke off, not at all sure of how to phrase what she meant. Her vocabulary was sorely lacking in certain areas. She could only hope that he would understand without words.

Through the haze of his passion, Storm became aware that something about what she had just said troubled him. What was that about everything not happening? Lifting himself far enough away from her to be able to gaze into her eyes, he said, "Erin, are you absolutely sure you know what you're doing?"

"No," she admitted honestly, "but I want to learn. I'll do anything to make you happy."

Storm swallowed thickly. It was doubtful any man had ever had a more enticing offer. He was not about to turn her down, even if he couldn't quite shake the vague feeling that something was wrong.

Moving over her gently, he gave in to the

driving temptation to taste her breasts with his mouth. Erin moaned softly as he tongued first one nipple and then the other before drawing her into him with warm, sucking motions that sent spirals of flame shooting through her.

By the time he raised his head long moments later, her eyes were cloudy with passion and her body arched to his in undisguised need. Hoarsely he muttered, "Touch me, Erin. Let me feel your hands on me."

She complied instantly. Her caress was tentative at first, but grew quickly bolder as his moan of pleasure gave her the confidence she needed. Petal-soft fingers stroked the broad expanse of his chest, relishing the rough silk texture of his skin. Guided by instincts as ancient as humanity itself, her breasts rubbed against him, each separate strand of the hair on his chest teasing her nipples unbearably.

Determined to make it absolutely clear to him that she would do anything he wished, Erin urged him onto his back, letting the luxurious length of her hair trail across him. "Teach me, Storm," she whispered. "Tell me what you need."

With his heart threatening to pound right out of his chest and his breath coming in tortured gasps, he was hard pressed to answer. Erin had to strain to make out his words when he at last muttered, "Only you. That's all I need. God, you're so much a woman!"

Though she could hardly fail to be gratified

by such sentiments, Erin was nonetheless dismayed by his reluctance to instruct her. Instincts were good enough up to a point, but she was afraid her ignorance would prove too much for them. Without his guidance, she might well fail to arouse him sufficiently, much less actually satisfy him.

The tumult of her emotions had become so intense as to be painful. Tears glistened in her clear blue eyes and her lower lip trembled helplessly. "You must tell me. Otherwise I won't know. And if I do something wrong, or don't do something I should, then you won't be able . . . I mean, you might not . . ."

As the full impact of her words reached him, Storm's rugged features stiffened in shock. He told himself he must have misunderstood; she couldn't possibly mean what she seemed to. Yet if she did, it would explain a great deal, including her extraordinary willingness to take the initiative in their lovemaking and her apparent concern that he would somehow not be satisfied by her.

Gently cupping her face in his big hands, he sat up slightly, enough so that they were looking at each other directly. When she tried to turn away, he compelled her to meet his gaze.

"Erin, would you please explain to me what you are talking about?"

"I'm not . . . that is, I didn't mean anything. Just that I want you to be happy." Acutely embarrassed as much by what seemed at that moment to be her own overwhelming clumsiness as by the acute intimacy of their situation, she blushed fiercely. Her thick lashes were wet with tears that trickled slowly down her high-boned cheeks.

Gently he said, "And I want the same for you, but I don't understand why you are so concerned. Why do I get the impression that you have some idea there might be a . . . problem?"

Erin opened her mouth to speak, but no words came out. The touch of his huge body against hers unleashed a deluge of sensation that overwhelmed rational thought. As his hands slid tenderly down her back to cup the ripe curve of her hips, she trembled. Aware that she was making very little sense, she was still compelled to try.

"The war . . . I cared for a lot of men who were wounded . . . I didn't realize then what the effects of some of the injuries might be. . . . But when Odetsu explained . . ."

"Odetsu? What did she tell you?"

"Nothing, exactly. She just said that sometimes when a man is hurt, there might be some difficulty for him when he . . . wants a woman." Unable any longer to restrain her anguished sympathy for him, she blurted, "It doesn't matter. Can't you understand that? I love you far too much to care if you aren't able to do what you once could. Anything that happens between us will just be all the more precious for that."

The slate-gray hardness of Storm's eyes softened to quicksilver flames. He gazed at her in astonishment, mingling with tenderness beyond anything he had ever known. What an incredible woman she was! Innocent herself, she was still able to put aside her own inhibitions and fears in order to do whatever she could to express her love for him.

A hard core of anger and hurt that he had carried within him for years melted as he contemplated devotion greater than any he had ever imagined. Already he sensed that no matter how long he lived, he would not know what he had done to deserve her. But he wasn't about to question that now. All the driving, pounding urgency of his manhood demanded that he yield graciously to her care.

Tenderly smoothing her hair back from her heated face, he wiped away her tears with a gentle hand. His voice was husky as he said, "You are a remarkable woman, Erin. You make me feel quite unaccustomedly humble and not at all worthy of what you so generously offer.

"But," he hastened to add as she began to interrupt, "that doesn't mean I intend to turn my back on what looks very much like paradise. All it means is that before anything more happens between us, there is something I want you to know."

Glancing around the chamber, which was rapidly becoming chill, he laughed softly.

"This is hardly the setting for such a discussion. I want you weak with passion, not a fever."

His laughter deepened as he took in her enchanting blush. Standing quickly, he wrapped her in the copious folds of the silk kimono laid out for his use. It covered her so completely that she looked little more than a child, except for the delightful wanton gleam of her eyes and the swollen fullness of her ripe mouth.

With rapid strides he carried her down the deserted corridor to his room. The glow of charcoal braziers welcomed them. His bed was made up with extra pillows. A tray of plum wine sat on the sleeping platform. The wooden shutters leading to the garden were firmly closed.

Storm shook his head wryly. "I must congratulate Odetsu on her thoroughness. Once she makes up her mind to intervene in a situation, she doesn't miss a single detail."

Erin did not understand him, but that hardly mattered. Snuggled against his chest, she felt at once safer and more vulnerable than she ever had in her life. When he set her down gently on the smooth wood-plank floor and loosened the kimono, slipping it from her slender shoulders, she raised her arms to him in a gesture of innocently open need.

Storm waited barely an instant before gathering her to him. Carefully, so as not to put too much of his weight on her at once, he lowered her to the soft down-filled mattress. Gazing tenderly into her eyes, he said, "I love you, Erin. More than I ever thought it was possible to love anyone."

Much as she longed to believe him, she could not help but suspect that he spoke less from his heart than from the heat of the moment. Still, she was willing enough to turn his avowal to her own ends.

"Then, if you truly love me, you'll trust me . . . and let me . . ."

A slashing male grin lit his bronzed features. "Whatever you wish, my sweet."

With mingled trepidation and elation, Erin pressed him gently onto his back. The caresses begun so tentatively in the bathing chamber grew bolder. Inspired by his declaration of love, she overcame the last remnants of her shyness to delight in the discovery of his body.

A purr of sheer womanly pleasure rippled from her as her hands stroked the bulging muscles of his arms, upward to his sculptured shoulders. Feather-soft fingers roamed down his chest, tracing the thick mat of hair across his flat abdomen.

Tempted beyond endurance, she bent her head, tracing the same path with her lips and tongue. His skin tasted faintly salty, his scent crisply clean with a hint of muskiness that touched some hidden chord deep within her.

Not even the protection of her great innocence could make her oblivious of the effect of her caresses. The hot urgency of his manhood pressing against her thighs sent a little shiver of fear coursing through her, but it faded instantly as Storm groaned with pleasure, his big body arching to hers.

Though his stamina was greater than most men's, he suspected it had reached its limits. Erin's natural skill astounded him. Dimly in the back of his mind he realized that it was his love for her that made him so susceptible to her touch, but he still could not help but marvel at what she would be like when she gained some experience.

Already she put the most adept courtesans to shame. A wry grin touched his mouth as he considered that a man might well die of such pleasure, and not mind at all.

Much as he was enjoying himself, he knew the time had come to correct her misapprehensions, before his body did it for him. Grasping her shoulders, he pulled her up to him. His eyes were gently teasing as he said, "You know, it's an interesting thing about the Japanese. They're a little hard to get to know, but once one of them considers you a friend, there's nothing he—or she—won't do for you."

"That's nice," Erin muttered, far too enthralled by what was happening between them to engage in a discussion of cultural characteristics.

"Odetsu, for example . . ." Storm went on, gritting his teeth against the mounting waves of pleasure that threatened to make speech impossible. His voice was low and thick as he said, "She isn't above bending the truth a bit when she thinks it's in the best interests of a friend."

"Do we have to talk about that now?" Erin whispered dazedly, bemused by the flames licking along every inch of her body.

"I think we'd better." A wry laugh broke from Storm just as his hands slid down to her waist and he turned suddenly, tipping her under him. Erin gasped at the sudden reversal in their positions. The molten glitter of his eyes took her by surprise. She sensed, more even than saw, some drastic change in him. The driving determination he had held in careful restraint during her enraptured explorations abruptly broke loose. There was no mistaking the full arousal of a man intent on claiming the woman he loved.

Grinning at her shocked look, he said, "Odetsu didn't actually tell you I had problems being with a woman, did she? She just dropped some none-too-subtle hints and left you to your own conclusions. But I'm afraid she misled you, my sweet. There is absolutely nothing wrong with my virility, as you are about to discover."

Before Erin could do more than yelp in astonishment, his heavily muscled leg pressed between her slender thighs, opening her to him. Strong, skilled hands stroked the length of her, from her high, full breasts to her slender hips, tapered legs and the tangle of dark curls that sheltered her womanhood.

Wave after wave of exquisite rapture pounded through her.

When his mouth claimed her nipple, suckling her urgently, Erin cried out. Stunned by the sudden realization of just how wrong she had been, overwhelmed by the unexpected domination of her body and senses, she could only yield to his mastery.

Taking a firm grip on his patience, Storm schooled himself to go slowly. Mindful of her virginity, he was determined to bring her to a peak of yearning so intense that she would not feel the first painful instant of his possession.

Heedless of his own burning need, he trailed gentle kisses down the silken length of her abdomen. Erin moaned brokenly, shocked by the ardor of his caresses, yet unable to restrain her desperate need for more. A raging hunger was building inside her, threatening to devour her from within.

When his mouth followed the path of his hand to nuzzle at the cluster of curls between her thighs, she grasped his head frantically, uncertain as to whether she wanted to stop him or urge him on.

Storm gave her no choice. Seizing her hands, he held them flat at her sides as he satisfied his own ravenous craving to know her in every way possible. The hidden place of her womanhood unfurled for him like an exquisite blossom. He lapped at her tenderly, coaxing precious drops of sweetness from her inner secrets.

Radiant shimmers of light pierced her. She was swept into a fiery vortex that whirled her far from consciousness. A star as bright as the sun itself exploded within her. Erin cried his name, writhing under him as the full force of sensual fulfillment struck her. Storm held her tenderly through long, convulsive moments until at last she slid slowly back to earth.

He let her rest barely a moment. Before the tremors racking her body could subside, he moved above her, gently spreading her legs and easing the tip of his hardness into her hot, moist womanhood. His mouth closed over hers, filling her with the taste of herself, before he thrust slowly and deeply. A soft cry of surprise broke from her as the barrier of her maidenhead yielded easily.

Waiting just long enough to let her become accustomed to his possession, he began to move inside her. With infinite skill and patience, he drew out their shared climb to the peak, varying the rhythm of his thrusts until Erin thought she would go mad from the sensations he aroused in her. Grasping his taut hips, she arched against him, begging him wordlessly to unleash the full power of his manhood.

A sheen of perspiration glistened over them both. The harsh sound of their breathing filled the room. The musky scent of unbridled arousal perfumed the air more potently than any incense.

Heeding her silent plea, Storm slid his

hands under her, cupping her small buttocks. Careful to make absolutely sure he did not hurt her, he drew out almost completely before plunging hard and fast into the sanctuary of her body.

Glowing splinters of light exploded behind Erin's eyes. Far off in the distance she heard her own sob of release rushing away from her. Consciousness vanished down a spinning, tumbling chute ending in the blissful haven of utter fulfillment.

Chapter Twelve

"I'M NOT SURE I SHOULDN'T BE UPSET WITH Odetsu," Erin said. "After all, she did take advantage of my ignorance."

"That she did," Storm agreed amiably, munching on a Japanese-style sandwich of rice rolled in sheets of seaweed and stuffed with thin slices of raw tuna and cucumber. Washed down by the potent local beer, it made a pleasant if belated lunch.

After a languorous night and early morning spent in ardent lovemaking interspersed with brief periods of rest, both were ravenous. Erin could not remember food ever tasting so good. Drops of juice from a crisp apple clung to her lips as she said, "But you were much worse. You actually let me believe you were . . . What's that word you told me?"

Storm grinned, reaching for a shrimp

wrapped in deep-fried noodles and stuffed with sweet chestnut. "Impotent."

"That's it." She shook her head dazedly. "I can't believe I was so gullible. I'll bet you've never had that problem in your life."

"On the contrary. I find myself with precisely that affliction right now."

Erin laughed sympathetically. Considering the erotic excesses of the last few hours, he could hardly be blamed for needing a rest. Her body glowed with radiant fulfillment and her eyes sparkled with wonder at the marvelous discoveries she had made. From the tip of her toes to the top of her head, she felt at once content and elated. The world was suddenly an enchanting place, full of delights she had never before even imagined.

With Storm as her patient, loving guide, she had wandered down glittering pathways of pleasure leading to rapturous fulfillment. His skill was endless, his desire unbridled. Together they had explored the ultimate in ecstasy, waking from exhausted sleep to make love again and again.

His concern that they might be overdoing, given her recently virgin state, vanished before her ardent longing. Even so, he never lost sight of her needs and responses, always being absolutely certain that he was not hurting or frightening her in the slightest.

Such gentle coaxing brought its own reward. As the night owls hooted in the pine trees outside and the full moon dipped into the indigo sea, Erin reveled in joyful celebration of her womanliness. Enthralled by their intimacy and by the rapture she could give him, she left the last of her girlhood behind without regret.

By the time the flaming sun rose above the mist-shrouded hills, she was transformed into a woman of infinite passion and tenderness, capable of both giving and receiving the ultimate in loving union. Storm's woman.

A tiny satisfied smile curved her mouth as she thought of that. Just a short time before, she would have bridled at the idea of belonging to any man. Now she gloried in it, knowing that he was as much hers as she was his.

One of the best parts of their loving closeness was that she felt secure enough to ask him things that would have once been unthinkable. Blushing only slightly, she said, "Do women always recover more quickly from lovemaking than men?"

Storm nodded ruefully. "Unfortunately, they do. That seems to be one of nature's little jokes. We men like to think ourselves the stronger sex, but in truth you women have the edge when it comes to sheer stamina."

Propping himself up on an elbow, he gazed at her across the small expanse of down-filled mattress separating them. "Some men refuse to believe it, but a woman's capacity for pleasure is far greater than ours. As I think you have already discovered."

His teasing gaze deepened her flush but did

not convince her to desist. "That hardly seems fair."

"Oh, I don't know. There's a great deal of satisfaction to be had simply in giving pleasure. In fact, when a man and woman truly love each other, their intimacy doesn't have to be restricted to sexual expressions."

Erin could hardly deny her interest in that provocative statement. Beneath the thin quilt, her body stirred languidly.

Storm watched her with tender amusement. He reached out a hand to gently trace the curve of her cheek down along her alabaster throat to the scented hollow between her breasts. The quiver that ran through her made him chuckle.

Drawing her closer, he nibbled gently on an earlobe as he murmured, "You enchant me. Was there ever a more delightful woman?"

The soft purr that broke from her seemed to be all the answer he required. Slipping an arm beneath the cover, he wrapped it around her slender waist and turned her onto her stomach. Erin gasped as he pulled the quilt back, baring her to his gaze.

Before she could move, Storm had straddled her, his hair-roughened thighs holding her firmly in place beneath him. "Relax. Believe me, you'll enjoy this."

Placing both hands along her spine, he pressed in slowly and firmly, manipulating the sensitive nerve endings just beneath the surface of the skin. Gradually drifting downward toward the dimpled curve of her buttocks, the deep, relaxing massage made Erin moan. Carefully applied pressure trod a fine line between pleasure and pain. Shocked by the intensity of her response, she tried to stop him. But Storm would not allow her to move.

His big hands grasped her shoulders and the nape of her neck, thumbs moving in deep, circular motions. By the time he turned her over, Erin was far too limp to protest further. She lay docilely beneath him as he kneaded each separate toe, the calves of her legs and her thighs. Pressing his palms into the flat plain of her abdomen just above the cluster of dark curls he had explored so thoroughly, he smiled devilishly.

"Stop looking so aroused, Erin. This is a strictly therapeutic massage called *shiatsu*. The Japanese acclaim it for its healing benefits."

"Among other things," she groaned, unable to repress the undulating waves of pleasure spreading through her. Her nipples tautened as her breasts swelled temptingly.

"As nearly as I can figure out," Storm continued huskily, "its major effect is to banish fatigue and restore certain energies."

"Hmmm."

"It certainly seems to work well."

Following the path of his eyes, Erin laughed softly. His claim that she had worn him out was no longer valid. As his manhood rose hard and urgent, she opened her arms joyfully.

They tumbled across the bed, far too eager to allow for long, drawn-out lovemaking.

Grasping her narrow waist, Storm lifted her above him. She had barely a moment to wonder what he intended before he lowered her slowly, inch by inch, onto his maleness. Erin's head fell back, her lips parted in a cry of aching delight.

Enthralled by the power he gave her to move as she chose, she relished the feel of him inside her. Her steadily increasing rhythm made Storm groan. His eyes narrowed to quicksilver slits, his breath coming in harsh pants as she brought them both to an ecstatic culmination shattering in its intensity.

Passion spent for the moment, they fell back in a tangle of arms and legs. He laughed throatily as he cradled her head against his sweat-dampened chest.

"You make me feel like a randy youth again. How did I manage to get along without you all these years?"

"I can ask the same myself. It seems as though everything that has gone before was only a dream. My life has at last begun, here in your arms."

Storm's arms tightened around her. "Our life together, my love. For now that I have found you again, I will never let you go."

He paused, wondering if she would object to his unbridled possessiveness. If she did, he would have to find some way to bring her around, for he could not conceive of existence without her. She had become as necessary to him as air and water. Perhaps more so, for the lack of those things would bring only physical death, while the very survival of his soul seemed to depend on her.

But far from protesting, Erin delighted in the knowledge that she was necessary to him. Nonetheless, she was still not prepared when he matter-of-factly announced, "As soon as the political situation calms down a bit, we must see about getting married."

"M-married . . . ?"

"Yes, of course. You didn't think I had anything else in mind, did you?"

Tilting her head back, he read the silent admission in her clear blue eyes. Storm shook his head in amazement. "You did. You actually thought I would be content to have you as my mistress."

"What else could I think?"

"Yet you still agreed to come here."

Erin smiled unrepentantly. "I suppose after the way I behaved last night, you must think me a shameless hussy."

"Not just last night. I seem to recall you working your wicked ways all morning."

"Too true. I'll just have to repent and re-form."

"Not if I have anything to say about it," Storm assured her. He cupped her head gently, drawing her close for a long, tender kiss. Their bodies entwined languorously. Cradled in his massive arms, Erin drifted off to sleep, a contented smile following her into her dreams.

"Are you sure you are not angry with me?" Odetsu asked the next day when Erin at last bestirred herself to venture into the garden. She found her friend gathering fallen pine cones, which would undoubtedly end up in delicately artful arrangements around the house.

The Japanese woman looked so genuinely concerned and contrite that Erin could not help but laugh. "I'm sure," she admitted ruefully. "You did me a great favor and I thank you for it."

Odetsu smiled in relief. She had thought that morning as she heard Davin-san whistling when he went off to join Takamori that her instincts had been correct. But it was good to know for sure.

"I am pleased that you are happy," she said shyly. "In such difficult times, people must find all the joy they can."

Erin nodded somberly. Although Storm had said very little to her about the progress of efforts to overthrow the shogun, she had the impression that the crisis was coming to a head.

All morning men had arrived at the house, coming in quietly through the back door. Most were Japanese, but a few were Western—men like Storm who wanted to do whatever they could to prevent widespread bloodshed. The low rumble of their voices reached her as she went about her own tasks. They sounded tired and worried, but undeniably determined.

Watching her, Odetsu saw the sorrow that darkened her eyes, and she wondered at its source. Softly she said, "Takamori has told me of the terrible civil war that ravaged your own country. I know that Davin-san was caught up in it, but were you also?"

"Not as much as he. Many of the people in the South, where he lived, lost everything. In the North, where my home was, we were more fortunate. But I still saw much suffering and death. It is bad enough when such things happen between people of different countries, but when brothers fight each other, it is terrible beyond belief."

"There was a time here in Japan when the daimyo warred almost constantly. That is how the shogun came to power. The people were so tired of violence that they were willing to accept the rule of one man, no matter how tyrannical."

"But conditions have changed now, haven't they?" Erin asked. "The coming of the Westerners saw to that. With men like Takamori traveling outside the country and being exposed to different ways, it was inevitable they would bring great reforms to their own land."

"The shogun does not consider it inevitable. He is fighting against every effort at change.

It doesn't seem to matter to him that we are in danger of losing our ability to determine our own destiny. He is living in a fool's paradise, yet that does not make him any the less dangerous. Even those who most despise him admit that he is wily and clever."

"But so far he has done little to stop the reformers," Erin pointed out. "Didn't he even offer to resign a few weeks ago?"

"He did more than just offer. In the presence of the emperor, he signed what was supposed to be a document yielding all his powers to the throne. But it was only a formality. Neither the emperor nor the royal court is in any position to actually administer the country, which the shogun knows full well. He did it just to throw his opponents into disarray, and to some extent he succeeded. That is why Takamori had to come here to confer with other reform leaders. They must decide what to do quickly or the shogun may succeed in destroying them."

"So I am right in thinking the situation has become critical?"

Odetsu nodded, her delicate features tense with concern. "Takamori and Davin-san believe the shogun intends to take some action to precipitate the crisis. It is only a question of how soon he will act. Tomorrow, the next day, next week. Surely it will not be very long."

Gazing down into the stone pool where small light-gilded fish swam lazily, Erin shivered. The last scarlet leaves were falling from the branches of the miniature maple trees scattered throughout the garden. The wisteria arbor was bare, leaving only the skeleton of bleached wood embraced by sere vines. A chill wind blew out of the north, carrying hints of the snows that would soon descend from the peak of Mt. Fuji to envelop the land.

Her eyes closed reflexively on the image of a world smothered in white and stained blood red. Odetsu was right: joy was precious and must be held tightly lest it slip through careless fingers and vanish into the maelstrom of great events.

A sound at the edge of the garden penetrated the dreary fog of her thoughts. She looked up to see Storm coming toward her. The golden light of late afternoon cast shadows over his rugged features, making him appear uncustomarily weary and vulnerable.

Rising quickly, she met Odetsu's understanding smile with her own. Moments later she was in his arms, sheltered by the enchanted circle of their love, which, strong though it was, could not quite conceal the tempest about to engulf them.

Chapter Thirteen

"To the samurai," Storm said quietly, "his sword represents his soul. He won't speak of it to strangers, much less let them see or touch it, except in battle. If he does show the sword to an honored friend, the blade must be handled only indirectly, with a cloth wrapped around the hand."

Erin nodded unenthusiastically. She was happy enough to accompany Storm on his errand to the swordsmith, simply because she enjoyed being with him under any circumstances. But she would just as soon not dwell on these reminders of both her own near-death and the violence that might soon descend on them.

Yet she could not deny a certain fascination with what she quickly realized was far more than simply a means of enabling warriors to hack each other to bits. The forge they visited bore no resemblance to the blacksmith's she remembered from home.

A low cluster of wood-and-tile buildings surrounded a meticulously clean yard. Young men in neat, somber kimonos hurried about their tasks. They spoke rarely, and then in the low, reverent tones of temple acolytes. The apprentice who admitted Storm spoke no English. But in response to Storm's fluent Japanese, he bowed to him deeply, concealed his surprise at Erin's presence and led them both to a small hut half-hidden by a bamboo overhang.

"The swordmaster," Storm explained, "is Tokukatsu. He is revered as both a great artist and a holy man who translates the will of the deities into steel."

The small, wizened man who approached them from the hut hardly looked like such an august personage. He wore an austere length of brown fabric draped over one shoulder and tied at the waist by a twisted piece of cloth. On his head was a small peaked hat held in place by a cord secured beneath his chin. His feet were shod only in thin sandals.

"Doesn't he mind the cold?" Erin whispered. She could feel the sharp wind even through her wool dress and cloak. The mere sight of the swordmaster's poorly clad form was enough to make her shiver.

"He has been inured to physical discomfort from childhood."

Looking into the weathered, expressionless face, Erin could believe him. She remained silent as Storm and the swordsmith bowed to each other and spoke briefly. At length, Storm turned back to her.

"Tokukatsu has agreed to allow you to witness the creation of a blade. It is a very rare honor for a woman."

Though she was tempted to point out that she could well do without such privileges, Erin did not. Such behavior would be unforgivably churlish. Sensitive now to the vital importance of "face," she was not about to embarrass Storm.

Instead, she quietly accompanied the men to a small shrine set up nearby and watched as the swordsmith offered his prayers to the deity whose spiritual power infused his blades. This done, they returned to the forge, where a raging fire was being kept well stoked by assistants.

As a chunk of iron was shattered into many pieces and placed inside the forge, Erin's polite curiosity began to give way to genuine interest. The manner of the master swordsmith and his apprentices made it clear that she was witnessing an ancient, revered tradition, part of the living history of the country she longed to learn more about.

"How does he know when the fire is hot enough?" she asked quietly.

Storm smiled. "The first time I watched Tokukatsu make a sword, I wondered about that too. He told me the fire is ready when it is the color of the rising moon about to set out on its journey across the heavens on a June or July evening."

"Was he serious?"

"Absolutely. The techniques for sword-making have been handed down over so many centuries that they bear no resemblance to modern technology. Formulas, temperatures, even precise measures of time have no meaning."

Erin could well believe that. There was an eternal gracefulness to the movements of the men as they removed the fused iron and repeatedly subjected it to heating and pounding. Before she would have thought it possible, the ordinary chunks of iron were transformed into a long length of metal that was then carefully dabbed with clay.

"The pattern of the clay," Storm said softly, "controls how quickly the blade cools. If it is not done absolutely correctly, the weapon will be useless."

Placed back in the forge until the clay had baked to a stone-hard consistency, the blade was then carried to a trough of water set just outside. The swordmaster tested the temperature with his hand.

"It must feel like the sea in August," Storm said. "If it is too cold, the metal will shatter. Too hot and it will not solidify quickly enough to be sufficiently strong."

Erin's breath caught in her throat as she

watched the wiry swordmaster lift the blade and without a moment's hesitation plunge it into the quenching liquid. Steam rose from the trough, hanging for a fragment of time before vanishing into the cool air. As the blade was removed and the clay chipped away, the swordmaster permitted himself a tiny smile of satisfaction. Proudly he held the blade up for Storm's inspection.

"Takamori will be very pleased. This promises to be a magnificent sword."

"It is for him?"

"Yes, that is why we came today in time to see it made. Ordinarily, Takamori would have been here himself. But since it is not safe for him to have his presence in Yokohama become known beyond the small circle of his supporters . . ."

Erin nodded her understanding. Gazing back at the blade that was being carefully dried with a length of pure white cloth, she struggled to reconcile the undoubted beauty of the ritual with the purpose of its creation. The sword would bring death, perhaps very soon. But it would also protect life, and the vision of men who were determined to make something better of their world.

As they were bowed from the swordmaster's domain and remounted the horses waiting for them outside, Storm touched her hand gently. "I know you can't help but worry, my love, but believe me, men like Takamori understand what they are doing. Every possible precaution is being taken to secure the reformers' safety and success."

"But they are caught between two sides, aren't they? On the one hand, the shogun stands ready to crush them. On the other, the traditionalists oppose anyone who advocates closer relations with the West. It seems to me that with so many enemies, the odds of surviving are slim."

"I don't agree. Being something of an expert on the subject of survival, I think Takamori and his associates have a better-than-even chance of overthrowing the shogun, defeating the traditionalists and taking power for themselves. If I didn't, I wouldn't be helping them."

Erin glanced at him skeptically. "There you go trying to sound cynical again. It doesn't work. I know perfectly well that even if you thought Takamori didn't have a chance, you'd still feel compelled to assist him because you believe in what he's trying to do."

His abashed grin made her laugh. "Don't worry," she assured him, "I won't tell anyone. If asked, I will insist you are the epitome of ruthless pragmatism, interested only in achieving your own ends. I'll never let on that you have even a nodding association with principles, let alone actual morals."

"If you are asked anything at all about this subject, I hope you will say nothing at all and come to me at once," Storm said wryly. "I don't delude myself into believing the shogun is unaware of our activities, but I still prefer for them to be kept as quiet as possible."

Erin tried not to let his quiet admonition worry her. It was only to be expected that in a hotbed of political intrigue such as Yokohama, friends were difficult to tell from enemies. At least she could take comfort from the fact that Storm was hardly an innocent about such matters. As he had said, he had ample training in survival. She had a feeling her own education in that area was soon to be broadened.

Takamori was delighted with the description of his sword's creation. Dinner lasted well beyond the usual hour, as he and Storm spoke of it and other weapons with which they were all too familiar. Erin was not surprised by either man's wide-ranging knowledge, but she could not help but be a bit dismayed by their enthusiasm. They might have been speaking of toys, for all the concern they showed.

Odetsu shared her unease. The women spoke rarely during the meal, contenting themselves with watching the men they loved. As the last dishes were finally cleared away by sleepy-eyed serving girls, the couples rose and said their good nights. Erin felt only the slightest twinge of self-consciousness when Storm's proprietary arm around her waist made it clear that they were headed for the same destination.

Once in his room, the last remnants of

bashfulness fell away as easily as the riding skirt and blouse he so expeditiously stripped from her. A sigh of pure bliss rippled through her as he gathered her into his arms, bending his tall head to trail gentle kisses from her brow to the dimple beside her mouth.

"This day has seemed at least a week long," Storm groaned, stepping back far enough to begin unbuttoning his shirt.

Erin laughed softly as her hands closed over his, taking over the task. The trembling of her fingers made her a bit clumsy, but she managed before too long to undo each button and reveal the sun-bronzed width of his chest. Her indigo eyes rapidly darkening with passion, she stroked the warm, hair-roughened skin, marveling in the perfection of his form.

Storm shuddered beneath her touch. His big callused hands slipped beneath the lacy edge of her camisole, exploring the delicate line of her back before gently urging the garment from her.

The blush that stained her cheeks and moved downward over her throat to the very tips of the full, high breasts he was admiring so unrestrainedly made Storm laugh. He watched in fascination as her nipples hardened and her skin glowed with the intensity of her arousal.

Chuckling wryly, he acknowledged that his own need was at least as great. The straining tautness of his trousers made that only too clear. Gently grasping her hips, he moved her against him, letting her feel for herself what she did to him.

Erin gasped softly. Their earlier lovemaking had not dispelled her fascination with the mysteries of male sensuality; on the contrary, she was more enthralled by him than ever. Of their own volition, her fingers gently traced the power of his virility. She delighted in the growl that broke from him.

With boldness that surprised them both, she unfastened the button at his waist and the first two below it. But beyond that she could not go. Storm laughed indulgently as he finished the job for her and slid the snug trousers off. Her pantaloons followed quickly, leaving no barrier to the impassioned touch of skin against skin.

Lifting her swiftly, he strode across the room and lowered her onto the sleeping mat. The glow of smoldering embers cast passion-twined shadows on the wall above them. Their bodies came together eagerly, reaching as one for the shimmering peak of fulfillment.

Drawing out her pleasure to the utmost, Storm waited until she was writhing beneath him before at last entering the silken haven of her body. Erin accepted him joyously, arching to meet each thrust. They moved in perfect unison, the very rhythm of their heartbeats merging. As the world shattered around them, their souls soared together, finding a freedom beyond all boundaries of human existence.

Deep in the night, they woke to make love again slowly and languorously, exploring each other's bodies with near-worshipful intensity. The hush of the dark hours shimmered with the force of their joining.

Storm's whispered words of carnal passion and loving need would have shocked Erin in any other circumstances. But wrapped in the cloak of gentle darkness, she responded without restraint until, inevitably, they drifted to sleep again in each other's arms.

The moon had long since set, and no pale hint of light yet marked the line between sky and sea when she stirred reluctantly. A wind rank with foreboding rippled through her dreams. She moaned softly, burrowing closer to the warm security of Storm's hard body.

He woke instantly, gathering her to him. "Erin . . . are you all right?"

Befuddled by sleep, she blinked dazedly. "I think so . . . I must have had a nightmare. Something . . . frightened me."

Work-roughened hands caressed her soothingly. "Hush, now, there's nothing to be scared of. Everything's all right." Whatever painful phantasms had been conjured up by her secret mind fled beneath his gentle touch. But she was still grateful for his protectiveness and the feeling of utter safety he imparted to her.

"Would you like a drink of water?"

Erin nodded sheepishly, only too aware that she was acting like a little child. Storm didn't seem to mind. Oblivious of the cool night air penetrating the room, he left the bed and went over to a small table near the door, where a stone pitcher and cups were laid out.

Barely half-awake, Erin lay back against the pillows. Her eyes fluttered in a futile effort to stay open. She was almost asleep again when Storm returned, but without the water. Dropping down on the mat beside her, he pressed an urgent hand to her shoulder. "Don't move. There's someone in the corridor."

Erin's eyes shot open. The tender, gentle man of moments before was gone. In his place was a ruthless warrior whose taut body radiated strength and whose pewter gaze shone with grim determination.

When she tried instinctively to speak, he covered her mouth with his hand. "Stay quiet. He's coming this way."

Though she could hear nothing but the thudding of her own heart, Erin obeyed. She shrank down under the covers as Storm moved swiftly back to the door. There was no time for him to reach his swords before the panel slid open and a dark figure enshrouded in black entered silently.

Icy shivers of terror raced through Erin as she struggled against the almost irresistible urge to scream. Any hope that the intruder might simply be a servant vanished instantly. No member of the household would dare to enter Storm's room without permission, much less do so in the dead of night.

The man, whoever he might be, had only violence on his mind, as evinced by the short length of chain stretched out tightly between his hands. Only her absolute trust in Storm allowed her to lie unmoving beneath the covers as the would-be assassin approached.

He was barely a yard from the bed when Storm moved. Hurling himself across the room with a speed and agility that would not have seemed possible in so large a man, he seized the intruder in a grip of steel. Caught off guard, Storm's target still managed to react instantly. Dropping the chain from one hand, he struck out with it, catching Storm across the back.

Erin screamed as the blow tore open his skin. She leaped from the bed just as Storm grabbed for the chain and managed, only because of his immense strength, to rip it from the man's hand. They faced off in the center of the room, both crouched like wild beasts.

The intruder moved first. With a blood-chilling cry, he leaped at Storm, slashing out at him with hands and feet studded with razor-sharp metal points. Evading the deadly weapons, Storm counterattacked with a kick that landed squarely in the man's chest, momentarily knocking the wind out of him and throwing him off balance.

Recovering quickly, the man lashed out with one black-shrouded arm, at the end of which glittered a small, lethal knife. Storm only just managed to avoid having a vein or artery slashed before he landed a chopping blow with the side of his hand. The sickening sound of a bone breaking reverberated through the room.

As the man reeled back, reaching with his remaining arm for yet another of the arsenal of weapons apparently secreted on his person, Takamori and several guards raced in with their swords drawn. Erin hastily scrambled back under the covers as the intruder was seized and roughly bound, his black mask stripped away to reveal a young, feral-eyed Japanese who spit defiance at his captors.

Takamori shouted a warning to the guards holding him, but it was too late. Before anyone could move to prevent it, the attacker bit down hard on something concealed in his mouth. An instant later his body writhed in its death throes as the potent poison did its work.

Storm gazed dispassionately at the slumped body of the man who moments before had come close to killing him. Glancing at Takamori, he said, "Ninja, I presume?"

Takamori nodded glumly. "No one else could have gained entrance to such a well-guarded house or carried such weapons as we see here. I should have expected this. My lack of foresight has seriously endangered you."

Storm shrugged dismissively. "I'd hardly call this little scratch serious."

"Well, I do," Erin insisted. Rising from the bed, thoroughly wrapped in a quilt, she marched over to him. "I want you to sit down right now and let me take care of it."

Takamori grinned sympathetically as Storm glared at her. Though she came no higher than his shoulders and should have been overpowered by his rampant nakedness, Erin didn't bat an eyelash. Settling himself with poor grace, he yielded to her ministrations.

Odetsu, who had hurried into the room just as the ninja's body was being removed, sent servants scurrying for hot water and bandages as Erin slipped behind a screen to pull on a robe. She returned with the quilt in her hands and insisted on tucking it around Storm despite his protests that he was not an infant to be coddled.

"Just be quiet and let me take care of you," Erin hissed, out of patience with his male bravado. The gray tinge beneath his tan worried her, as did the steady seeping of blood from the gaping slash across his back.

Horror at his injury almost overwhelmed her. She had to take several deep breaths before her hands were steady enough to clean and stitch the wound. As gentle as she was, she knew she must be hurting him. But Storm neither moved nor made a sound. When she finished securing the bandage in place, he smiled at her reassuringly.

"Don't worry, love," he said softly. "It takes a damn sight more than that to lay me low."

Erin wasn't convinced. She felt he was underestimating the effects of his struggle with the ninja and wanted him to get back into bed to rest. But Storm vetoed that at once.

"No time. We've got to be on our way."

At her bewildered look, Takamori explained, "The ninja was part of an elite group of paid assassins hired for their immense expertise in finding and destroying their quarries. Davin-san is too modest to admit it, but very few men have ever survived an attack by one of them. Nor is it often possible to elude them. They are renowned for being able to penetrate any fortress, no matter how well-guarded, and if necessary, they can kill using only their bare hands or ordinary objects you would never guess might be lethal."

"Do you know who hired him?" Erin asked shakily. Though she fought to remain calm, she could not hide the trembling of her slender body.

Odetsu put an arm around her comfortingly. "There is little doubt he was sent by the shogun. Failure is unacceptable to the ninja. Once word of Davin-san's survival gets out, more will come. Instead of trying to defend against them here, we would be far wiser to withdraw to a safer, more secret location."

"But where? If the ninja are so adept at

reaching their victims, what place would be safe?"

All eyes instinctively turned to Storm. Bare-chested, with a sheen of perspiration showing against his burnished skin and a lock of chestnut hair falling across his forehead, he managed to look rakishly confident.

"I think it's time we put the *Rising Sun* to sea."

Chapter Fourteen

"ARE YOU WARM ENOUGH?" STORM ASKED, wrapping his arms more snugly around Erin and drawing her back against the wall of his chest.

She nodded contentedly. Since he had deemed none of her own clothes adequate to protect her from the frigid onshore wind, she was engulfed in one of his greatcoats. The lapels framed her face beneath a saucy knit cap, while the sleeves completely engulfed her hands and the hem fell well below her ankles. She could not walk with any degree of grace, but then, she had nowhere in particular to go.

The steady swaying of the deck beneath her feet was reassuringly familiar. Above her she could hear the rippling thrum of the *Rising*

Sun's sails. When completely raised, the more than an acre of canvas required three masts to hold it and was supported by miles of rigging.

Under full sail the sleek clipper ship could attain a speed of sixteen knots an hour, making her one of the fastest cargo carriers plying the Pacific trade. But the magnificent vessel that had been their home for several weeks was going far more slowly, with only the jib and mizzen sails in place.

Off in the distance, in between the bulks of the other vessels sailing in their convoy, Erin could make out the rocky coast of Kyushu, the southernmost island of Japan. This early in the new year, the ground was dotted with snow and even the water looked forbiddingly gray.

She supposed the bleak scene and their uncertain circumstances should dishearten her. But instead she felt adrift on an island of peace and serenity. The impression was deceptive, as she well knew, but she intended to cling to it as long as possible.

"Is Odetsu with Takamori?" she asked, watching the flight of a seagull toward its evening's nest.

Storm nodded. "The last time I saw them, they were both putting Saido to bed. Takamori was telling him a story about one of the legendary samurai."

"He treats the boy like his own son."

"I hope before too much longer he will be."

"Would Odetsu's family object to their marrying?"

"I don't see how they could," Storm said. "Ever since she fled from them before Saido was born, they have considered her to be dead. Since they're allied now with the Satsuma clan, I suppose an effort will be made at reconciliation. But Takamori won't let their feelings influence him one way or another. He is determined to have her for his wife."

"More determined than ever, from what I can see. Since we learned of the murders of his brothers and uncles, Odetsu has been the only joy in his life."

Storm nodded somberly. News of the killing of leading members of the Satsuma clan caught in a trap of the shogun's devising had reached them shortly after they sailed from Yokohama. Takamori bore his grief stoically, but there was no mistaking the fact that his need for the beautiful young noblewoman who loved him so devotedly was greater than ever.

"Takamori is not the only man in a hurry to marry," Storm reminded her gently. His chin rested against the ebony silk of her hair as he breathed in her fragrance. The thought of the small but comfortable bunk waiting below in their stateroom flitted through his mind.

He smiled as he remembered how he had awakened that morning to find her satiny nakedness snuggled against him, her face still slightly flushed from their lovemaking and her moist lips temptingly parted.

For a man who prided himself on his self-control, he had embarrassing little around her. Despite the knowledge that he was expected on deck, the temptation to kiss her awake had proved too much for him. Half an hour later he had ruefully slipped from the bunk while she turned over as contentedly as a well-stroked kitten and went back to sleep.

Rather to his surprise, he had found her napping that afternoon. At dinner, she had skipped the usual raw fish and deep-fried vegetables, apparently struck by a craving for pickled ginger and soybeans.

He was about to ask if she thought she might be coming down with something when Erin turned in his arms. "I am glad to hear you are still interested in making an honest woman of me, sir."

"Of course I am," Storm declared. Frowning slightly, he asked, "You haven't really been concerned that I might not?"

Erin shook her head, reaching up a hand to gently trace the hard line of his mouth. She trusted him far too much to have any doubts about his intentions. But she still couldn't resist the urge to tease him. "Meg always told me that gentlemen had only one use for ladies of easy virtue, and that had nothing to do with marriage."

"The redoubtable Mrs. Gilhoully is not what

I would consider an expert on the behavior of gentlemen, or for that matter, men of any sort." Skeptically Storm asked, "Was there ever a Mr. Gilhoully, to your knowledge?"

"I don't know," Erin admitted. A giggle escaped her as she added, "But between the two of us, I rather doubt it. You see, once, when I was sixteen, I got up the nerve to ask her about what is generally referred to as 'the marital act.' Meg was plainly horrified by my curiosity, but nonetheless felt compelled to reply, if only to keep me from asking anyone else. What she told me bears little resemblance to what you have so kindly instructed me in these past weeks."

"Ah, you see, it's all a matter of having the right tutor. Now, I happen to be an unusually patient, forbearing man, more than ready to indulge a promising student."

"Only this student," Erin reminded him tartly. "The rest of the world will just have to get along without your expertise."

"Is that a possessive note I hear?"

"More than that. It is plain old-fashioned jealousy. I would happily scratch out the eyes of any woman who did more than glance at you."

Storm shook his head in mock dismay. "Let it never be said I was responsible for a lady being injured. I will just have to devote myself to you heart and soul."

Erin laughed softly, burrowing her head

into his shoulder. "And body, too. Don't forget that part."

His chuckle followed them downstairs to the cabin they shared. Nestled into the prow of the ship, it was small and compact, but surprisingly well-appointed.

Paneled in mahogany with brass and copper oil lamps carefully secured to the walls, the cabin boasted a double bunk, ample storage space for clothes and books, and a large table secured to the wood-plank floor near the portholes. There was even a potbellied stove to provide some warmth on the frigid winter mornings. But Erin preferred the more dependable heat of Storm's long, hard body.

"I hope Odetsu and Takamori are as comfortable," she murmured as he gently removed his coat and hung it back in the closet. Because the *Rising Sun* occasionally carried passengers, there were several cozy cabins available. Takamori was accustomed to the Western furniture and outfittings, but for Odetsu they were both novel and a bit disconcerting.

"She's much too polite to say so, but I suspect she's finding it awkward to sleep in a bed raised off the floor and to sit on chairs."

"Saido, on the other hand, is delighted by everything. I think he spends every waking hour on deck learning the arts of seamanship."

"He has less trouble communicating with my crew than I do," Storm admitted ruefully, referring to the difficulties of dealing with a roster comprising Japanese, Americans, and Europeans of all nationalities.

Unfastening the pearl buttons of her blouse, Erin glanced up at him. "You seem to like children."

"I haven't been around them much."

"But I see you with Saido, talking to him and teaching him things."

"I enjoy doing that." Sitting down on the edge of the bunk, Storm began to pull off his boots. "Maybe because he really isn't my responsibility. Actually having a child dependent on you for everything must be rather frightening."

In the midst of removing her skirt, Erin hesitated. "Does that mean you aren't anxious to have children of your own?"

"I never thought about it one way or the other. Before the war, I guess I just presumed that I'd marry and have a family. Everybody did. But since then, there hasn't been any opportunity." He broke off, looking at her cautiously. "Do you want to have children?"

"Very much."

"Oh . . . well, then, maybe we'd better give it some consideration. After we've been married awhile, of course." A rueful laugh broke from him. "Come to think of it, I'd forgotten about doing anything to prevent you from conceiving. I'll have to start being more careful."

Erin's eyes widened. Wrapping a warm robe around herself, she asked, "You mean there's some way to avoid pregnancy?"

"Several. But you needn't be concerned about that."

"Why not?"

"Why, because . . . it's up to the man. A lady needn't worry about such things." Storm sounded pompous even to himself. He was hard pressed to handle the situation. The sudden seriousness of the conversation surprised him. He sensed there was something going on under the surface that he couldn't quite catch.

"I don't like the idea of you having sole responsibility for what happens to my body, but we can come back to that. If you felt it was up to you, why didn't you take any of those precautions?"

"How would I know? I just didn't think of them."

"But you must have used them before or you wouldn't be familiar with them."

Standing stiffly, he frowned at her. "Do you really want to discuss my previous experiences with women?"

"No," Erin admitted hastily. "I just wondered why you haven't bothered to use precautions with me."

"Because I didn't think of them, that's all. Around you I have trouble thinking of anything."

"Are you sure it wasn't because you really wanted me to get pregnant?"

Storm suspected that might be the case, but he wasn't willing to admit it. He was embarrassed enough to realize how careless he had been of her well-being. There was no reason to complicate the issue by acknowledging that he might have used a primitively male tactic to bind her to him.

"Of course I'm sure," he claimed. "I want a few years alone with you before we even think about having children."

The sudden loss of color from her face startled him. His stomach plummeted as understanding at last pierced the fog of his male ignorance. "Erin . . . are you trying to tell me you're already pregnant?"

She bit her lip, unable to look at him. "I think so. I'm not sure."

"Damn!"

The word, torn from him so spontaneously, could not have been more ill-chosen. Erin jerked away as though burned, her hands flying to her abdomen in an instinctively protective gesture.

"If you didn't want this to happen, you should have thought of it sooner. Even I know that babies are a natural outcome of what we've been doing so much of."

"Of course I want it. I just . . ."

"You certainly don't sound that way."

"I was surprised. You can hardly blame me for—"

"You're surprised? How do you think I feel?"

"I don't know," Storm admitted somberly. "How do you feel?"

"I . . ." Erin broke off. She turned away from him, staring sightlessly at the gray sea beyond the porthole. Despite her robe, it felt very cold in the cabin. She shivered and wrapped her arms around herself.

So softly that he could barely hear her, she murmured, "It's all so strange to me. The thought of a baby growing inside my body is miraculous . . . but frightening."

Storm longed to comfort her, but he sensed she would not accept his touch just then. Not while his angry denunciation still rang between them.

"That's why I wanted us to wait," he said quietly. "But now that it's done . . ."

Erin's back stiffened. Her indigo eyes glittered dangerously as she faced him. "Since you're obviously displeased by what's happened, just forget about it. I can take care of myself."

That was so patently absurd that Storm could not help but laugh. "Don't be stupid. Of course you can't."

"Oh, so now I'm stupid, am I? Last night I was the joy of your life. What a difference learning about the baby makes!"

"Don't throw my words back at me," Storm growled. "You're deliberately misunderstanding."

"No, I am not. Maybe I have been stupid. All that talk about loving me and being so eager to marry me lulled me into believing you would want the baby. But now I can see that I made a mistake."

"The only mistake you're making is right now." Her behavior bewildered him. He was torn between the desire to chastise her—impossible under any circumstances, but especially in her present condition—and the desperate need to hold and reassure her.

"Are you saying you're happy about the baby?"

Storm balked at resorting to an outright lie. The thought of a child coming so soon stunned him. After all the turmoil and tragedy of the last few years, he was ill-prepared to cope with the responsibilities of fatherhood. For the moment, it was all he could do to realize that he had found a woman he could happily spend the rest of his life with.

The fact that her pregnancy was his fault only heightened his dismay. How had a man of his experience managed to be so oblivious of the need for precautions? Unaccustomed to questioning his own feelings, he was bewildered by them. It was as though a stranger had suddenly taken control of his actions.

His refusal to answer seemed to confirm Erin's worst fears. In her anguished state, she could only conclude that the child who should have been a precious gift was instead unwanted by its own father. The love he had so ardently professed was hollow and meaningless. She had been a fool to be taken in by him, especially since he had every reason to want to punish her for her actions eight years before.

That thought reverberated through her sickeningly. Was all the joy and tenderness of the last few weeks nothing more than a trick? Had he intended from the beginning to hurt her like this?

Something of her fears must have shown on her ashen features, for Storm took a quick step toward her, grasping her by the shoulders. "I don't know what's going through your head, but whatever it is, you're dead wrong. I love you and I want you to be my wife. Yes, the baby is something of a shock. But I'll get used to the idea."

"Don't bother," Erin snapped. Her pride could not bear the thought that he would merely tolerate the child she already cherished. "I told you I can take care of myself, and I meant it. As soon as the *Emerald Isle* and the *Nantucket Moon* are ready, I'll sail home with them. You can just forget about me and the baby." A painful sneer distorted her soft mouth. "Even the most cautious men occasionally make mistakes. Chalk it up to experience."

Under any other circumstances, the look on Storm's face would have frozen her with fear.

But she was too enmeshed in her own anguish to even notice the suddenly feral glitter of his eyes or the savage tightening of his mouth.

Rage such as he had never known before in his life roared through him. Her willful refusal to admit his love and her maddening threat to leave him were more than he could endure. His big hands were clenched into fists as he grabbed his boots and strode over to the door.

Slamming it open, he growled, "For your sake, and the baby's, I'd better not remain in the same room with you. At least not until you learn to curb your tongue and rein in your pride." Ominously he added, "Don't think for a moment that I will let you get away from me, Erin. Even were you not carrying my child, I would stop you. If I have to hold you prisoner, I will do so."

With a final damning glance at her rigid form, he stepped out into the corridor and yanked the door shut. Too late, she hurled herself after him. A harsh laugh reached her from the other side as the key turned in the lock and she was securely sealed in.

"Erin," Odetsu called softly, "are you feeling well enough to eat some breakfast?"

Turning over in the bunk where she had shed so many tears the night before, Erin moaned. A wave of nausea struck her. Dimly she remembered hearing that expectant women were prone to such upset. But having not yet experienced it for herself, she was unprepared for the intensity of the dizziness that assailed her. The slightest effort to raise her head made her want to retch.

"I don't think so, Odetsu," she called weakly. "Anyway, the door is locked from the outside."

"Davin-san gave me the key," her friend explained. The next moment she was bustling into the room, inspecting Erin's wan features with concern. "I will tell the cook to make tea and plain rice for you. That will settle your stomach."

"I doubt it. It seems to be doing cartwheels."

Odetsu smiled gently. "I've never heard that word before, but I can guess what it means. When I was carrying Saido, the mere thought of food was enough to make me ill."

"Then you know about . ... ?"

"Davin-san told us." At Erin's surprised look, she explained, "Takamori found him on deck late last night. I'm afraid he had drunk a bit more rum than is good for him. Anyway, after he settled down, he explained why you were locked in the cabin." A stern look touched her delicate features. "I am surprised at you, Erin. You and Davin-san love each other. How can you talk of leaving him when you are carrying his child?"

"But that is exactly why I have to leave," Erin said sadly. "He doesn't want the baby."

"Nonsense, of course he does. He just needs time to get used to the idea."

"I wish I could believe you. But he told me he wanted to wait several years before I got pregnant."

Odetsu smiled wryly. "He should have thought of that sooner."

"I'm sure he's sorry he didn't."

"Are you? It seems to me that Davin-san is far too intelligent and sensible a man to make such a mistake. But like most men, he has trouble understanding his own feelings. Just give him time and he'll come round."

As she spoke, Odetsu took a cool cloth and gently wiped Erin's flushed face. She was privately concerned about the younger girl's condition. Being confined to a small cabin with only her own unhappy thoughts for company was hardly good for an expectant mother. Added to that was the fact that the sea had turned unexpectedly choppy during the night. Her nausea was likely to worsen unless she could get up on deck and breathe fresh air.

"Erin, I must lock you in again while I go talk with the cook, because I promised Davin-san I would do so. But I will find him and tell him you cannot remain in here. You need exercise and sunshine. I'm sure he will understand."

"I don't want any favors from him. If he won't let me on deck, fine. At least I won't have to see him."

Odetsu shook her head ruefully. "We certainly know one thing about the baby already. With you for a mother and Davin-san for a father, he is guaranteed to be stubborn."

"I am not stubborn," Erin groused. "It's Storm who's so bullheaded he can't unbend an inch. He's the most obstinate, recalcitrant, infuriating man I've ever—"

"Do you have to talk so loud?" a deep voice inquired peevishly. Both women looked up, surprised to find the object of their discussion tottering into the room.

Erin's heart turned over. He looked decidedly the worse for wear. A night's growth of beard could not obscure the gray tautness of his features or the shadows beneath his red-rimmed eyes. His shirt and trousers were rumpled and his hair clung in an unruly mass.

He had every appearance of being a man who had waged a long, hard conflict with himself. But Erin was determined not to be misled by that. She told herself his only struggle had been with a bottle of rum, and the bottle had clearly won.

"To what do I owe this unlooked-for honor?" she demanded icily.

Storm winced. Several dozen hammers were banging away inside his head. A furnace burned where his stomach had been and his legs felt as though they might give way under him at any moment.

Sitting down heavily at the foot of the bunk, he eyed her cautiously. "If you're going to keep shouting, I'll have to leave. As Odetsu may have mentioned, I had a drop too much to drink last night."

Erin laughed heartlessly. She couldn't deny a certain enjoyment of his condition. It made her own seem far pleasanter. "A drop? More like an ocean. You reek of the stuff."

"I'll take a bath after we talk. First, how are you feeling?"

"Marvelous. On top of the world. Topnotch."

"That bad, huh?"

Odetsu giggled. She put a hand over her mouth and tiptoed out of the room. Such a moment called for privacy.

Erin straightened up in the bed, ignoring the peculiar gyrations of her senses. "I told you. I am perfectly all right. Now, kindly go away."

Storm glared at her. He had spent an agonizing night berating himself for being such an unfeeling lout before being finally driven to drown his remorse in a rum bottle. He was in no mood to bandy words with the devastatingly beautiful woman he adored. "This happens to be my cabin too. Move over."

Erin gaped at him in disbelief. "I will not. If you think you can come in here and take over after what you said to me—"

"Sweet Lord, woman, have you no more compassion than to argue with a man in my condition?"

Now that he mentioned it, he did look as though he was about to collapse. Still reluctant, but unable to refuse him, Erin inched over to the other side of the bunk.

"All right. But don't you get any ideas about touching me. That's all over."

"Believe me," Storm groaned as he flopped down next to her, "if I tried, I'd only disappoint us both."

"You flatter yourself. It will be a cold day in hell before I seek pleasure with you again."

From beneath furled brows, baleful eyes glared at her. "Now it's my turn to give you a piece of advice. Don't think for a moment that you will have any chance to satisfy yourself with other men. I intend to keep you on a very short rein until we get this matter cleared up."

"*How dare you!* You're even more witless than I thought if you imagine you can keep me imprisoned. I'll escape you, no matter what it takes."

"Then maybe I'd better make sure you don't want to," Storm growled, turning over swiftly to trap her beneath his body. The surge of pain that tore through him was a small price to pay for the satisfaction of feeling her slender form helpless in his arms.

"Witless, am I?" he taunted. "Then why is it you're on my ship, in my cabin"—a lean finger toyed with the gossamer thinness of her sleeping gown—"more or less naked in my bunk with my child growing inside you? It seems to me, my sweet, that if one of us has been foolish, it is you."

At the mention of the child, Erin flushed. She told herself she must be mistaken about the fiercely possessive gleam in his eyes. It was only the aftereffects of the rum. But there was no mistaking his intent when he abruptly pushed the covers aside and laid both his big hands on her abdomen.

Shivering beneath his touch, she could only stare in wonder as he murmured huskily, "You said it was both miraculous and frightening to be carrying a baby. But I want to know more than that. Tell me what it feels like."

"I don't understand what you mean."

"Can you feel him moving?"

Despite herself, she laughed softly. "No, it's too early for that."

"Oh . . . that reminds me. When do you think he will be born?"

"He?"

"Or she," Storm amended. The thought of a daughter pleased him easily as much as that of a son. Despite the vast quantities of rum he had swallowed, or perhaps because of them, he had managed to confront his true feelings on a previously unattained level. While he would hardly recommend the method, and had no intention of ever repeating it, he could not deny it had served its purpose.

With the arrival of morning, every throb of his head seemed to be telling him what an idiot he had been. Takamori's assurances that men were frequently such fools were small comfort. He had his work cut out for him if he were to have any chance of winning Erin's forgiveness. Reminding her that he could easily hold her prisoner was hardly the way to begin.

Gazing into her eyes, he repeated gently, "When do you think our child will be born?"

Erin tried to look away but could not manage it. Her throat was tight as she said, "In about seven months."

"Will it bother you if people guess he was conceived before we were married?"

"That's hardly an issue. I'm not going to marry you."

"Yes, you are."

"No, I'm—"

"Erin, we are both tired and not at our best. What do you say we postpone this discussion until a later time?"

"I don't see what there is to postpone. I will not marry you simply to give my child a name."

"Our child."

Reluctantly she conceded that point, but added, "When I get back to the States, I will present myself as a widow. If people don't believe me, too bad."

"You aren't going back to the States. At least, not without me."

"Are you about to tell me again that I can't get away from you?"

"No," Storm conceded. "That will only make you angry, which is the last thing I want to do. But it's still true."

His frankness won a reluctant smile from her. She studied him for a moment. "Do you really intend to stay here in the cabin?"

Storm nodded, bracing himself for another demand that he remove himself. But Erin surprised him. She merely sighed tiredly and snuggled further into the mattress. "Then would you please pull up the covers? I'm cold."

He complied instantly, too relieved to question why she was willing to put up with his presence. Despite the generous width of the bunk, it was impossible for them to keep from touching, especially since Storm insisted on sprawling out in all directions. Erin finally gave up trying to evade his arms and settled into them with poor grace.

Did she imagine the gentle brush of his lips against her hair? Perhaps not, for his voice was undeniably tender as he asked, "Will you be able to eat the breakfast Odetsu is getting?"

"Let's not talk about food."

"Just a little. Surely you could manage that."

"If I do, will you leave me alone?"

"No, but at least I won't nag you for an hour or two."

Erin shook her head in bewilderment. "For a man who yesterday didn't want a child, you certainly are full of surprises. How can I be sure you won't change your mind again?"

"Because I tell you I won't. Yesterday I was shocked and guilt-ridden. So I behaved badly. If you will forgive me, I assure you it will never happen again."

He glanced down at her hopefully, but Erin wasn't about to be so easily cajoled. Dubiously she asked, "Why should you feel guilty?"

"For getting you pregnant, of course."

"Didn't I have anything to do with that?"

"Yes, but it was up to me to prevent it."

Propping herself up on an elbow, she gazed down at him with what looked suspiciously like the beginnings of a teasing smile. "What makes you think you're the only one who knows how to avoid pregnancy?"

Storm's eyes narrowed. "Are you trying to tell me—?"

"I'm much better informed than you think."

"Oh, really? Then suppose you describe to me exactly how one prevents conception."

"That's easy," Erin announced smugly. "There's a magical incantation I learned long ago."

As Storm chuckled, she recited, "'Unhand me, you brute. I am not that sort of woman.'"

"Works, does it?"

"It must. After all, look what happened when I forgot to use it."

The tension eased out of his big body as he

gathered her closer. A burnished hand traced the petal-soft curve of her cheek with infinite gentleness. "Thank you."

"For what?"

"For being so much more sensible than me."

"Is that why you say you love me, because I'm sensible?"

"Of course. You didn't think it was because you're ravishingly beautiful, delectably responsive, marvelously intelligent and a good businesswoman to boot, did you?"

"I'm not."

"Which?"

"A good businesswoman. If you hadn't agreed to help me, I'd never have gotten the *Emerald Isle* and *Nantucket Moon* outfitted."

"Putting aside for the moment the matter of your overwhelming modesty, I wondered if you were ever going to admit that."

"I just did."

Storm yawned. He was worn out from his rum-sodden night and drained by the realization that she was willing to forgive him. Later he would be more than happy to properly celebrate their reconciliation. But for the moment he was in desperate need of sleep.

"Let's consider it a wedding present," he suggested.

"I'm still not sure we should get married."

"We'll discuss it later."

"When?"

"After we're wed."

Erin sighed. He was the most stubborn

man. But then, she really wouldn't want him any other way. A satisfied grin curved her mouth as she nestled closer to him. Storm grunted contentedly, one big hand lying over her abdomen with the other tangled in the silken skeins of her hair.

They were almost asleep when shouts from the deck brought them suddenly upright. As the meaning of the words sank in, Storm flung himself from the bunk. He was reaching for his swords as Takamori burst into the cabin with the news that their sanctuary had at last been discovered. The shogun's fleet was rounding the point near them, under full sail, with gun portals opened.

Chapter Fifteen

"How could we be taken by surprise like this?" Erin exclaimed as she and Odetsu hurriedly loaded rifles and handed them one after the other to the sharpshooters stationed on the deck.

Storm had tried to prevent her from taking on that task, but she had made it quite clear that it was either that or let her go below to help the men arming their dozen cannons. He had relented reluctantly, only after being assured by Odetsu that she would stay close to Erin's side.

"It was the fog that came up last night. We could not even see the ships in our own convoy. I would not be surprised if the shogun's forces were as startled as we are to discover us here."

"If they are," Erin muttered, "they're certainly making the most of the opportunity."

Although the attacking fleet was comprised solely of Japanese ships, which were slower and less maneuverable than Western counterparts, the captains clearly knew how to get the most from their craft. Already they had managed to come close enough to fire several cannon salvos, one of which had just missed taking off a chunk of the *Rising Sun*'s mainmast.

"Why do they all keep firing at us?" Erin gasped. "Shouldn't they pay some attention to our other ships?"

"Not if their commanders are as smart as they seem. If they can sink or incapacitate the *Rising Sun*, they will gain an immense advantage in the battle."

Erin lifted her head slightly to get a better look at what was going on. As she did so, a grizzled seaman caught sight of her and swiftly pulled her back down. His muttered curse was accompanied by the sound of a bullet whizzing past her.

"Begging your pardon, ma'am, but you've got to stay out of the line of fire. This ain't no time for gawking."

Murmuring her apologies, Erin got back to work. She lost count of the number of rifles she loaded, pausing only long enough to help fill buckets of water to snuff out the flaming arrows fired onto the deck by samurai archers. Like the samurai of the Satsuma fleet, their code of Bushido made them despise guns in favor of more traditional weapons.

Though Storm's sharpshooters succeeded in picking off many of them, they continued unrelentingly. Each time a man fell, another quickly replaced him. The *Rising Sun*'s Japanese forces were every bit as determined. They managed to fire the sails of several ships in the shogun's fleet and started a major blaze on one of the smaller vessels.

The frigid morning air was soon black with acrid smoke. Cries from the wounded rose on all sides. As the ships moved so closely together that the sharpshooters no longer had any advantage, the women turned their attention to caring for the casualties.

Erin mobilized a makeshift dispensary staffed by the servants brought from Storm's Yokohama house. Since they were the only people who could be spared from the fighting, they were kept busy bandaging gunshot wounds, digging out arrowheads, stanching bleeding, and offering what comfort they could to the wounded and dying.

In too many cases, the injuries were so severe that nothing could be done. The stores of laudanum were quickly depleted. Bodies covered by blankets began to line one wall of the dispensary. As a young boy grasped her hand, crying out in pain and fear, Erin shook herself dazedly.

It was as though time had rolled back and

she was once more in the war hospital, surrounded by shattered men. The differences in appearance and language were insignificant. They were all part of the same humanity devouring itself in some obscenely cannibalistic rite.

The *Rising Sun*'s cannons had begun to fire constantly, the force of the blasts reverberating throughout the ship. Word filtered down of several sinkings among the shogun's fleet and the disabling of more vessels. Two Satsuma war junks were crippled, but managed to make for shore after transferring to other ships all of their crews that could still fight.

Storm appeared occasionally below deck to offer a word of encouragement to the men at the cannons and check on the wounded. Despite the near-freezing temperatures, he wore only the same wrinkled shirt and trousers in which he had spent the night. His swords were buckled around his tapered waist and a pistol was stuck into his belt.

All signs of the rum's aftereffects were gone. His slate-gray eyes glittered with determination and his mouth was drawn in a hard, thin line. The burnished planes and hollows of his face were shadowed by a night's growth of beard and something more.

Erin did not doubt that he was also torn by anguished memories of other battles. Yet the mere sight of him was enough to bolster her flagging strength and renew her courage. They exchanged a quick look, full of tenderness and understanding, before hurrying on about their tasks.

As the battle raged on into midday, the shogun's forces resorted to a desperate gamble. With courage and skill that had to be admired even in an enemy, they brought several of their war junks close enough to the *Rising Sun* to fire a cannon salvo that took down her mizzenmast. It crashed to the deck, trapping several seamen beneath.

"All but one of them's dead, ma'am," a white-faced cabin boy reported to Erin. "We can't get the poor sod who's still alive out from under. He's caught fast and screaming something horrible."

Pulling a blanket over the samurai who had just died in her arms, Erin hastily gathered medical supplies and followed the boy on deck. As she stuck her head through the hatchway, she froze momentarily, unable to credit the scene before her.

The *Rising Sun* was completely surrounded by the shogun's war fleet and Satsuma vessels fighting to help her hold them off. The ships were so close together that their sides thumped and scraped against each other repeatedly. Storm was at the wheel, using the boom as a battering ram to smash through the prow of an enemy junk.

The ploy worked, but only just. He had barely a moment to turn at a precariously steep angle to avoid a cannon blast that would have taken out their midsection. The clipper pitched low on its side toward the water's edge, and for a sickening moment came close to capsizing. But the ship's superb construction and Storm's magnificent handling prevented it. They righted quickly, in time to see water flowing through the smashed prow as the junk began to founder.

"That'll show them bastards," a crewman muttered. "The way they build those ships, they're damn near watertight. But they didn't figure on the captain, here. He can sail or sink anything afloat."

Erin prayed the man was right. They were still surrounded by enemy vessels, several of which were now close enough to hurl boarding lines toward them. As she made her way across the deck, she was dimly aware of others scrambling to cut through the lines and at the same time throw their own. The battle was reaching its peak even as all her attention focused on the sailors trapped under the fallen mast.

Quickly confirming that only one was still alive, she knelt down beside the seaman who was writhing in pain from his shattered leg. The laudanum she poured down his throat helped somewhat. By the time the mast was heaved out of the way by straining men, he was mercifully unconscious.

Erin's hand trembled slightly as she examined him. She took a deep breath, forcing her emotions back under control. One of the steel bits that held the rigging in place had cut almost all the way through his leg. There was no possibility that she could save the limb. Blood pumped from severed arteries. He was bleeding to death before her eyes.

Turning to the cabin boy, she ordered, "Bring me water and towels, then get a torch and stand by until I need to use it."

He nodded and raced away, returning moments later with another young boy he had enlisted to help and the supplies she needed. Erin almost wished they had taken longer. She was not at all prepared for what she had to do, but time was running out and she had no choice but to act at once.

The white apron covering her blouse and skirt was soaked through with blood as she knelt beside the man again. Checking to make sure he was still completely unconscious, she removed a razor-sharp surgical blade from her satchel. Mercifully, the steel bit had already done almost all the work for her. Only a few quick cuts were needed to finish severing the leg.

Blood flowed over her hands to pool on the deck at her feet. There was but one way she knew to stop such a hemorrhage. Taking the torch from the boy, who turned away to retch, she applied it to the stump. The putrid stench of burning flesh filled the air.

If the man did not succumb to shock or infection, he had a chance of surviving. Erin was well aware he might not thank her for that. Her face was ashen as she watched him being carried below to the dispensary. For long moments she could not move or think. Overwhelmed by the horror all around her, she drew inward, trying frantically to find some safe place for her spirit to hide.

But there was no such sanctuary, as she realized an instant later when a fierce roar alerted her to the fact that despite the heroic efforts of her crew, the *Rising Sun* was being boarded. Within seconds Erin was surrounded by men fighting in hand-to-hand combat. She turned to flee, only to be stopped by the sight of Odetsu, her kimono caught up into impromptu pantaloons and a sword grasped firmly in her hand, clearing a path toward her.

The young Japanese woman was obviously no novice. She wielded the sword with deadly efficacy, dispatching several opponents. Dimly, in the back of her mind, Erin remembered hearing that the daughters of samurai families were also trained in the martial arts. But she had never expected to witness such forceful proof of that custom, especially not from gentle Odetsu.

"Come on," her friend commanded, "we must get below deck."

Erin obeyed instantly. Seizing her precious supplies, she followed Odetsu toward the hatch. Along the way, she thought to pick up a heavy length of wood. Compared to the glittering swords flashing all around her, it didn't make much of a weapon. But it proved unexpectedly useful when a samurai thought to make short work of Odetsu, only to find himself caught between the young woman's slashing blade and Erin's club. She brought it down smartly on the back of his head, sending him sprawling to the deck.

"I didn't think Western women were trained to do such things," her friend commented when they at last fell gasping into the passageway.

"We're not," Erin admitted breathlessly. "But it's amazing what we can do when we have to."

Odetsu nodded, gesturing toward the men suddenly streaming onto the *Rising Sun*'s deck from other Satsuma vessels. "Reinforcements, and not a moment too soon. If Davin-san can just hold on, we may make it yet."

Erin glanced toward the prow. A low moan escaped her as she spied him surrounded by samurai, fighting fiercely but being pressed back relentlessly toward the railing. She took a quick step forward, only to be stopped by Odetsu, who had also seen the unequal contest and knew Erin could do nothing to help.

Takamori was nearby, frantically trying to fight his way to his friend's side. But it was too late. A soundless scream tore from Erin as Storm lost his balance, teetered for a moment and fell headlong into the remorseless sea.

Chapter Sixteen

"YOU MUST COME INSIDE," ODETSU SAID SOFT-
ly. "It will do you no good to stand out here."

Erin shook her head numbly. Oblivious of
the freezing wind, she continued to scan the
beach in front of the village of Myuga where
they had taken shelter, and beyond to the icy
waters where men in longboats were still
searching for survivors of the battle, which
had ended hours before.

Takamori's superb leadership had saved the
Rising Sun and won the battle, but had not
been able to help Storm. Despite frantic efforts, no trace of him had been found. Erin
knew the search might well be futile, but she
was grateful that it had not yet been called off.
When that happened, her last hope would die.

"At least put this warmer cloak on," Odetsu
pleaded. She slipped it around Erin's shoul-

ders gently and managed to guide her over to a small stone bench overlooking the sea. They sat together for some countless time without speaking.

Tormenting images flashed through Erin's mind. Storm as he looked in Ned Carmody's office and again on the night of the dinner party. Their arguments about the *Emerald Isle* and *Nantucket Moon* that merely cloaked far more personal conflicts. The ferocity with which he had fought the samurai who tried to kill her in the market, and the tenderness he had shown her afterward. The days in his house when he selflessly refrained from touching her until the old wounds between them were truly healed and they could forge a new life together free of shadows.

She closed her eyes against the bittersweet memory of their lovemaking. How gently he had brought her to the full realization of her womanhood. How generously he had taught her to relish her capacity to both give and receive pleasure.

Only a strong, tender man could so encourage her to accept her own passions without fear or restraint. Storm was both. It was impossible for her to believe that a spirit which had triumphed over so much could be snuffed out by capricious fate.

She refused to accept what all the evidence insisted must be true. Every ounce of conviction she possessed told her she would know if Storm were dead. Just as she had known of his child growing inside her before the physical signs were manifest. But far from believing him lost to her, she was utterly certain he still lived. Where and how, she could not say, but that did not weaken her faith.

The sun was beginning to dip beneath the snow-fringed pine trees when she at last looked up. Takamori was standing over her. For the first time since she had met him, his stoic expression was gone. In its place was anguish and deep, abiding sorrow.

In a gesture that was at once a plea for understanding and a revelation of overwhelming compassion, he knelt down before her and took both her hands in his. "There is nothing more we can do."

Erin knew he was telling her the truth. The men were exhausted, night was coming, and the water was too cold to allow anyone to survive in it for very long. If any hope had remained, Takamori would have moved heaven and earth to continue the search. Not only did his honor demand that he do so, but he was also Storm's friend, a man with whom he had shared both the burdens and the rewards of their search for a new, better world. If he said it was over, then it must be.

Yet her heart continued to insist Storm was still alive. "Perhaps in the morning . . ."

Takamori and Odetsu glanced at each other. Both were extremely worried about Erin. In her anguished condition, she might well lose the child. If that happened, her final link to the man she loved would be gone and she could well feel that life had become unbearable.

Neither believed there was anything to be gained by deliberately misleading her, but they still wished to protect her from the full realization of the tragedy until she had a chance to regain her strength.

Rising, Takamori gazed down into her drawn face. Her eyes were fathomless pools of sadness. Her soft mouth trembled slightly. She seemed somehow smaller and more fragile, as though a vital part of herself had been stripped away.

Quietly he nodded. "In the morning."

With Odetsu's help, he got her inside the fisherman's house where they were sheltering for the night. The family, awestruck by such revered visitors, had gone off to stay with a neighbor. The small, one-room structure was austere by any standards, but Erin did not notice. She was barely aware when Takamori lowered her onto a mat and covered her carefully. Sleep came in a great dark wave that hurled her so far from consciousness that not even dreams could reach her.

She woke abruptly in the dead of night. All weariness was gone. In its place was a fierce if incomprehensible urge that propelled her out of bed. Tiptoeing carefully around the half-dozen or so people sleeping nearby, she left the hut and headed toward the twisty, rock-strewn path leading to the beach.

A full moon rode high in the sky, pale as an ancient shell marooned on some eternal shore. Its ashen light bleached out what little color remained in the winter-bare landscape. Stark silhouettes of trees marked the edge of jagged cliffs. Below, the sea pounded endlessly. Only scattered clusters of debris cast up by the waves testified to the great struggle that had raged scant hours before.

Survivors of the shogun's fleet were under guard in the village. Satsuma loyalists held what had been the enemy ships, as well as their own. The Japanese dead were laid out in readiness for the cremation ceremony the following day. The bodies of Americans and Europeans who had perished in the battle were wrapped in canvas shrouds in preparation for transport back to Yokohama and burial. Messengers from Takamori were on their way to the capital at Edo to inform both the emperor and the rebel leaders of the great victory.

It was a time of immense rejoicing. The shogun's power was finally crushed, civil war was averted at the cost of relatively few lives. But none of that touched Erin. She thought only of Storm, and her absolute conviction that he was alive somewhere out there, calling to her.

In her anxiousness to find him, she slipped several times on the steep path. By the time she reached the beach, her hands were cut and bloodied. The wind whipped her cloak around her legs. Her ebony hair blew out in a stream behind her as sea foam lashed her face.

She began to walk, drawn by a power she could not deny. Heedless of her direction, she scrambled over boulders and squeezed through narrow defiles in the cliffs that often ran straight down to the water's edge. The tide was coming in, soaking through her shoes and turning the bottom of her skirt and petticoats to a sodden mass.

Chilled to the bone, she trembled uncontrollably. Several times her knees buckled, sending her sprawling onto the cold, wet sand. But she kept going, driven by sheer instinct and desperate need.

The moon drifted behind a cloud, momentarily blinding her. Erin leaned against the face of the cliff, trying to get her breath. Straining for any sound, she could hear only the pounding surf and the murmurings of the wind whipping around the ancient stone.

The cloud slid by. Silvered moonlight spilled across the sea. Fingers of light illuminated the beach. Almost overcome by weariness and despair, Erin nonetheless moved on.

Doggedly putting one foot in front of the other, she gave up trying to keep track of how far she had come or how she might get back. Instead she concentrated utterly on answering the primeval cry echoing within her.

A black shape swam within her vision.

Tossed up on the beach, it looked at first like a large chunk of driftwood. Not until she got closer could she make out the shape of a man, lying facedown in the sand.

She began to run. Her feet caught in her hem and she stumbled, but kept going. Almost there. He wore a white shirt and trousers. Tall black boots still hugged his legs to the knees. An unruly mass of glistening hair clung to his head. Though his features were turned away from her, she had no doubt of who he was.

"Storm!"

No answer. He might have been dead for all his awareness of her presence. But Erin never even considered that possibility. When she slipped to her knees beside him, her hand feeling for the pulse at his wrist, it was only to confirm what she already knew. The beat was slow and weak, but still unmistakable. He was alive, though badly injured.

The chunk of a mast lying beside him gave mute testament to how he had managed to survive. Destruction of the huge oak timber had cost several men their lives, but saved Storm's. By holding on to it, he had managed to stay afloat in the sea long enough to be washed onto shore.

Erin could never remember afterward how she got back to the fisherman's hut to awaken Takamori and Odetsu. Once they understood her incredible discovery, men were rapidly dispatched to bring Storm to the village. Erin tried to go along with them, but Takamori forcibly stopped her.

As Odetsu hurried to get water boiling and stoke up the charcoal braziers, he carried Erin to a quiet corner of the house and spoke to her firmly. "It is a miracle that you found him and that he is alive. But you will do him no good if you exhaust yourself. Save what strength you have left to help care for him."

She nodded mutely, knowing he was right. Her endurance had been pressed as far as it could go. For her own sake and the baby's, she had to rest, if only for a few minutes. Obediently she sat back on the mat and sipped the tea Odetsu brought her.

By the time Storm was carried into the hut, some color had returned to her face. Far from being weakened by her exertions, she felt stronger and more vigorous than she ever had in her life.

As Odetsu stood by with heavy blankets, Takamori and Erin stripped Storm's salt-encrusted clothes from him. His body was blue with cold and he did not stir. Wrapping him in quilts, Erin checked quickly for injuries.

He had suffered several minor slashes during the fighting, but none of them was still bleeding. There was a bruise on his forehead just beneath the hairline that did not seem serious enough to be contributing to his unconsciousness. His breathing was shallow but regular.

"We can't do much for him," she said softly, "except to keep him warm and watch him carefully. There's no way of telling right now how much water he swallowed or whether his air was choked off for any length of time. Until he comes to, I won't be able to assess the damage."

"I will sit with him," Odetsu offered.

Erin thanked her but shook her head. "I can rest later, when I'm sure he will be all right." Now that Storm was found, she had lost her confidence that he would not die. Every breath he drew was precious to her.

She gave in to Odetsu's pleading only long enough to slip away and change into dry clothes. Back within minutes, she sat down beside him and reached beneath the covers, her hand grasping his.

For hours she remained like that, not taking her eyes from him. Toward daybreak, he was seized by a fever that made him toss and turn restlessly. Takamori's help was needed to keep him from rolling off the bed.

Over and over, Erin bathed his heat-infested body. Holding his head, she urged him to drink. Her low, urgent voice whispered to him of her love and her determination that he would not die.

In midafternoon Takamori found her curled up asleep at Storm's side, her hand still holding his. He covered Erin with a blanket but did not disturb them. Storm was sleeping more peacefully, as though calmed by her nearness.

Erin woke in early morning and swallowed the bowl of food Odetsu brought her, without tasting a morsel of it. The moment it was done, she resumed the task of bathing Storm in melted snow.

There was no end of people willing to do that for her, but Erin persisted. She sensed, and they all agreed, that her touch strengthened him in some indefinable way no one else could match.

That night, when he began suddenly to shake with chills, she hesitated barely an instant before slipping beneath the blanket. Wrapping her arms around him, she cradled his head to her breast, her hands running over his lean, hard body as she strove to impart her warmth to him.

Storm muttered something she could not make out and grasped her closer. His beard-roughened chin rubbed against the softness of her neck. Even through the heavy wool of her skirt, she could feel the muscular power of his limbs.

Impatient with the barriers between them, she lifted her head and glanced around. They were sheltered from the other people in the hut by a bamboo screen taller than her own head. Disentangling herself from him briefly, she stripped down to her thin chemise and pantaloons, then crawled in again beside him.

The icy touch of his skin against hers made her gasp. She resumed stroking his body until slowly but steadily it lost its chill and grew warm. As the coldness fled from him, Storm seemed to grow more relaxed. His limbs lost their rigidity and wrapped naturally around hers. His breathing grew deep and steady.

As Erin listened to it, she allowed herself the first tentative stirrings of hope. He would be all right; he had to be. Fate could not be allowed to separate them like this, not when they had endured so much to find each other again. The vitality she felt radiating through him reassured her. A tentative smile curved her lips as she drifted into sleep.

Takamori found them like that in the morning when he peered behind the screen to see how Storm was doing. Blinking in surprise, he grinned down at the pair. They both looked considerably better than they had the night before.

He was about to leave them to their privacy when a movement caught his attention. Storm had opened his eyes. His friend glanced first at him, then at Erin. As Takamori struggled to restrain an understanding laugh, Storm slowly but unmistakably winked.

Chapter Seventeen

"I DON'T THINK I WANT THIS BOOK AFTER ALL," Storm said. "Would you mind bringing me the ship's log instead?"

Erin rose at once to fetch it. She was greatly relieved by his willingness to follow her instructions and not try to rush back to work before completely recovering. Never mind that he was a rather demanding patient who became restless if she strayed out of his sight. She was far too happy to begrudge him anything.

"Here it is," she said, handing him the journal. "How are you feeling this afternoon?"

"Better," Storm allowed. "But I still think it would be a mistake to overexert myself."

"Oh, I agree. After what you went through,

you need a great deal of rest." Cozily ensconced in their cabin on board the *Rising Sun,* she was more than content to look after him. But she realized their quiet interlude could not last forever. The weather was fair and they were making good time back to Yokohama.

"When does Takamori think we will make port?" Storm asked.

"Tomorrow, if the wind holds. He said to tell you not to worry; everything is under control."

She didn't mention that their friend had grinned when he said that. Takamori smiled frequently of late. Odetsu had agreed to marry him as soon as they were received by the emperor in Edo.

The formal announcement of the new government was due within a matter of weeks, after which they would be wed. Erin hoped to be at the ceremony, but she didn't want to go without Storm and she wasn't certain he would admit to being up to it.

He was taking longer than she'd expected to recover from his ordeal. His appetite was fickle, he didn't like being left alone, and if she so much as stirred from their bed at night, he woke instantly. Still, he seemed cheerful enough and except for wanting her constantly at his side, showed none of the impatience she had encountered before in sick or injured men.

"Do you think you might feel well enough to take a turn on deck?" she asked, glancing outside at the clear blue sky. Except for those days when it was extremely cold or snowing, she had managed to coax him outside regularly.

"Perhaps, if you will come with me."

"Of course, but you must promise to tell me the moment you begin feeling tired."

"I will," Storm assured her solemnly. Erin missed the devilish gleam in his eye as she went to fetch both their cloaks. Wrapped up snugly against the wind, she tucked her arm around Storm's as they left the cabin.

At that hour of the day, the ship was very quiet. Only a few seamen kept watch while the first mate manned the helm. They all nodded cordially as Storm and Erin passed, restraining their humorous comments about the captain's talent for handling women until they were safely out of earshot.

Odetsu and Saido joined them briefly. The little boy, who with the innocence of children had managed to sleep through the battle that changed the course of his country's history, overflowed with enthusiasm for everything around him. He had already announced his intention to become an admiral when he grew up.

Erin helped him assemble the pieces of a wooden ship one of the seamen had carved for him. Having never spent much time with children before, she found Saido a delight. He was an intelligent, happy little boy secure in the love of his mother and his father-to-be. Seeing what pleasure a child like him could give made her all the more eager for the arrival of her own baby.

While she was too occupied to notice, Odetsu glanced at Storm and smiled wryly. An unrepentant gleam lit his eyes, only to be quickly masked as Erin turned back to him.

After a sedate stroll around the deck, she was feeling just a bit sleepy. The steadily increasing demands of pregnancy sapped her strength more than she cared to admit. When Storm announced he was fatigued and wished to return to the cabin, she offered no demur.

The steward arrived with dinner shortly thereafter. Though Erin had no great inclination for food, she had learned that unless she made a sincere effort to eat, Storm would not do so.

His tastes had changed since his accident, causing him to prefer plain broiled fish and chicken, a few lightly seasoned vegetables and quantities of milk obtained from the cows brought on board before they left Hyuga. The menu suited Erin well enough. It did not upset her uncertain stomach and it seemed to meet the changing needs of her body.

When the remnants of the meal were cleared away, she accepted Storm's help in unfastening her dress. He insisted that since she did so much for him, he had to be allowed to assist her.

"You're becoming a passable ladies' maid," she teased as he undid the last button and slid the dress from her shoulders. Beneath it she wore only a chemise, pantaloons and warm petticoats. Pregnancy gave her the perfect excuse to abandon her stays entirely. She was convinced they could not be good for the baby and therefore refused to wear them.

"I think I'll stick to seafaring," he growled as the rest of her clothes drifted in a lacy heap at her feet. "It's much easier on the nerves."

Erin laughed softly. The fire of his gaze wandering over her warmed her most effectively. He made no secret of the fact that he found her ripening body beautiful. Yet he also made no attempt to renew their intimacy. Their nights were spent sleeping chastely in each other's arms.

Wrapped in her robe, she sat down to brush her hair. Storm watched her silently. The grace of her movements coupled with the loveliness of her face and form stirred him to a desire so intense as to be painful. He longed to feel her slender length beneath him, to hear her cries of rapture, and find within her sweetness fulfillment beyond anything he had ever known with another woman.

Yet he was absolutely resolved not to take her again until they were married. Shrewdly he realized that her desire equaled his, and she could not long remain content with any arrangement that denied her the most fundamental expression of their love.

Besides, he worried that a resumption of their intimacy might endanger the baby, especially after all Erin had been through. Until he could get her safely back to Yokohama, he was determined to exercise the greatest self-control, whatever the cost.

Gritting his teeth, he managed to return her smile as she stood up, removed her robe and with a delicate shiver pulled on her nightgown. Her arm tangled in the sleeve, much delaying the process. By the time she was once again covered, a sheen of perspiration had broken out on his forehead.

Erin eyed him with concern. "I think you may have done too much today. You look quite pale."

"I'm fine. Just come to bed."

She obliged as willingly as any man could ask, cuddling into his arms. Within minutes she was fast asleep, a contented smile curving her delectable mouth.

Storm sighed softly. Gathering her closer, he reconciled himself to yet another uneasy night.

They reached Yokohama the following morning, to great rejoicing by the populace. In honor of the occasion the gates of the Black

Star Trading Company were thrown open and celebrants allowed to stream onto the docks to welcome the proud clipper ship home.

In a city founded on the sanctity of trade, there was immense relief that a protracted war had been averted. Businessmen who had previously professed loyalty to the shogun had no problem switching their allegiance, such as it was, to the new regime.

A few were presumptuous enough to believe the reform leaders could be convinced to take a smaller share of the profits than the shogun had demanded. But most realized that was not likely to be the case. They understood that men such as Takamori would not tolerate the expropriation of their nation's wealth by anyone, Westerner or Japanese.

Instead of being content with quick gains for a few, the reformers would insist on a much longer-term view of what was best for the nation as a whole. To all but the most exploitive hucksters, that was a welcome change.

Leaning over the railing, Erin waved eagerly to Meg and the Carmodys, whom she had spotted on the dock. She tugged on Storm's sleeve, calling his attention to them.

"You're in luck. Meg doesn't have her umbrella with her."

He laughed confidently. "It's not me who needs to be concerned about the formidable Mrs. Gilhoully. Unless I'm very much mistaken, you're in for an earful about all the worry you've caused her."

"She should talk, after believing your blarney about having no disrespectful designs on my person."

"I wonder if she really did believe me," Storm mused. "After all, hasn't she been trying to get you married off for some time now?"

Erin made a face at him. Provoked by his suggestion that she was hard up for a husband, she said, "Are you starting that marriage business again?"

Storm scowled. "I wasn't aware I had ever dropped it."

"Just don't expect me to do anything about it soon. After all, we still have to finish buying cargoes for the *Emerald Isle* and the *Nantucket Moon,* find crews for them and see them safely on their way home. There'll be plenty of time after that to think about getting married."

"Your priorities leave much to be desired, madam. Before you finish dreaming up reasons to delay our wedding, our child will have arrived."

"Would that be so terrible?"

"Erin . . ."

The warning note in his voice alerted her to the fact that she was treading perilously close to the edge of his temper. But before she could attempt to make amends, Storm sighed dramatically. "You have me at a great disability.

Being still so weakened from my ordeal, I can hardly compel you to obey me."

Erin managed to look immediately contrite. "I am sorry, dearest. That was thoughtless of me. Just put the whole issue of marriage out of your mind. We'll discuss it when you're completely recovered."

That was not what Storm had wanted to hear. He was still scowling as they made their way down the ramp and were engulfed by the joyful crowd.

"Praise God you're back safe and sound," Meg declared, hugging Erin to her ample bosom. "Many the night I've lain awake praying to the Blessed Virgin to return you to us."

"Now, Meg," Ned admonished, "you know perfectly well it was you who kept telling us they'd both be all right."

"Only because I trust Captain Davin here. God love you, sir, for taking such good care of her."

Erin snorted disparagingly, but didn't get a chance to comment before Elizabeth swept her out of Meg's embrace and into her own. "I'm so relieved you're all right. When we heard you were on board the *Rising Sun* during the attack, I'm afraid I imagined all sorts of terrible things."

"Exactly what you shouldn't be doing in your condition."

Blushing attractively, Elizabeth glanced down at her protruding stomach. "That's what Ned kept telling me, but I just couldn't help it. Even though we haven't known each other very long, I feel that we have become good friends. The thought that you might be harmed horrified me."

Deeply touched by her words, Erin put an arm around her comfortingly. "As you can see, I'm right as rain." Glancing at Storm, who she felt was taking unseemly enjoyment in the scene, she added, "But the captain is still feeling the effects of his ordeal. We really should not linger on the dock."

"Of course not," Ned agreed, giving Storm no chance to object. "Allow us to escort you home and then we will leave you. A celebration dinner is planned for tonight, but I'm sure you both want to rest up before that."

He hesitated, uncertain of how to bring up a delicate point, but finally asked, "Uh . . . Erin . . . if your business with Captain Davin is concluded and you prefer to stay with us . . ."

"She does not," Storm said firmly. Glowering at her, he dared her to contradict him.

Erin shrugged as though it wasn't important. "Thank you, Ned, but since the captain is still convalescing, I think I should return with him."

"How kind of you," Storm muttered. So quietly that only Erin could hear him, he added, "When we get home, my sweet, we will discuss this ridiculous idea you have about postponing our marriage. It's time we settled that once and for all."

Glancing up at him through her thick lashes, she refrained from answering. The carriage ride passed quickly as they exchanged all the latest news and caught up on the changes already being enacted by the new government. Servants were waiting outside Storm's house to welcome them.

Meg cast him a sharp look as he helped Erin down. "I trust this business of yours will be settled shortly, Captain?"

He nodded calmly. "That is my intention."

Mollified, she gave Erin a final peck on the cheek. "There's a fancy-dress ball tonight. Have you something to wear?"

Stepping out of the carriage, Erin nodded. "My blue silk, I suppose."

Meg sniffed doubtfully. "Don't count on it fitting much longer."

Storm and Erin glanced at each other in guilty surprise, then back to the group in the carriage. Elizabeth laughed outright and even diplomatic Ned chuckled indulgently.

"It might interest you to know," he told Storm, "that the Reverend Blakely will be in attendance this evening. Loves a wedding, does the reverend."

Before his startled audience could reply, he gave the horses their rein. The carriage pulled away, leaving them to stare after it in befuddlement.

"I am afraid," Erin said as they entered the house, "that we have no secrets."

"All the more reason to settle the issue

now," Storm growled. If Meg and the Carmodys had realized Erin's condition, it was only a matter of time before the entire community did, too. He was determined she would not subject herself to the censure that was bound to come, even if he had to drag her to the altar.

"I'm willing to discuss it."

"How forbearing of you."

"But not if you intend to be sarcastic."

"Oh, very well. We'll talk about it calmly, and then you'll agree to do things my way."

"Perhaps," Erin allowed as she accompanied him onto the enclosed veranda overlooking the garden. A servant brought the customary tea and cakes. Storm remembered to alert the staff to the fact that Odetsu and Takamori were journeying on immediately to Edo and therefore should not be expected. That done, he turned his attention to Erin.

His eyes locked on hers as he said quietly, "I thought you had forgiven me for responding so thoughtlessly when you told me about the baby. Was that not the case?"

Such frankness surprised her. Unwilling to have him believe she nurtured any sort of grudge against him, she blurted, "Of course it was. If I had been less fatigued and confused at the time, I would never have taken your words so seriously. But as it is, they are certainly forgotten."

"Then why don't you want to marry me?"

Storm demanded, striding over to her. Seizing her by the arms, he fought against the urge to try to shake some sense into her.

"I do," Erin said hastily, "but I must be sure of your feelings." Her eyes darkened with anguish as she at last revealed her most deeply held fear. "You say you love me, but how can you be certain it is me you love and not the girl you remember from eight years ago?"

Storm stared at her in dawning comprehension. His grip loosened, becoming gentle, as he said, "What I felt for you eight years ago was nothing compared to what I feel now. If I can spend the rest of my life at your side, I will only be able to begin convincing you of how much I treasure and adore you."

Yearning to believe him, Erin did not yet dare to. "How can you care for me so much when I behaved so selfishly and turned my back on you when you needed me most? I was shallow and insensitive and—"

She meant to go on, but Storm stilled her with a gentle kiss. "I was thinking only of myself when I asked you to marry me on the eve of the war. If you had agreed, you would have been separated from your family and the only way of life you had ever known. Once I rejoined the army, you would have been left on your own, subject to all sorts of dangers. No, I realize now that it was my callousness that I have fought against admitting all these years, preferring to think badly of you instead. But at last I can freely admit the truth, knowing that what we have found this time is infinitely more precious."

"You really don't just feel obligated because of the baby?"

A throaty laugh escaped him. His big hand spread gently over the curve of her hip to settle on the satiny skin of her abdomen.

"My love, what I feel for you is a great deal less decorous than obligation. I want you in the most primitive way possible. I want to tie you to me in every way devised by man and God."

Softly his lips trailed over her delicate throat to nuzzle in the sensitive hollow behind her ear. "And I want to watch you swell with the child we have made together, to see you with our son or daughter at your breast."

Looking up, he saw the sheen of tears in her eyes and smiled tenderly. "Most of all, I want to be there when your hair becomes streaked with silver and the bloom of youth leaves your cheeks, to be replaced by the serenity and grace that come to an older woman when she is truly loved. I want to share all the years with you, every precious day of them."

A teasing note entered his voice as he asked, "Now, does that really sound as though I merely feel obligated?"

Erin shook her head mutely. She had to swallow several times before she could speak. "It sounds as though you mean to fulfill my most precious dream."

Despite her immense happiness, she could

not quite suppress the urge to gently tease him. "But are you sure you aren't doing this just because you're scared of Meg? She packs a mean umbrella, you know."

"Oh, it isn't only Meg. Elizabeth Carmody may look small and delicate, but I'd hate to ever get her mad."

Erin took a playful swat at him. "Just what did you tell them all to get them to agree to my moving in here?"

Storm had the grace to look a bit abashed. "That day I took you back to the Carmodys' house after the attack in the market, I told them I was in love with you and wanted to convince you to become my wife, but that there was much in our past we needed to overcome. I thought the best way to do that was to have you living here. At the time, I honestly believed I could be near you without taking you to bed. How I ever got such a crazy idea, I'll never know."

"Even then you knew you loved me?"

Storm nodded. "From the moment I saw you in Carmody's office, I was overwhelmed by the need to make you mine. But I kept fighting it, because wanting you so much made me acutely vulnerable. The worst moment of my life was when I saw the samurai attack you. Seeing you standing in front of him, with no way to escape or protect yourself, I knew all my anger and hurt for what had happened between us eight years before was gone. In its place there was only the desperate need to save you."

"I know this will sound strange, but in a way, we owe that man our thanks. Coming so close to death forced me to realize how foolish I had been to let pride stand between us. I made up my mind that if I somehow miraculously survived, I would do everything possible to win your love."

"You have it. Now, will you please agree to marry me?"

Erin grinned, happiness spilling out of her. Tilting her head back, she gazed into the quicksilver eyes whose loving warmth mirrored her own. "I suppose I'll have to, what with a party already planned and all."

A heartfelt sigh of relief escaped from Storm. Taking a firm grip on her hand, he headed toward the bedroom.

"Where are we going?" Erin inquired, though she already had a fair idea.

"To put you into your blue silk," Storm informed her. A mischievous smile lit his rugged features. "While it still fits!"

Chapter Eighteen

ERIN TOOK A CAUTIOUS BREATH, WILLING THE buttons of her dress not to give way. A sigh of relief escaped her when she realized they were holding, if only just. Managing a smile for the Reverend Blakely, who had conducted the brief but moving wedding ceremony, she was grateful the clergyman could not read her thoughts. Married barely an hour, and she could hardly wait to get her clothes off.

Beside her, Storm grinned devilishly. He raised her hand to his lips, brushing a gentle kiss just above the gold ring he had slipped on her finger barely an hour ago. "How thoughtful of Elizabeth and Ned to invite the entire diplomatic and business community. I thought the congratulations would never end."

"It wasn't entirely their doing. When I mentioned it to Meg, she said something about wanting to make sure there were plenty of witnesses."

Storm laughed appreciatively. "And not because she harbors any doubts about me, I'll wager. No, she was determined you'd be locked up good and tight with the key thrown away."

Erin gazed up at him laughingly, hardly daring to believe that the compelling man who hovered over her so protectively was actually her husband. "Speaking of keys, you don't have any more ideas about keeping me a prisoner, do you?"

Storm appeared to give that some serious thought. "There's no denying you're headstrong and impulsive. Left to yourself, you'd probably get into all sorts of mischief. For the sake of our baby, I'll have to find some way to drain off all that excess energy."

"Helping you in your business will be a good start," Erin assured him sincerely. Storm had taken the occasion of their wedding to announce, with her full approval, the merging of the Black Star Trading Company and Conroy Shipping. He had also made it clear that he expected Erin to be a full and active partner.

Their conversation broke off briefly as Captain Foster came over to offer his congratulations. The white-haired seaman positively beamed as he wished them a long and happy life together.

"You're fortunate there's no need for you to

be separated by long voyages," he pointed out a bit wistfully. "I wish that was true for the missus and myself."

"Is there no way she could come along?" Erin asked sympathetically. Her love for Storm made her abhor the thought of even the briefest parting. To go for months without seeing a dearly loved spouse seemed intolerable beyond belief.

Captain Foster shook his head regretfully. "It's against the regulations of my shipping company. I've tried to convince them otherwise, but they won't be persuaded."

Storm and Erin glanced at each other. An instant of silent communication was all that was needed to bring them to agreement. Quietly Storm said, "You may be interested to know that the Conroy-Black Star company has no such regulation. Furthermore, we are looking for an experienced captain to take two ships back to the States. Perhaps you would care to come by our office next week to discuss it."

When Captain Foster realized Storm was serious, his grizzled features lit up in an ear-splitting grin. "Well, now, I'd be right pleased to do that. Imagine if I could tell the missus she'd be coming with me from now on. Why, that'd be about the best thing that's happened to us since our own wedding day!"

Delighted to have been able to truly share their happiness with someone else, Erin and Storm spoke awhile longer with the captain before he took himself off to ready his reports and log. If he was going to leave one company for another, he wanted to make sure everything was shipshape for his successor.

"I think we may have found the right man," Storm said when he was gone.

"I'm sure of it. Remember, I sailed over here on his ship. Not only did he make the crossing in excellent time, but he did so without ever losing the affection and respect of either crew or passengers."

"Then it's settled. Now, I believe we were discussing how I can keep you busy . . ."

The sensual flare of his eyes warmed Erin all the way through. She swayed toward him slightly, only to quickly pull back when Meg suddenly appeared before them.

"Don't be seeing how much of that champagne you can drink," she scolded, ignoring the fact that Erin's glass was untouched. "I declare, Captain, you've got your hands full with this one." Her stern words were undermined by the sheen of tears in her eyes and the audible sniffs she could not hide.

Erin put an arm around her shoulders consolingly. "I'll be fine. Don't you be worrying about me." With just a touch of wickedness, she added, "After all, you've got to save your strength, what with not one but two babies coming soon."

Meg snorted disparagingly. "No one could ever accuse you of being a slave to convention, Miss Erin. But at least you're safely married now and are the captain's problem. The best of luck to you, sir. You'll need it."

Storm accepted her good wishes cheerfully, ignoring Erin's pout. "Wouldn't you agree, Meg, that the brand-new Mrs. Davin is looking a bit peaked? It can't be wise for her to be standing around like this."

"If you say so, sir. Why don't I just find the Carmodys for you and you can make your farewells?"

"Splendid idea, Meg. Thank you."

As the Irishwoman bustled off, Erin shook her head resignedly. "I should have known the two of you would team up against me. Like as not, I won't be able to take a step without hearing about it."

Not at all misled by her tartness, Storm asked gently, "Are you sure you don't mind about Meg staying here instead of coming to live with us?"

Erin did mind, but she was too unselfish not to want what was best for her old friend. "Meg wouldn't be comfortable sleeping on the floor and eating raw fish. But at least she'll be able to come over part-time to help with the baby."

"You couldn't keep her away," Elizabeth said gaily as she beamed at the newlyweds. "It's a good thing we're not due at the same time, or poor Meg would be run ragged."

"Due?" the Reverend Blakely, who happened still to be standing nearby, repeated. He smiled benignly at the startled group. "Don't tell me you're talking schedules and suchlike on a wedding day. Ned, my boy, surely you won't permit that?"

"Uh, no, of course not, sir." Under his breath, he added, "This might be a good time for you two to pull out. My guess is it'll be hours yet before anyone else leaves."

"Just what we were thinking," Storm murmured. He and Erin offered their sincere thanks to the Carmodys, who accepted them graciously while promising to come to dinner the following week.

Easing toward the door, they hoped to make a quiet exit, but the other guests wouldn't hear of it. Showered with rice and well-wishes, they stepped quickly into their carriage. Storm took the reins while Erin waved happily. She had greatly enjoyed her wedding, but she was also glad it was over. As they rounded the corner and started toward home, she snuggled against Storm contentedly.

"I had no idea it was that easy to get married. Back in Boston, all the girls I knew spent months agonizing over their nuptials."

"Probably with good reason, if some of the local swain I met were anything to go by."

"You know that's not what I meant. It was marvelous of Meg and the Carmodys to do all the organizing."

"I wouldn't be surprised if they started planning for it the day you moved in with me."

Erin giggled softly. Glancing at him out of the corner of her eye, she murmured, "How fortunate we are to have friends willing to take care of all that for us, especially since I know you are still feeling so weakened by your ordeal."

Storm winced. He had spent a good part of the evening trying to think of some way to convince Erin it was time to put an end to his convalescence. A discreet word with the understanding physician who served the Yokohama community had assured him there was no reason to delay the consummation of their marriage. Provided, of course, he could convince her he was able to do so. The ploy that had served so well both to keep her near him and to persuade her to follow a healthy regimen for a pregnant woman just might be about to rebound on him.

"Uh . . . about that . . ."

"Now, don't you give it another thought. Heavens, we've got all the time in the world now." Hesitating a moment, she added, "Would you like me to drive?"

"No! That is, thank you, but it isn't necessary. I really feel quite recovered."

"Don't be misled by an unusually good day. Why, the moment you start to exert yourself, all sorts of things might happen."

"I've been rather counting on that," Storm muttered. He kept prudently silent the rest of the way home. Not until the horses and carriage were led away by a beaming servant and he and Erin stood in the entranceway pulling off their shoes did the matter of his disability come up again.

"I believe," Storm said softly, "it is customary to carry the bride over the threshold."

He was about to lift her when Erin demurred. "Perhaps we'd better skip that. After all, we wouldn't want your strength to be taxed any more than it has already been today."

"Indulge me," Storm muttered. Gathering her into his arms, he strode into the house and headed straight for the bedroom.

"I just wanted to have a word with the new housekeeper," Erin cautioned.

"Later."

"You really shouldn't carry me all this way. You'll hurt your back."

"My back is fine."

"Perhaps you'd better take me to my room."

"That is where I'm taking you."

"I mean the room I used before we—"

"Forget it."

"But, Storm, you really are not being sensible about this. It was only a few days ago that you were almost killed. What kind of wife would I be if I tried to insist that you do your duty under these circumstances?"

"A good one. Go right ahead and insist."

Erin shook her head primly as he sat her down in their room. "I wouldn't dream of it. We've spent several chaste nights together. There's no reason we can't continue to do so for however long it takes you to recover completely."

"I can give you an excellent reason." Turning her around, Storm began to briskly unfasten her dress.

"What's that?"

In answer, he seized her hand and pressed it to him. The blatancy of his gesture shocked her even as his obvious need sent spirals of pleasure racing through her.

Nonetheless, Erin continued to insist that for the sake of his health they should put off resuming their intimacy. Storm listened to her patiently, removing her clothes as she spoke. By the time she finished, she was stripped down to her camisole and pantaloons and he was busy unfastening those.

"Now, wait just a moment," Erin protested a bit breathlessly. "You haven't heard a word I've said, have you?"

"Every one of them. You said you would love, honor and *obey* me. Isn't that right?"

"I wasn't talking about that. I was talking about—"

"That's right, isn't it?"

"Yes, but—"

"No buts. Let's see some of that obedience you promised."

"I knew that part was a mistake," Erin grumbled. She shivered as the last of her covering was tossed onto the floor and she stood naked before him.

Storm's quicksilver eyes wandered over her lingeringly. The enriching of her body by pregnancy enthralled him. Her breasts were fuller and heavier, the velvety nipples darker than before. Her waist was still small, but beneath it her belly swelled slightly. He reached out a gentle hand to touch her there, letting his caress drift downward to the dark nest of curls that hid her womanhood from his impassioned gaze. Thickly he ordered, "Undress me."

"Let me get a robe first. I'm cold."

Storm grinned. He knew perfectly well she was warm enough. Charcoal braziers kept the room at a comfortable temperature despite the frost-laden night. Gazing down at her, he shook his head. "No."

"You're so stubborn. If I do what you want, will you get into bed?"

"Absolutely."

"Then I suppose I'll have to. Hold still."

Storm obeyed with alacrity. As Erin slipped the jacket from his massive shoulders, he shrugged it off along with his waistcoat. Her small fingers fumbled with the buttons of his shirt, but at last they too were undone. The breath caught in her throat when the hair-roughened width of his torso was revealed to her.

Erin inhaled deeply, letting her hands stroke the bulging contours of his chest and back. Bemused by the flares of passion darting through her, she was only dimly aware that Storm was urging her on to the buttons of his snug-fitting trousers.

"The last time you did this," he muttered huskily, "you lost your nerve before you were through. Is that likely to happen again?"

"Wives," she informed him pertly, "are much more daring than mistresses."

Her actions proved that claim. Storm gasped softly as her fingers brushed against him enticingly. Freed from its confines, his manhood rose hard and urgent into her welcoming hand.

"Oh, my," Erin murmured. "It seems part of you doesn't realize you are still convalescing."

"It has a will of its own," Storm growled, drawing her to him. In the glow of the oil lamps, his skin was burnished copper, hers polished ivory. His huge, heavily muscled body seemed to engulf her. She looked so small and fragile next to him, the top of her ebony hair reaching barely to his shoulders.

His big hands cupped her face, tilting it to him. Her cheeks were flushed and her eyes glowed with inner fires. The moist ripeness of her lips beckoned his. A low groan broke from him. He was just bending toward her when she smiled tenderly. "Now, if you'll get into bed, I'll bring you a nice cup of warm milk."

"*What?*"

"You drank so much of it on the ship, I naturally assumed you were quite fond of it."

The pewter sheen of his gaze darkened. "Erin, there's something I have to tell you."

"Hmmm."

"I hate milk. If I drink any more of it, I will turn into a suckling whelp."

Indigo eyes widened in innocent surprise. "But then why did you insist on having it on the ship?"

"Because that was the only way to get you to drink it. You're supposed to, you know. Being pregnant and all." Hesitantly he added, "The fact is, I only pretended not to be fully recovered so that you would stay near me and take proper care of yourself."

"Really?"

"Yes, you see, I . . ." Storm broke off abruptly. Erin's enticing mouth was curved in a devilish smile. Her body began to shake from her futile effort to hold back the laughter his contrite confession sparked.

Grasping her shoulders, he stared down at her in disbelief. *"You knew."*

"I couldn't resist the urge to go along with the act." Erin giggled unrepentantly. "But there were times I really thought I'd give it away. All that milk!"

"Gallons of it, not to mention all those days of staying in the cabin to keep an eye on you." A pulse beat in the corded column of his throat as his hands tightened. "And those nights . . . those damned endless nights. I thought I'd go mad if I had to lie beside you once more without touching you."

Erin's eyes met his as her laughter abruptly died. Her soft fingers tangled in the thick mat of hair covering his chest. "There, at least, I can sympathize." She moved closer, and her ripening breasts brushed against him enticingly. "Do you think, husband, that we might conclude this discussion? After all, we have quite a bit of time to make up for."

Storm needed no further encouragement. He swept her into his arms and covered the distance to the sleeping platform in half a dozen rapid strides. Without releasing her, he set her on the mattress and came down swiftly beside her.

Warm male lips nuzzled her throat as he muttered, "Not only that, sweet. You will pay for allowing me to be so gullible."

Erin gasped softly as he nibbled at her lower lip, coaxing it open. His tongue traced the moist outline of her mouth before plunging inward in a slow, demanding thrust that made her writhe beneath him.

Cupping her breasts in his callused palms, he gently brushed his thumbs across the straining peaks. "Are you tender here?" he demanded huskily.

She nodded mutely. Her nipples, swollen by pregnancy, were ultrasensitive. The merest touch sent spirals of exquisite delight coiling through her. When he bent his proud head, his tongue lapping at her tenderly, she moaned deep in her throat.

"S-Storm . . ."

Determined to draw out her pleasure to the utmost, he ignored her implicit plea. His hands and mouth awakened her to a firestorm of desire more intense than any she had ever experienced. His lips traced a burning path down the length of her body to the nest of curls between her thighs. Gently his knee nudged her legs apart, giving him access to the moist sanctuary where their child slept.

Despite the throbbing inferno of his own need, Storm forced himself to go slowly. The hot length of his phallus lying against her left no doubt that his desires were ready to burst all bounds. Yet Erin still could not persuade him to end his loving torment of her body.

His tongue traced the silken skin of her inner thighs upward to the unfolding petals of her womanhood. Reveling in the honeyed sweetness he unleashed within her, he brought her again and again to the peak of fulfillment, until her alabaster length shone with perspiration and repeated moans broke from her.

Only then did he at last lower himself to her, entering slowly and gently to be absolutely certain he caused her no discomfort. Natural changes wrought by her pregnancy made her even tighter than before. Storm gasped as moist velvet undulated around him, drawing him farther and farther into her.

Holding himself perfectly still, he allowed her to set the pace of their consummation. Her slender hips arched rhythmically against him as powerful inner muscles brought him swiftly to the edge of rapture.

Convinced at last that she could accept all

of him, Storm slid his hands beneath her to grasp her buttocks and hold her for his deep but careful thrusts. Kittenish purrs broke from her as the world turned swiftly to shimmering fire and exploded around them both.

Barely had they begun the slow descent to earth than each realized that their celibacy of the last few days had an unexpected benefit. Storm grinned roguishly at her startled look.

"Did you really think you would get off this easily, my love?"

Before she could answer, he moved within her again, giving eloquent demonstration of his manhood's resurgent power. Driven to the edge of rapture and beyond, Erin cried out helplessly. Her hands grasped his massive shoulders as they began another, even faster ascent.

Storm's breath came in harsh gasps and his huge body shook with the force of his passion. Still he waited until he saw rapture seize her and felt the exquisite contractions of her body swept by ecstasy. Only then did he release himself, her name an exultant cry on his lips.

Briefly drained of strength, he slumped against her. Erin's hands stroked the sweat-dampened expanse of his back lovingly. Despite the utter satisfaction of her body, she could not get enough of his taste, scent, and feel. A thoroughly feminine smile curved her ripe mouth as she murmured, "I think I'm going to like being your wife."

Storm raised his head, blinking to clear his

passion-fogged senses. The loving intensity of her gaze was matched by his own. "I'm delighted to hear it. But just in case you're ever in danger of changing your mind, I intend to keep convincing you."

"Whatever you wish, my husband," Erin murmured with uncharacteristic docility. At his surprised look, she added wryly, "Not that it's necessary. For I love you with all my heart and will for eternity."

Storm glanced away for a moment, embarrassed despite himself by the effect of her words. When he looked back, his quicksilver eyes glowed with a sheen she had never seen before. Smiling down at her tenderly, he murmured, "Is that all?"

Erin laughed, matching his teasing mood. "It's a beginning."

"So it is." Drawing the quilts over them both, he gathered her closer. She snuggled against him contentedly, their bodies gently entwining.

Night settled softly over the ancient land swept by the winds of·change. But in their hearts the glowing sun of love burned on forever.

About the Author

MAURA SEGER is the fourth generation of her family to pursue writing as a career. Her first historical romance, *Defiant Love*, helped to launch the Tapestry series. Since then she has written three more: *Rebellious Love*, *Forbidden Love*, and *Flame on the Sun*. A Connecticut resident, Maura credits the support and encouragement of her husband, Michael, for enabling her to fulfill the lifelong dream of becoming an author.

POCKET BOOKS
PROUDLY INTRODUCES
TAPESTRY
ROMANCES

POCKET BOOKS

If you've enjoyed the love, passion and adventure of this Tapestry™ historical romance...be sure to enjoy them all, FREE for 15 days with convenient home delivery!

Now that you've read a Tapestry™ historical romance, we're sure you'll want to enjoy more of them. Because in each book you'll find love, intrigue and historical touches that really make the stories come alive!

You'll meet brave Guyon d'Arcy, a Norman knight ... handsome Comte Andre de Crillon, a Huguenot royalist ... rugged Branch Taggart, a feuding American rancher ... and more. And on each journey back in time, you'll experience tender romance and searing passion ... and learn about the way people lived and loved in earlier times.

Now that you're acquainted with Tapestry romances, you won't want to miss a single one! We'd like to send you 2 books each month, as soon as they are published, through our Tapestry Home Subscription Service.℠ Look them over for 15 days, free. If not delighted, simply return them and owe nothing. But if you enjoy them as much as we think you will, pay the invoice enclosed.

There's never any additional charge for this convenient service— we pay all postage and handling costs.

To begin your subscription to Tapestry historical romances, fill out the coupon below and mail it to us today. You're on your way to all the love, passion and adventure of times gone by!

HISTORICAL *Tapestry* ROMANCES

Tapestry™ is a trademark of Simon & Schuster.